TIME TRAVEL SWAP

Connie Lacy

Wild Falls Publishing

~ ~ ~

Atlanta, GA

For the music makers

~~~

Also by Connie Lacy

The October That Changed Everything
Livvy and the Enchanted Woodland
A Suffragette in Time
The Time Capsule
The Going Back Portal
The Time Telephone
VisionSight: a Novel
A Daffodil for Angie
The Shade Ring, Book 1 of The Shade Ring Trilogy
Albedo Effect, Book 2 of The Shade Ring Trilogy
Aerosol Sky, Book 3 of The Shade Ring Trilogy
~~~

1

Mid-July 2024

The familiar melody echoed in her mind. Carly sang the lyrics in a whispery voice as she got ready to go. "It was fate, baby, that brought us together. Not happenstance that brought you to me." It was her big song, the song she couldn't wait to perform tonight at the album release show. She was pumped. Stoked.

Swaying to the music, she grabbed her shawl from where she'd draped it over the sofa. The color of wine, it was vintage and flowy with fringe along the bottom and would conjure the nineteen seventies vibe she was going for.

In tight black pants, a brocade crop top and a pair of ankle boots, she had the look of a rock musician. But it was more than just her clothes. There was also the strawberry blonde hair that reached halfway down her back, intense eyes and an expressive mouth. She moved with assurance like she could hold her own in a profession dominated by men.

Immersed in her music, she jumped when she heard what sounded like an intake of breath behind her. Whirling around, she scanned the living room. No one there. Funny, she'd had fleeting sensations since she moved in this spring that she wasn't alone in her apartment. Still, she didn't believe this old mansion had a ghost. That's what some of her gullible neighbors claimed. She felt that weird itch to write a song about it. But she couldn't take time right now to scratch that itch. She would circle around to the ghost idea later. Dictating a quick voice memo on her phone, she got back to work.

She rolled up the shawl and tucked it into a pillow case before packing it in a wheeled suitcase with the other things she'd laid out – makeup case, curling iron, brush and hand mirror. She had already loaded her keyboard into the back of her SUV. Thankfully, the new Roland was smaller and lighter than her old keyboard and easier on her back.

Although she was doing her best to remain calm, there was no denying she was nervous. The Triple Vee, a venue in New York's West Village where the good bands performed, had decreed that Hawke & Carly could grace their stage. She hadn't been this keyed up since she first got into the music business. Why now? She'd debuted plenty of songs. In fact, she'd contributed half the band's catalog. Of course, Hawke said this tune was special, that "Happenstance" had the potential to be a breakout hit that would catapult them to the big time. God, she hoped he was right.

They'd spent a wad at the recording studio and worked hard to make sure everything sounded top-notch, that the mix was perfect, that the master was flawless. When they released the single a couple of weeks ago, a prominent music podcaster went on and on about it, saying that "despite having a driving rock sound, it has unexpected lyricism." He also praised her voice. "Carly Munro has a woman's voice. Unlike so many female rock singers today, she doesn't sound like an emo thirteen-year-old."

She slung the strap of her purse over her shoulder and grabbed the handle of her suitcase. When she was on edge like this, it was best to get there early. That way she'd have time for vocal warmups while doing her makeup and hair. She was about to make tracks when a text pinged her phone.

"Carly, baby! Let me pick you up."

It was Hawke. His idea of arriving early meant showing up in time to load in, do a soundcheck and toss back a shot of whiskey. At least he was already dressed in his stage duds when he got there, often a pair of leather pants and a sleeveless shirt to show off his tattoos.

"Already on my way," she replied, preferring to be in the driver's seat.

"OK. Gonna be an epic show tonight, babe! Love you up one side and down the other."

He added a winking emoji – his way of alluding to sex. She answered with a goofy face emoji – her way of avoiding any words she didn't mean.

It had been three years since they met, two years since they formed the band, a year since they first had sex, and a few months since they started throwing the L-word around like it might mean something more than "we're good in the sack." But the night before a major gig, they each slept in their own bed and drove to the venue separately. Tonight was definitely a major gig.

Her eyes swept the room to make sure she wasn't forgetting anything. There was nothing left on her blue sofa or the pub table. In fact, the place was tidy enough to invite Hawke over to celebrate after the show. Scarves were draped over the lamps to soften the lighting, tasseled mauve curtains covered the window and colorful throw pillows were arranged just so. She liked the Boho feel of her little corner of the galaxy. It suited the place with its oak floors and eleven-foot ceilings. A modern look would be all wrong for a ramshackle nineteenth century mansion converted into apartments.

But what was she thinking? Hawke didn't give a damn how the place looked. He was a world-champion slob. He wouldn't want to come over tonight anyway when he could hang with the guys after the gig and drink shots until he had to order an Uber to take him home. In his mind, that's what rockers did. Being cool was a top priority. Which is why he ditched his white bread name – Marc Williams – to rebrand himself as Hawke.

A sigh near her right ear made her flinch. Could there be an old steam radiator behind the wall making those sounds? No time now to investigate.

She turned off the lights, opened the door and backed into the hallway, key in hand. Sensing movement close behind her, she spun around once again. No one there. Yet the prickly sensation lingered as though someone was watching her.

"Natalie?"

There, a few feet away, a tall slender man had just exited a door she'd never seen before. In chino shorts and a polo shirt, he looked like he was heading out for a round of golf.

"You're not Natalie," he said, his head tilting to the side – a human question mark.

He studied her as she studied him. He was a good-looking Asian-American guy with dark hair – a little spiky on top –

and large, inquisitive eyes. More European than Asian, she decided.

He pulled his door to, triggering a soft buzz and a click as the door locked.

"You must be Natalie's younger sister? A niece?"

She had no clue what he was talking about or why he was standing beside a door that didn't exist yesterday. What the hell!

Squinting in the bright light, she was baffled to find the hallway transformed. The antique ceiling globes were gone, replaced by modern light fixtures. The deep green walls were now pale cream and the wainscoting had been removed. Plus, the hallway was longer now with eight doors instead of four.

"I didn't know she had company," he said, as though trying not to alarm her. "I live here in one eleven." He gestured at the door from which he'd emerged. "The name is Ian."

She glanced from his door to hers, discovering the heavy wooden door to her apartment had been replaced with a smooth white door. No beveled panels, no woodgrains.

Was this a virtual reality projection? If so, it was the most realistic VR she'd ever seen. Must be Hawke's idea of a prank. She would kill him later. Pranks were not welcome on what could be the most important day of her life. Right now she had to get going.

She gripped her key, ready to lock the door and be on her way. But the doorknob no longer had a keyhole.

The man moved closer. He seemed so real! This was like an amazing hologram. Where was the projector?

Touching the door, it was the same as the door her eyes were seeing – smooth and featureless. And the doorknob definitely had no keyhole.

"There's a keypad," the man said, pointing.

She couldn't resist touching his arm, but yanked her hand away like she'd burned her finger. Not virtual reality.

His expression turned wary, as if he was standing too close to a buffalo in Yellowstone Park that was about to gore him.

So if this wasn't a virtual reality gag, then where was she? And how did she get here? This was not the converted mansion she lived in.

"I don't have time for this!" she cried.

She touched the keypad on the wall by her door but there was no buzz, no click. She tried again. Nothing. Withdrawing her phone from her pocket, she cursed under her breath to find it dead. She marched down the hall looking for the front entrance but the entryway wasn't where it was supposed to be.

Some other time this might be amusing. Right now it was exasperating. There was an elevator on her left. Beside it was a door that opened onto a stairwell. She trotted down the stairs, her suitcase thumping along behind her, coming out in a well-lit underground parking deck. Where was her car? She left it in the small parking lot out front, not here in a random parking deck she'd never seen. She was about to retrace her steps to the first floor when the stairs door opened. It was the guy from the hallway.

"What did you say your name is?"

"Ian. Ian Stewart."

"Right," she said, thinking that was an unexpected name for an Asian-American guy, "So Ian, I don't know what's going on here, but I've got an important show tonight. I can't afford to be late. I need to find my car. What's the quickest way to the parking lot out front?"

"I can give you a lift." He gestured at a small white vehicle that looked like a melted Volkswagen Beetle.

"I'd rather drive mine, thanks. How do I get to the parking lot?"

His stare was like that of an alien waiting for permission from the ET-in-charge to kill and eat her on the spot.

Shaking her head to erase that thought, she left him standing there, a bewildered expression on his face.

She found the exit ramp, making her escape on foot. When she emerged into the hazy sunshine, she could feel her body break into a sweat. It was a good thing she could freshen up tonight at the venue before taking the stage. If for some strange reason she couldn't find her car, she'd take a bus to the transit station. She used to take the subway to gigs, but got tired of struggling to pull a keyboard through the gate and onto the train. Then it hit her – if she didn't find her car, she wouldn't have a keyboard for tonight's show. She groaned.

"Let me drive you," Ian called out as his odd little vehicle zipped out of the parking deck, soundlessly pulling even with her.

She scoured her surroundings. Where were the trees, the grass and the old homes? The neighborhood was gone, replaced by apartment buildings resembling giant grey and tan Legos stacked one on top of the other. What a contrast with the big Victorian home that she lived in with its pale blue exterior, white shutters and wraparound porch.

"I know the city," he said.

She took stock of him. He didn't look like a serial killer. In fact, there was something about him that made her trust him even though he was a suburban guy who likely wasn't used to navigating the city at night. This was Westchester County, after all – a suburb.

With no sign of the tree-shaded parking lot, she stowed her belongings in the back of his car and hopped in beside him. She gave him the name of the venue and the address. He repeated it as if dictating to someone, then touched a screen on the dash. Meanwhile, she pulled her phone out again. She would ask Hawke to rent a keyboard on his way. She couldn't haul one in this dinky little car. But her phone was still dark.

She'd ridden in a self-driving car before. Even so, she found it a disagreeable experience. She would've preferred getting to the venue as fast as possible. Ian busied himself adjusting a map screen to get a better viewing angle as the car crawled through the city. The busy streets looked familiar, yet different somehow. The cars looked odd, like Ian's car. And they were disconcertingly quiet. When they pulled to the curb nearly an hour later, irritation got the best of her.

"This is not the Triple Vee! God, I feel like someone slipped me a mickey." She looked in all directions but had no idea where they were.

"Slipped you a—"

"I'd call for an Uber but my phone is comatose."

"A Nuber?"

"Can you Google the Triple Vee?" she said, aggravation front and center. "I suppose it's possible there was damage to the building and I didn't get the message?"

It would be just like Hawke not to pass along that kind of information if the bar contacted him instead of her.

When Ian didn't find a listing, she closed her eyes, holding one hand over her face.

"We invited everyone," she moaned. "Media people, music industry people, a booking agent, a record company rep."

He asked his phone to search for a bar called Triple Vee.

"No hits," he said. "Type your band name in for me." He handed her an ultra-thin phone that unfolded to create a larger screen.

"Why?"

"To check your website for tour dates and venues."

"You think I don't know where we're playing tonight?" she snapped.

He held up his hand in a 'calm down' gesture. "Thinking it would help to verify the—"

She didn't wait for him to finish, entering Hawke & Carly in the search bar and slapping it into his hand.

"No hits," he said.

"Impossible!"

She was seething. After a few seconds of silence she asked him to drive to another venue the band had recently played.

"How will that help?" he said.

"Managers know the competition. They'll know about the Triple Vee."

"So you're Carly?" he said as he took control of the car, making an illegal U-turn.

"Yes." She drew the word out like he was a dimwit for asking.

"Who is Hawke?"

"He's my partner in the band. We write the songs, do the vocals, the arrangements, line up gigs, manage the money."

"I'm guessing you have his number?"

"In my phone. But, as I mentioned, my phone has turned into a brown bear and gone into hibernation."

She tried to hide her anger, and yes, her deep disappointment. She'd worked so hard. Tonight was supposed to be their big break. Instead, she seemed to be trapped in an episode of *Black Mirror*.

She wondered about Hawke and the guys. Would they muddle through the set list? Would Hawke call someone to sub for her? Would they cancel the show? Surely, he wouldn't debut her song without her. Granted, he'd be pissed. Understandably so. She imagined his eyes shooting bolts of lightning as he attacked his Stratocaster. The E string would break when he played his solo in "Not Going Back."

When they arrived at the second address to find no bar there either, her hands balled into fists.

"What. Is. Going. On? Are you positive we're in the East Village?"

"Of course I'm—"

"I want out!" she roared.

Leaping from the car, she took a few steps in one direction, then turned the other way, completely disoriented. Across the street, she spied a building with bushes and vines covering its exterior. She'd seen plant-covered buildings in pictures but not in person. But there was no time to investigate.

Ian rolled the window down, calling out to her. "Let me help you!"

"You're in on the joke!"

"Joke?" He raised his hands, all innocence.

"Hawke has a sick sense of humor. He hired you, didn't he?"

He paused to rub the back of his neck. "Let's visit the Neon Biome. My friends were there last week. It's a live music bar not far from here."

"Never heard of it!"

"You can ask the manager about the Triple Vee."

The words "go screw yourself" were on the tip of her tongue but she stifled them. It dawned on her that he was as clueless as she was. There was no amusement in his eyes at her expense. The last thing she should do was take her fury out on the one person in her corner. Whatever plans he made for tonight had been shelved so he could participate in the wild goose chase she was leading him on. That's how he must see it anyway. He was twisting himself into a pretzel to help her even though he probably thought she'd broken out of a mental hospital.

She got back in the car.

~

The Neon Biome was the most outrageous bar she'd ever seen. And she'd seen plenty. The flashing colors were blinding. The floor vibrated with the beat like it was designed for the deaf so they could feel the music through their feet. The people were all sizes, all colors, and half of them were dressed – if you could call it that – in bits of shiny fabric attached to strategic areas of their bodies while they spasmed to the music. Her clean-cut escort did not fit in.

A band cranked out overdriven hard rock with a machine gun beat, the high-decibel sound caroming off the walls. A drone drifted above the crowd unnoticed as it hugged the ceiling like an inverted robot vacuum cleaner. She pointed it out to Ian who said some bars used them to keep an eye on customers.

When they cornered the manager, he was irritated at being interrupted.

"Triple Vee? What's that? A hallucinogen?" He chuckled as he started toward the back, Carly close behind.

"It's a well-known live venue," she said, indignant. "Standing room only for big name bands."

"*Was*. Past tense. Triple Vee died of natural causes, like, fifteen years ago."

His answer knocked the air out of her. Ian touched her elbow, guiding her from the darkened backstage area, through the packed, gyrating club to the busy sidewalk outside.

Finding her voice, she sputtered as they climbed in the car. "I don't get it. Triple Vee packs them in every weekend. It took us a year – and my new song – to get a booking."

Ian murmured, "mm-hm," giving her a sympathetic nod.

"Triple Vee didn't close down years ago. He's full of it."

There was another "mm-hm."

"He must be high. Either that or he's an ass!"

They returned to the cookie-cutter apartment building, the historic mansion nowhere to be seen. She followed him inside, watching as he sat down at a desk with a flat keyboard and a wafer thin black box. There were two large screens so thin, they looked like sheets of Saran Wrap clinging to the wall.

It didn't take long to find what he was looking for. He pointed to a web page on the screen above him, reading aloud: "The rock band known as Hawke & Carly peaked as they recorded their debut album in 2024."

"That's ridiculous!" She was insulted that her band was written off so casually, giving him a rapid-fire list of their accomplishments to prove her point. "My new single has been out for two weeks and it's already been picked up by more playlists and podcasts than I can keep track of! I mean, you can hear my song on the radio! And it's selling like gangbusters and racking up streams on Spotify, Apple and other platforms! Our music video is trending on YouTube and there are loads of videos with my song on TikTok. We've been invited to play two big festivals next spring. And get this – we have a meeting next week with a major record company interested in signing us! If that's not enough, my song has made it on the Hot One Hundred chart! We haven't peaked! We're just getting started!"

Ian turned to her then, a gentleness in his expression. He seemed to weigh his words before speaking.

"They're talking about a band that almost made it big back in twenty *twenty*-four."

"What do you mean *back* in twenty twenty-four?" She gave him a frosty stare. "This *is* twenty twenty-four!"

He hesitated a beat before responding. "This is twenty *fifty*-four. Twenty *twenty*-four was thirty years ago."

He navigated to an online news site, pointing to the date at the top of the page: Friday July 16, 2054.

She shook her head in disbelief.

He clicked on a weather site. It said Friday July 16, 2054.

She continued shaking her head.

He jumped to another website.

She squeezed her eyes shut, refusing to look.

<u>2</u>

Feeling dazed, she pulled her knees to her chest, seated on a small grey sofa in Ian's tidy living room. He set a glass of cold water on the lamp table, then sat in a chair opposite her. He seemed to be waiting. For what, she didn't know. Possibly for her to explain. But Carly couldn't explain anything. And she was too drained to give voice to the panic metastasizing in her body.

Despite her best efforts to ignore the mounting evidence, she could no longer deny that she was now filling her lungs with air thirty years in the future. Which meant those thirty years were gone. Not gone like they would be if she'd coasted along day by day as time slipped away. No, those thirty years were gone like she'd never lived them at all. In point of fact, she had *not* lived them. Her hair was still strawberry blonde. There were no wrinkles creasing her face. No arthritis in her knees. She was a thirty-one year old woman. If she'd arrived in 2054 in the usual manner, she'd be sixty-one. She was used to improvising – handling whatever was thrown in her path – but this? She couldn't wrap her head around this incredible turn of events. Incredible in the original sense of the word – too extraordinary to be believed, not possible. The very idea of traveling through time was outlandish, ridiculously sci-fi. It made her feel unsteady, like she'd lost her grip on a whirling merry-go-round to be flung off into the distance, landing in uncharted territory.

She snuck a glance at him as he sipped his water. If he was perturbed by the evening's events, you couldn't tell by looking at him. Perhaps he wasn't waiting for her to explain. From all she'd seen, he was a good guy. It was possible he was sitting there to provide a sympathetic ear. But she didn't want to talk. Instead, she let her eyes wander around his apartment, which was even smaller than hers.

Funny, the room was done in grey and tan, like the exterior of the building. Grey walls, tan rug, grey sofa, tan chairs. Unlike the exterior, there were splashes of blue and green, which added some human warmth. Hanging on the walls was evidence that a music lover lived here – a couple of framed album covers by performers she didn't recognize, along with an old acoustic guitar and a brass Zildjian crash cymbal.

He cleared his throat softly as if alerting her that he was about to speak.

"You know," he began, his voice reminding her of a cup of honey lavender tea, "when I first saw you, I mistook you for Natalie. You don't truly look alike, but you both have long blonde hair, although hers is darker."

She lifted her glass, needing to wet her throat.

"Then," he went on, "I had you pegged for a burglar who'd broken into Natalie's apartment. But you stomped around trying to figure out where you were rather than escaping with your haul, so I tossed the burglar theory. Next, I was convinced you must have mental problems. You were doing some crazy stuff, like touching my arm as if checking to see if I was real, and then there was all that business about the Triple Vee." He paused, gauging her reaction. "I discarded that theory too. My gut tells me you're sane, that something genuinely weird happened to you." He chuckled. "Although, who knows, I could be wrong."

He was one of those people who talked with his hands. Lots of gestures as he spoke, his hands punctuating the words as though words weren't quite enough to convey his meaning.

She suspected he wasn't expressing his real opinion though. He was going along with whatever she said. More than likely, he would place a call tomorrow to get his unexpected guest some psychological counseling. She would do the same if she were in his shoes.

The thought hit her – from his vantage point she did look a little crazy. Dressed for the big show, her long hair was now splayed over her chest and shoulders like straw sent flying in all directions during a hurricane. With her eyes wide in panic, she must look a fright after dashing around like a maniac, working up a sweat.

She wanted to say something to reassure him that she was of sound of mind, but she was afraid her voice would tremble. Setting her glass down, she tugged her knees close again, wishing she could go to sleep and start the day over so it would play out like it was supposed to.

"Do you have family here?" he said.

She nodded absently.

"We could drive over to your parents' house," he suggested.

"My parents are dead."

"Jesus, I'm sorry."

She didn't want to talk about it. Her mom and dad were among the early victims of the pandemic. They attended the funeral of a close friend in March of 2020, unaware that the virus was already sweeping across the country. They did a lot of hugging and shaking hands, then sat in a crowded sanctuary with hundreds of people. Two weeks later, they were both in the intensive care unit. The pandemic hollowed out the very heart of her family.

It also gutted Carly's livelihood for a year. All her gigs were cancelled and her income evaporated. She found herself living in her parents' home after they died. Their passing created a black hole in her family from which no light could escape. The nightmare caused a rift between her and her brother and sister over how to handle the modest estate.

"My brother and sister both want the house," she said, giving Ian the address. "It's in the Bronx, north of the Harlem River."

He got results immediately, transmitting the page to the screen above him so she could see for herself.

The picture caused her to gasp. It hadn't been that long since she visited. At which time everything looked normal – speckled red brick, white shutters and a pin oak out front, along with the baby dogwood she'd given her dad for his birthday the summer before Covid hit. He planted it by the front walkway. In the photo she was staring at, a very large dogwood stood by the walkway to the porch. The sapling she gave him would've taken decades to grow that big.

As the truth began to sink in, she realized her priority since stepping through her door into that featureless hallway shouldn't have been getting to the Triple Vee for the show. Her priority should've been going home as fast as possible.

She needed to walk back through the doorway that brought her here.

Ian opened his mouth to speak but a chime sounded on his phone. He touched the screen and, as if by magic, the quiet was shattered as a buff Latino guy and a pretty Black woman with a soft halo of dark hair strolled in. They were flashy tropical birds, their arms wrapped around each other.

"Hey, compañero, you didn't show!" the man said, giving Ian a friendly shove. He moved like someone who found it hard to stand still.

"Now we know why," the woman said, eyeing Carly with amusement.

She had mischievous eyes and several colorful tattoos.

Before Ian could make introductions, they did the honors.

"I'm Ian's neighbor, Mona Durham from Atlanta, Georgia." Said with an intentionally cartoonish southern drawl. "This is my lover Jaxon Cruz who works with Ian but whose priority in life is yours truly." She planted a juicy kiss on her boyfriend's lips, sliding her fingers inside the waistband of his form-fitting pants.

"I'm from Jersey," the man said when they came up for air, using an equally cartoony pronunciation, making it sound like joy-zee. "Everyone calls me Cruz." He had a couple of tattoos as well and wore his black hair shaved on the sides and long on top.

"Yeah, well, everyone calls me Gorgeous," Mona said, pressing herself against him so that her perfect butt cheeks were on display in micro booty shorts.

"And this is my friend—" Ian started.

"Katie Gambill," Carly jumped in before he let her real name slip.

They stared openly, not bothering to hide their curiosity.

"Where'd you guys meet?" Mona asked.

"In the hallway," Ian said, picking up on Carly's reasoning. "She was arriving as I was leaving."

Carly ran with it. "I came to see Natalie but she wasn't home. Do you guys know her?"

Although Ian still looked his easygoing self, Carly sensed he was curious as to what she had up her sleeve.

"Boy, do we!" Mona said. "She's the music maven of the building. Always tipping us off to her latest finds from last century rock 'n' roll. She works at a store where they sell old tech, like vinyl albums, CDs, tapes, DVDs, you name it!"

"Any idea when she might be home, what her schedule is?" Carly asked.

"Nobody knows Natalie's schedule," Mona said.

"Even Natalie doesn't know Natalie's schedule," Cruz added.

"Pretty sure Natalie's never even heard the word *schedule*," Mona went on, sharing a knowing look with her boyfriend.

"Yeah," Cruz said, "if there's one thing we can all agree on, it's that Natalie is as unpredictable as the passing of wind at midnight during a heat wave."

Mona's big hoo-hah prompted a theatrical bow from her beau.

"If I had to guess, I'd say Natalie is bar hopping tonight," Ian said.

"Yeah, trying to turn a young guy on to some obscure band from the nineteen seventies," Mona said.

"While also trying to turn that young guy on to an older woman who plays her music on a turntable," Cruz added.

The two of them exchanged an amused look.

"We're headed to Hunter's party," Mona said. "You two should vámonos with us. That's right, isn't it, honey? Vámonos?" Said with doe eyes aimed at Cruz.

"Sounds good," he replied.

"He's teaching me to speak Spanish," she said.

Cruz smiled with pride.

"You guys go on," Ian said. "I think we'll pass."

"Good Time Gummies guaranteed," Cruz sing-songed like it was an opportunity too good to pass up.

Ian laughed and escorted them to the door.

There was some whispering as they said their farewells. Carly heard Mona say, "what if she's got a gun?" When the goodbyes were over and the door was closed, quiet reigned once more.

"Sorry about that," Ian said. "Mona's a great neighbor. She has a PhD in physical therapy and can work the knots out of your muscles like a five-star butcher chef." He placed his hands on his lower back, miming his ecstasy. "She's the only physical therapist I allow to needle me. Great technique!"

It was an amusing image – Ian groaning with pleasure while Mona stuck him with needles after working his body over like it was Silly Putty. Still, she couldn't quite manage a smile.

"You asked her to put me up for the night." She unfolded her legs, rising from the sofa as she pushed her hair off her shoulders so it fell down her back. "She's right to be cautious. She doesn't know who I am. Of course neither do you."

"I wasn't trying to get rid of you. I thought you'd be more comfortable staying with a woman."

"I don't blame you for being leery. Anyway, I've gotta go home now."

"How?"

"I think I need to go back through that door."

"Natalie's door?"

"It must be my door too – the door to my apartment."

He said nothing, eyes unfocused like he didn't want to be the one to tell her she was nuts.

"Can you text Natalie and see when she's coming home?" she said.

"Already did. No reply."

"Does anyone have a spare key to her place?" She recalled the keypad, realizing her mistake. "I mean, is anyone able to get inside her apartment?"

"Me, until recently. I had her passcode because I used to take care of her cat when she was out of town. But the cat died a few weeks ago and she reset the code on the security system."

"Management must be able to open the door."

"Yeah, but we can't exactly claim there's an emergency."

"Good point." She crossed to his door, studying it. "I'm guessing it's not easy to break in."

"Don't worry, she'll be back later tonight. Or tomorrow. You can spend the night here. Right now, I'm starving. Taco salad okay by you?"

She hadn't noticed she was hungry until he mentioned food.

They moved to the tiny kitchen that opened off the living room. It had a comfy feel to it with sage green cabinets and blue bar stools. A bamboo shade covered the window with an artificial vine trailing down one side. On the wall beside the window were a few framed family photos. In one, Ian and another guy who had to be his brother stood with a man who had to be their dad. In another one, there was a smiling Ian in cap and gown. And there was a group picture that included Ian at the Grand Canyon.

He cooked ground beef, adding taco sauce and beans while she sat at the kitchen bar shredding lettuce and dicing tomatoes.

His phone chimed. This time it wasn't the door. It was a call.

She noticed then that he was wearing nearly invisible earbuds.

"Hey, Dad. How about I call you back in half an hour? I'm having supper with a friend."

There was a pause.

"It's no big deal. I'll get it down for you after we finish eating. See you soon." He disconnected.

"My father hates texting. Plus, I think it does him good to hear my voice. He's disabled. Every once in a while something happens that he can't take care of on his own. Like tonight. He wants a can of peaches for his middle-of-the-night snack but it's in the highest cabinet and he can't reach it even with his grabber. He can't use a stool because his sense of balance is out of whack. And his neighbor is out of town."

When the food was ready, he pulled two brown bottles from the fridge, raising his eyebrows in question as he held them up for her to see.

"Don't think I need a beer tonight," she said.

"It's non-alcoholic."

"You don't look old enough to drink near beer."

"How old do you have to be?"

"At least sixty."

He chortled.

"Okay, I'll have one," she said.

He clicked his phone to stream some music while they ate, transmitting the audio to unseen speakers. It was pop music but had a synthetic sound that grated on her ears.

She asked more about his father.

"He's disabled because of back surgery that was supposed to fix a couple of major problems but ended up ruining his life." He raised both hands in frustration.

"I don't understand. How did it happen?"

"Dad's been asking that very question for five years."

"Can he walk?"

"Short distances with a helluva lot of pain. He used to be an active guy – played pickle ball, tennis, loved hiking, bicycling, enjoyed travel. Now? He lives his life mainly within the four walls of his apartment, except for doctor visits. The surgery shifted his center of gravity, wrecking his sense of balance. When he's walking, or even just standing still, he feels like he's on a boat that's rocking on the water."

"That pisses me off and I've never even met him."

"I don't want you to be any more pissed off than you already are, but thanks for caring."

When they finished supper he invited her to go with him to his dad's condo but she stayed behind, feeling drained. She also wanted a chance to wander around the building. Before leaving, he gave her a security code for his door. He cautioned her as he was leaving.

"Crime is low around here because of all the cameras inside and outside the buildings. Still, be careful."

Five minutes later, she stepped through the door to the hallway, poking along as she passed Natalie's door – apartment 113. It was hard to resist the urge to try again to get inside. It was Ian's heads-up about security cameras that stopped her.

She was going to take the stairwell to the parking deck, but spotted a door further down, on the opposite side. She'd been too agitated earlier to notice it. The door led to the building's front entrance. When she reached the lawn, streetlights and a couple of lampposts provided enough light to see where she was going. The old oak tree was the one thing that remained from before the mansion was demolished. It was the sole redeeming feature of the building's exterior. A couple of benches were positioned along sidewalks that crisscrossed the property. She chose one that gave her a view of the tree. Catching a glimpse of a lightning bug flashing his lonely light in the deep shadows, she felt sorry for him. He wasn't likely to find a mate this late in the summer.

She used to occasionally sit on the front steps and look at this same tree while enjoying a vape, a habit she gave up when she got serious about taking care of her voice. Now the mansion was gone and with it the quaint wraparound porch.

A crescent moon and a smattering of stars were visible in the night sky. Which took her back to a few nights ago when she cajoled Hawke into walking outside with her after they ate Chinese take-out and worked on a new song he was writing. He was the embodiment of a rock star with his rugged good looks and shaggy brown hair. There was also the ever-present three-day stubble, an earring in his left ear and an attitude that made him look cool no matter what he wore. He preferred loud bars with a glass of whiskey in his hand. Yet sometimes he would sit on the porch with her. He was a different kind of guy in those moments – a guy who didn't need to be the center of attention, who didn't have to preen or strut. That's when she liked him best, when he gave her his undivided attention. But those moments were few and far between.

They were tip-toeing around each other after a fiasco of a gig the night before. Although he denied it, she suspected he was drunk or high when he agreed to sub for another band at The Dugout Lounge, a venue they stopped playing months ago because of all the bullshit they had to put up with. The bar only paid a percentage of liquor sales, which meant they lost money every time they played there. An inexperienced kid ran the board on a worthless sound system. The men's bathroom reeked of urine so bad, the smell overwhelmed the area near the stage. She got tired of demanding they clean it up. On top of that, the location sucked. They were committed against their will, with Hawke failing to let her and the guys know about the show until the day of. Owen Keeler, their drummer, could make it, but Shawn Hightower, their bassist and backup singer, was already booked to play with another band. So she and Hawke spent that afternoon fruitlessly trying to find a bassist to sub for Shawn so the band could fill in for another band at a venue they swore they would never play again. Which meant she was stuck filling in the bass part on her keyboard on top of playing her own part and singing. She was ticked and he knew it. She wished they could've bailed on the whole thing but their band name was already on the bar's sign and website. And they didn't need any negative PR right before releasing their new album.

Hawke was trying to smooth things over and she was trying to let him.

"When we make it big, we'll hire a booking agent," he said. "I admit I'm not a born manager. A born rock star, that's all."

He flashed his trademark sexy smile and kissed her like he wanted to be with her for the rest of his life. Or at least the rest of the night.

She sighed thinking about him. But her wistfulness was short-lived, turning to dismay over her current predicament.

Muttering under her breath, she made her way back inside using the code Ian gave her to pass through the locked front door. When she reached Natalie's apartment, she stood in the spot where she was standing when this ordeal began after she left her apartment on her way to the most important show ever. She was desperate to see what was on the other side of that door. What if she opened it and her apartment was there? It sounded absurd, but not any more absurd than what she'd been through over the last few hours. She reached out, ready to grab the doorknob. No doubt an alarm would go off, alerting everyone, including Natalie, that an intruder was trying to break in. But what if this was an elaborate hoax as she suspected in the beginning? It made her wonder if Ian spouted all that mumbo jumbo about security cameras and crime to deter her from trying to leave. No, it couldn't possibly be a hoax. She'd seen the evidence. Like it or not, she had actually traveled to the future. And she needed to go home pronto. This was the door she came through. It had to be the time gate, or whatever it was called, that led to her own apartment in 2024. To hell with it! She grasped the doorknob and twisted. It wouldn't budge. She touched her palm to the keypad. No buzz. No click. Nothing.

At that moment, a door down the hall opened and a man stepped out holding a chubby baby in his arms. Dressed in athletic shorts and a T-shirt, he appeared to be Indian or

Pakistani with thick hair, neatly combed. The look on his face was friendly.

"Is your security system malfunctioning?" He spoke with a British accent and his tone was cordial. But then his arm tightened around the baby as if she needed protecting. "You're not Natalie!"

"I'm a friend of Ian's."

"Ah," he said, relaxing. "It's the door behind you." He pointed toward Ian's apartment.

She looked in that direction, pretending to get her bearings. "Thank you." She continued to Ian's door, tapped his security code into the keypad and entered the apartment. Once inside, she leaned against the closed door and mumbled to herself.

"Locked out of my apartment. Locked out of my life." She crossed to Ian's desk and used a pen to make a note of that idea on a slip of paper. There might be a song there, she thought, stuffing the paper in her pocket.

When Ian returned a few moments later he said he'd spoken with a neighbor who saw her trying to open Natalie's door.

"Management gives Raj a discount on his rent for keeping watch on the building. He's hooked up to a security system that sent him a notification that someone was trying to break into Natalie's apartment."

She felt like a rec league soccer player being reprimanded by an overzealous coach.

"Well what am I supposed to do?" she said, temper flaring. "Because I've traveled thirty years into the future, there's nothing in my purse that's of any use to me. My credit cards, my debit cards, my driver's license, my medical insurance card, all of them are from thirty years ago. Worthless! My phone has faded to black. I don't have an apartment anymore. In all likelihood, I'm listed as deceased by the Social Security Administration. My bank account has long since been closed. I have twenty-seven lousy dollars in my wallet!" Her voice cracked but she kept going. "I don't exist here. Which means I have one goal, and one goal only – to figure out how to get back to my own time!"

3

A sore neck was her alarm clock the next morning. She had refused to take Ian's bed. It was only fair that she sleep on the uncomfortable grey couch, not him. She'd burdened him enough already. On top of that, she let her exasperation spew forth like scalding water from an angry geyser when he got home from his dad's place the night before. It was fitting that she be punished this morning.

Hearing him in the kitchen, she slipped into the bathroom, still steamy from his shower. She followed his lead. Twisting her hair into a topknot, she showered, put the stage clothes she'd been wearing last night back on, brushed her teeth and applied a little lipstick. She left her damp hair up to keep it off her shoulders.

It smelled of good coffee when she sat down at the kitchen bar. Dressed in a black T-shirt and grey golf shorts, he greeted her with a quiet "good morning." Instead of the spiky style of last night, his hair was brushed back from his face instead.

Letting her choose which coffee she wanted, he brewed a cup of medium roast with his single cup coffee maker while preparing a bowl of fresh fruit.

"I'm sorry for losing my cool last night," she said.

"No need to apologize again. Three effusive apologies last night was plenty."

"Well, you've been generous to a fault helping the belligerent lunatic who barged into your life."

Which met with an appreciative chuckle.

"Here, have some tree-ripened summer peaches. It'll do you good."

He set two plates, silverware, the bowl of peaches and a mug of coffee in front of her. "I streamed your album last night lying in bed. Your songs are fantastic. Musically rich. Authentic lyrics. Not like all the soulless, AI stuff cranked out these days."

"See? Magnanimous Ian should be your nickname."

"I should put that on my virtual business card."

She laughed.

"It's a great album," he went on. "It's a cool mix of genres – classic rock, blues rock, some funk rock, with a little pop and R&B thrown in. But you're the best thing about it."

She inhaled the steam rising from her mug, bringing her voice under control. She was feeling a little trembly this morning.

"You really are a kind man."

"And you really have to taste the peaches."

He was right. The peaches were little slices of heaven on a crap day.

"I don't suppose you heard from Natalie," she said.

"Not a peep."

"God, I need to…"

She trailed off, the strain evident in her voice.

"Tell you what," he said, picking up his mug, "let's go knock on her door and see if she snuck back home in the wee hours of the morning."

She followed him into the hallway where the two of them stood outside Natalie's apartment. Ian touched the doorbell button, which sent a notification to Natalie's phone. A quiet chime also sounded inside the apartment. He sipped his coffee, waiting a bit before knocking. No one answered. He rang the bell again, then knocked again, calling out her name for good measure. There was no sound from within.

When they sat down at the bar again, he was busy on his phone for a moment.

"I messaged Raj, asking permission to go inside Natalie's apartment. I told him you visited her right before she left for parts unknown and left your phone behind. I said if he could open the door and let you search for it – accompanied by him, of course – it would only take a couple of minutes. He says he can't authorize something like that but he'll contact property management to ask permission."

"Brilliant. I owe you."

"No you don't."

"Last night most people would've called the cops first thing to report a suspicious character yammering like she had thirteen screws loose."

"Any average Joe would've helped you."

"But you – you not only didn't try to get rid of me, you took me to a live music bar that doesn't exist anymore, and then another bar that wasn't there. After that, you took me to a psychedelic venue that does exist and then back to your apartment to search online. As if that wasn't enough, you fixed me supper and put me up for the night. You're definitely not an average Joe!"

"Keep in mind, like a megaton of people these days, I lead a mostly virtual life. Very hum on your drum, if you know what I mean. I was venturing out last night to break out of my little cubicle for a while – go to a party that gets crowdier and crowdier – so I could hang out with some flesh and blood people where everyone competes to see who can drop the most F bombs without saying anything remotely interesting, where everyone buys into the stupidization of American culture. Then a time traveler shows up? Holy goat turds! It was like winning the lottery!"

She couldn't help smiling. "It's way too strange thinking of myself that way. As cool as time travel sounds to Trekkies and Whovians, I don't have time for a detour to the future."

"Trekkies and Whovians?"

"Fans of *Star Trek* and *Doctor Who*."

"Right. Classic sci-fi."

A chime sounded and Ian clicked on his phone to open the door. Cruz ambled through the living room, arriving in the kitchen, eyes half open.

"I need a cup of wake-the-hell-up," he muttered, brewing himself a cup of coffee like he was Ian's roommate. Then he rummaged in the cabinets until he found a breakfast bar, explaining that he and Ian were working on a project together.

When his coffee was ready, he filled a mug and joined them at the bar.

"You ever connect with Natalie?" he asked Carly.

"She's not back yet."

"Not reachable at all?"

"Not replying to texts," Ian said.

"If I know Natalie, she's gone to a retro cover show in some podunk town. You know, a cover band playing the biggest hits of a band like Fleetwood Smack."

"She likes Fleetwood Mac?" Carly said.

"I'll say! She loves seventies music. She likes the two women singers, Stevie what's her name and—"

"Nicks," Carly said.

"Yeah, Nicks. And somebody Mc-something."

"Christine McVie."

"You're a fan too?"

"You might say that."

She didn't explain that Fleetwood Mac was one of her musical influences, in large part because of those two women. What a coincidence that this Natalie person was a fan too.

"If you guys are friends," Cruz said, "I guess you know what a rabid fan she is of all that Stone Age rock n' roll."

"I'm a rabid rock fan myself. But I think the Stone Age of rock would've been the nineteen fifties. The nineteen sixties might've been the Bronze Age. So the seventies could've been – what? – the Iron Age?"

Ian snickered as he used his phone to stream some classic rock through ceiling speakers. She didn't know if it was his own musical taste or if he was bending to what he assumed was her preference. "I Can't Get No Satisfaction" was playing.

"Ah, the Beatles," Cruz said, nodding sagely.

"Dude, surely you know the difference between the Beatles and the Rolling Stones," Ian said.

"Of course I know the difference! The Beatles had four guys. The Rolling Stones had more than four. Plus the big tongue."

Ian rolled his eyes for Carly's benefit.

Looking chagrined, Cruz changed the subject.

"Saw Raj on the way in. He's in his happy place now that he has something to keep his eye on. Namely, you two." Said with a playful smirk. "He saw you walking around outside last night," he said to Carly. "Natalie does that sometimes."

Ian checked his phone then, giving Carly a secret look as he strolled into the other room for some privacy. She chatted with Cruz to keep him busy.

When Ian returned, he said it was time for him and Cruz to get to work.

"I'll clean up," Carly said.

"Cool."

Coffee mugs in hand, the men left her at the bar.

Cleaning up would take a few minutes. Then what was she supposed to do? She was still sitting on her stool, staring into space when Ian reappeared, whispering so Cruz wouldn't hear.

"The guy with property management gave Raj the green light for letting you into Natalie's apartment. He says tonight at seven-thirty works for him. He'll give us five minutes."

"Thank you," she whispered.

A little rush of optimism boosted her spirits for the first time since she arrived. Which made her value Ian even more. It also made her appreciate his smile.

She'd been so consumed with her own crisis, she hadn't paid that much attention to her new friend. He had an infectious smile and a quick sense of humor. Plus, it was refreshing to be around someone who wasn't obsessed with being a rock star. Which was mostly her world now.

For her, it was all about coming up with new songs, improving her songwriting, maintaining her voice and polishing her onstage presence. It was so important to have chemistry with the other band members, to have that certain something that attracted audiences, making them want to watch and listen. And being an independent singer/songwriter was not just a full-time job, it was a small business, but without employees to carry some of the load. It wasn't at all like the regular jobs so many people had. Most of them could leave the job at the office. Not so for her and Hawke. It was 24/7/365.

Friends made fun of her for sending herself emails with ideas for lyrics. She hadn't seen Ian send himself any messages. She also hadn't seen him look in the mirror. He didn't seem to worry about his appearance. Hawke, on the other hand, made sure he was "on brand" every day, meaning he always had to look like a stud. For him, it wasn't that big of a challenge. Hell, he was probably born sexy. She had to work on her brand too. Although she wasn't as concerned about her looks when she wasn't on stage.

Still, as demanding as it was being a performer, she couldn't imagine being tied down to any other type of work. Performing gave her a natural high. It was a gift being able to create and play her own music. Getting lost in the music filled her heart in a way that nothing else did. How many people could say that about their jobs? She knew she was lucky.

Right now getting back to Hawke was her top priority. Not because of their romance. She was desperate to get back to her life. She fervently hoped getting access to Natalie's apartment would be her ticket home.

She could imagine the tongue-lashing he would give her. Where had she been? How dare she miss their album launch? How were they going to recover from that disaster? Then again, who could blame him?

~

While eating homemade stir-fry that evening, Ian wanted to know what her plan was for visiting Natalie's apartment.

"Plan?"

"Yeah. What's your plan?"

"Well, my plan is to walk through the door. If all the stars align, I'll find myself in my own apartment where I'm supposed to be. If it works, I guess that's the last you'll see of me. Maybe I'll vanish into thin air."

The thought left her wonderstruck.

"What if nothing happens?" he replied.

She refused to answer.

"I have an idea," he said. "Keep your phone in your purse. If you travel back to your time, you'll have your phone. If you don't, you can pretend to *find* it on the bar or the couch when Raj isn't looking. It would be to our advantage for him to trust us. It could come in handy in the future."

"To be honest, I hope I end up in my place. That would leave you to explain what happened. Sorry to dump on you like that."

"I don't mind being the dumpee if you're the dumper."

Which made her chuckle in spite of herself. If she wrote novelty songs, that might go in the chorus.

Still wearing her stage duds, minus the shawl, she paced the floor waiting for seven-thirty.

When his phone chimed, he answered and said, "Okay."

"Raj says he's ready. We'll meet him in the hallway."

She grabbed her purse and suitcase. Taking a slow breath, she followed him out the door. This had to work. It just had to.

Raj stepped out of his apartment holding the baby again. He was wearing shorts and a polo shirt with deck shoes, a more professional look than last night. The baby was dolled up in a pink outfit and seemed happy in her daddy's arms. She had his big brown eyes and long lashes.

"Priya is working a long shift at the hospital," Raj explained. "I'm hanging out with Veda."

He was unapologetically a good daddy. Which Carly admired. She gave little Veda a warm smile. The baby lowered her head onto her father's shoulder and averted her eyes.

"Thanks for doing this, Mister Kumar," Carly said.

"Call me Raj."

She thought he'd ask some questions but he simply placed his hand on the keypad. The lock mechanism released and the door opened.

Her heart raced as she gazed into the darkened living room.

"After you." Raj gestured for her to lead the way.

She looked at Ian, realizing this could be the last time she saw him. She wished she could give him a hug. But that wouldn't do. A goodbye hug would make Raj suspicious. If she wasn't mistaken, Ian wanted to hug her too.

When she latched onto her rolling suitcase, that attracted Raj's attention.

"Better leave that here," he said.

She was about to make up a story about needing to take it with her but it wasn't worth giving him pause. She could replace everything. She parked the suitcase against the wall, then stood for a second in front of the open door. Ian flashed her a bug-eyed look that said she needed to get a move on before Raj changed his mind.

She braced herself, hoping with every fiber of her being that when she walked through the door she would be back in her own apartment. *Please, please, please, take me home.* She stepped gingerly across the threshold, gasping as her hands flew to her mouth. Her vision blurred as her eyes swept the room.

Hoping against hope had been a waste of time. Instead of seeing her bohemian living room with its scarves over the lamps and tasseled mauve curtains, she was now gaping at a modern red sofa, cold stainless steel lamps and white vertical blinds over the window. The layout was a mirror image of Ian's apartment with a tiny kitchen off to the left, whereas Ian's kitchen was on the right.

The baby began to fuss and Raj made comforting noises behind them.

"If you could make it quick, I'd appreciate it. My nose tells me it's time for an unexpected nappy change."

"Right," Ian said, giving Carly a verbal nudge. "Where do you think you might've left your phone?"

Her eyes began to sting. She couldn't move, couldn't form words.

"Why don't you look around the living room while I check the kitchen?" he continued. Which would sound innocuous to Raj. But Carly knew Ian was trying to help her function following the crushing disappointment at finding herself still trapped in the wrong time.

She sleepwalked into the room as he turned left toward the kitchen.

Raj took no notice, busy entertaining Veda with something on his phone.

Carly was devastated. She thought when she walked through the door she would find herself in her old apartment. Granted, there was always the possibility it might not work, but success was the only scenario she'd prepared herself for. Now what? She reached into her purse to retrieve her phone, ready to bring this charade to an end. But as she did so, familiar faces on a small black table behind the sofa caused her to do a double take. An album cover leaned against the wall beside a turntable. It was a slick cardboard album cover used for vinyl records in the twentieth century that made a comeback in the 2000s. It wasn't some random album cover though. It was her own band's debut album with the familiar photo of her, Hawke, Shawn and Owen on the front. *Happenstance,* the album title and title of her hit song, was printed across the top with the band name Hawke & Carly scrawled across the bottom in what looked like handwriting.

It was surreal. What were the odds of transporting thirty years into the future through the door of a woman who was a fan of Hawke & Carly? It had to mean something. It couldn't be coincidental.

"Nothing in the kitchen," Ian said, sweeping into the living room to stand beside her. "You find it?"

She pointed at the album cover.

"That looks like you," he whispered, his gaze fixed on the picture. He turned to study her face. "That *is* you." His voice was filled with amazement, as though he'd been playing along before, but now saw that Carly's outrageous story was true. He lifted the album with care and turned it over. The back featured another photo of the band, this one on stage. Carly's mouth was open wide as she belted out a song, holding the microphone, eyes closed. He pointed to a worn price sticker at the bottom that said Tootsie's Used Records & Movies.

"That's where Natalie works," he said.

Realizing it wasn't an empty cover, he slid the record out halfway.

"You find it?" Raj called, interrupting them.

Carly pulled her phone from her purse and leaned over the table, pretending to find it before turning around to show him.

"Yep," she said, sliding it back into her purse before he got more than a quick glimpse of her decades-old smartphone.

"Brilliant, because I need to deal with a nappy full of tinky winky."

Before taking her leave, Carly's eyes wandered from the record to a small microphone and other audio equipment on the table. This wasn't merely a listening set-up. As much as she wanted to investigate further, they had to go. And she couldn't load her arms with Natalie's audio equipment.

Raj locked up as they left.

"Can you believe that record collection?" he said. "Natalie is a vintage audio fanatic. Besides all those LPs, she's also got CDs, cassette tapes and eight track tapes."

"She's sort of a kook," Ian said. "In a good way, of course."

"That's an understatement. Did you know she used to live on the other end of the hallway but paid Mona to swap apartments?"

"Mona used to live in this unit?" Carly said.

"Yes, but Natalie paid her two months' rent to switch."

"Aren't all the apartments the same?"

"Identical! But she said this one has a better view."

"Of what?"

"The tree."

"You can see the tree from all the front apartments," Ian said.

"I know, right?" Raj replied.

"That sounds like a load of—"

"Like a load of tinky winky," Raj jumped in, glancing at his little daughter, protecting her from the word he knew was about to fly out of Ian's mouth.

4

With rather more force than necessary, she stowed her suitcase in the rack by the door, then resumed pacing the living room. If the doorway to Natalie's apartment wasn't a portal to her own time, then how was she supposed to go home?

She'd gotten her hopes up sky high, expecting to be home now and rushing to make it to the band's Saturday night gig. But no! She was still spinning her wheels in a time and place where she didn't belong. She wanted her life back!

She collapsed on the couch, her mind churning. She had a feeling that if she knew more about Natalie, she'd learn how and why she arrived here. What was the Hawke & Carly record album doing on Natalie's stereo table? And how weird that Natalie switched apartments with Mona.

"Do you suppose Mona would mind if we dropped by?" she asked Ian.

"Not if we bring pizza and beer."

A short time later they arrived at Mona's place with food and drink. She and Cruz were planning a night of bar hopping. While waiting until it was late enough to go, they had settled into a kill-or-be-killed virtual reality game with helmets on their heads and controller paddles in their hands. They laughed and shouted epithets and challenges at each other but didn't mind taking a break when the tantalizing smell of unhealthy food filled the room.

Cruz served the pizza and beer like he was the one who sprang for everything. Ian helped Carly question Mona.

"Raj told us something interesting tonight," he said. "That you and Natalie swapped apartments a couple of years ago."

"Yeah," Mona said. "That's when I knew that Natalie's as nutty as a cashew smoothie."

Cruz hooted. "I bet she tastes like one too!"

"I didn't take time to find out."

When the laughter died down, Carly jumped in.

"Raj said she paid you to do it."

"I thought she was joking at first," Mona said. "But she told me she'd pay my rent for two months, plus my moving costs. At first, I thought it was a scam but Raj drew up this contract."

"Why did she want to swap?"

"As crazyballs as it sounds, she wanted to look directly out on that big oak tree. She said one thirteen had the best view."

"And you believed her?" Cruz said.

"Okay, sometimes you have to go with the flow. I mean, she's like the mayor of Kookytown. I saw her out front one night measuring, like, the distance between the oak tree and the building, and between the tree and the property line by the driveway. You saw her measuring too, didn't you, cariño?"

"Yeah," Cruz said, "I was on my way here and saw her using a measuring app in the hallway."

"Measuring what?" Ian said.

"No clue. Like Mona said, I think she's into weird. Oh, and we saw her singing karaoke one night. It was at that upscale karaoke place where you have to audition before they let you sing."

"And boy, was she in rock star mode!" Mona said, "She was wearing a fringe shawl and belting it out."

"Like she was a world famous *Star is Born*, you know?" Cruz added. "She was doing a song I'd never heard before."

Mona held her beer like it was a microphone, closed her eyes, threw her head back and sang like she was a pop diva in need of autotune. "It was fate, baby, that brought us together. Not happenstance, that brought you to me."

"Woo, baby," Cruz sang out.

Mona caressed his cheek.

Carly had a stunned look on her face that didn't escape Ian's notice. He waited until they were walking back down the hallway to his apartment before saying anything.

"Was that your song?"

She nodded.

"I think I need a little more time inside Natalie's apartment. But fat chance Raj will let me back in there."

"What we need to do is engineer a power outage."

She shot him a confused look.

Once inside his apartment, he paced around the living room, head down as though working something out in his mind. "First of all, a little background. The security system for the apartment complex has a serious flaw. Neighbors filled me in right after I moved in. When a power outage hits, the apartment complex security system takes two minutes to reboot." He held up two fingers for emphasis. "During that time, exterior doors are unlocked, security cameras are offline and, very importantly, those door keypads are also offline." He pumped his eyebrows at her. "So all we have to do is knock the power out long enough for you to sneak in there and steal the audio stuff."

"*Borrow* the audio stuff."

"Right. Borrow."

"But how can we trigger a power failure?"

"We need to con Raj into doing it for us."

He gave her a conspiratorial grin.

Who knew someone could become your best friend overnight?

"My dad has a stash of cardboard boxes that'll come in handy," he said. "We can pay him a visit in the morning."

He began tapping away on his phone while she gathered her bedding.

Making up the couch, she noticed it was eight o'clock. If this catastrophe hadn't happened, she'd be warming up her voice as she freshened her makeup, getting ready to take the stage at a quality venue called The Lightfoot Café for the second night of their album launch tour. They'd gotten word before she left that it was a sold-out show.

She hated to think about it but wondered if Hawke had found someone to fill in for her. For tonight's show and for the rest of the month. If he had to cancel a bunch of shows, that would be bad for the band's reputation. And their finances. Sheena Christie had sung with the band before. She knew a lot of their songs. She also had plenty of covers in her repertoire as well as being good on harmony. They needed a female singer to share lead vocal duties with Hawke. After all, half their songs were written from a woman's point of view. Poor Hawke. He had a right to be mad. Even if he could sometimes be a prick, he didn't deserve to have the rug pulled out from under him. She had to figure out how to go home fast.

"I told Dad we're bringing breakfast in the morning," Ian said.

"What've you got planned for those boxes?"

"A little stage dressing."

She plopped down on the sofa wishing she was there tonight for the gig. Wishing she was there for all the gigs. There was nothing like being on stage when it was a fantastic show. When the band was cooking with gas and the crowd was into the music, it was exhilaration city! Like the Saturday night they played on the street shortly after creating the band. The crowd was hungry for connection, sick of pandemic restrictions and ready to dance and have a good time. She and Hawke and Shawn and Owen fed off the waves of energy coming from all those people. It was like she'd reached a whole new level. What a night!

Her eyes came to rest on the guitar and crash cymbal on the wall.

"Ian?" she called out.

"Yeah?" he answered from the bedroom.

She crossed the room to inspect them more closely. Both had been well used. The acoustic guitar had scratches and nicks. One of the strings was missing. The cymbal was heavily dented and needed a good cleaning.

Ian stepped into the living room.

"What's the story on these?" she said, pointing.

"I was hoping you wouldn't ask."

She responded with a puzzled look.

"In high school, I suffered from a common delusion that I was a budding rock musician," he explained. "Rockers were the go-to archetype for American boys, like cowboys used to be a century ago. Rebellious and independent with a generous helping of swagger. Not to mention, being chick magnets."

"You played guitar and drums?"

"You might say I majored in guitarology." He paused to play a little air guitar. "And minored in drumology." He performed a quick imaginary drum fill. "I was supposed to be focused on things like biology and geometry. Which means I played guitar and drums in a couple of stinko bands."

"Well," she said, "they look like they've got some mileage on them."

"But there's mileage put on a car by a top racecar driver and there's mileage put on a car by a guy who barely manages to get from point A to point B without having a head-on collision. If you know what I mean."

"So you didn't want to tell me you had aspirations to be a musician because?"

"Because I could strum chords on the guitar and I was a passable timekeeper on the drums. When I realized I was destined to be on the pit crew rather than the driver of the Formula One race car, I sold my electric guitar and drum kit. Then I hung up my old acoustic and the crash cymbal to impress people." He shook his head. "They've been collecting dust ever since."

"You know Elvis Presley could just strum some chords on the guitar. And I don't think he played drums at all."

"So I'm in good company."

"Did you write any songs?"

"A few. You'll be relieved to learn I didn't save any of them."

She smiled, trying to imagine Ian rocking out on stage.

~

A large philodendron was the first thing she noticed when they arrived the next morning, its long tendrils dangling from a macrame planter hung from the ceiling. It was one of three hanging plants that graced the window on the left wall. A tall banana palm was positioned by another window on the far side of the room. It was a space filled with sunshine.

Ian's father had pasted a smile on his face to welcome them to his humble abode, as he put it. Ian popped into the kitchen to warm the scones and perk some coffee, leaving Carly and his dad to get acquainted.

Tom Stewart wasn't what she'd pictured. Dressed in loose cotton slacks and a solid blue Hawaiian shirt, he was trim and good looking. Streaked with grey, his black hair was shorter than Ian's but just as thick. Although the corners of his mouth turned up, a deep furrow between his eyebrows appeared to be set in concrete.

"You're not ugly," he said.

So much for her expectation of a quiet, disabled older man.

"Sorry to disappoint," she said with a joking shrug.

He motioned her toward a vintage restaurant booth by the window beneath the hanging plants. It was upholstered in green leather and looked like something in a 1960s diner. Plates, mugs and silverware were already arranged on the table.

"Don't get me wrong. Ian didn't say you were ugly. But when I asked what you looked like, he told me, 'looks aren't important, Dad.' So I drew my own conclusions."

Which made her chuckle. She hadn't expected to enjoy herself this morning.

Ian had told her his dad was a semi-retired history professor at NYU, now teaching one online course a semester because of his condition. Half Asian and half European, he was about Ian's height and looked more Asian than his son. At first glance he didn't look the least bit disabled. Then she noticed his cane. Making his way to the booth, he moved as though walking through water, wincing as he lowered himself.

"By the way, call me Tom."

"And you can call me Katie."

"Short for Katherine?"

"Short for Katie Didn't Do it."

He responded with laughter, placing his hand on his ribs.

"Hey! What's going on in here?" Ian called out, returning from the kitchen.

He carried a tray loaded with scones, slices of honeydew and a carafe of coffee, with a pair of ice pack slippers under his arm.

"Here you go, Dad," he said, leaning down to put the slippers below the table at Tom's feet. Then he pulled a pair of sport socks from his pocket, handing them to his father.

Tom put on the socks, then cringed as he slid his feet into the cold slippers.

As they served themselves, Ian clicked an app on his phone and soft jazz filled the room.

"Have we met before?" Tom asked.

"I doubt it," Carly replied.

He cocked his head, looking preoccupied.

Wanting to change the subject, she asked him about the watercolor paintings on the walls. There were three small paintings of flowers opposite the booth, and a larger watercolor of a golden hickory tree in autumn above the sofa.

"I assume you're the talented artist?" she said.

"You're too kind. I'm still learning. But I enjoy painting and it's something I can do at home."

"I like them."

"Dad is too modest," Ian said. "He's a natural. He even sold some paintings recently."

"If we haven't met, then you remind me of someone," Tom said, eyeing Carly. "I've been trying to remember who."

"A couple of people have mistaken me for Ian's neighbor Natalie. Including your son."

She gave Ian a sidelong glance. He responded with a humorous lift of the eyebrow.

"Perhaps superficially," Tom said. "You know I ran into her recently."

"How recently?" Ian asked.

"Last Thursday. Asher drove me to Terra Mart and pushed me in my wheelchair to do a little shopping." He turned to Carly. "Asher Blum is a good friend of mine. He's a local honcho with the Anti-Defamation League in addition to being a history professor at NYU. Anyway, after we finished shopping, we stopped for a bite at their café. Then – boom! – Natalie sat down across from us drinking a coffee milkshake. She looked different from the last time I saw her. For one thing, her hair was longer. For another thing, she'd had a lot of blonde highlights added so it almost looked like your hair." Said with his eyes on Carly. "She said she was picking up a few things for a weekend vacay. To make conversation, I asked where she was going and she snorted like I'd said something funny. In the few times I've been around her she seems like a crooked painting that won't hang straight no matter how many times you fix it."

"Interesting," Ian said. "She hasn't been home in a couple of days. She used to let me know when she'd be out of town because I took care of her cat while she was gone. But Boots up and died a few weeks back."

"She said something odd when she stood to leave," Tom went on. "She said she should look me up. Then she chuckled and walked away slurping that mocha."

"Yeah, there's something about Natalie that keeps me on edge," Ian responded. "She can say 'thank you' and you suspect she actually means, 'kiss my ass.'"

Ian made a conversational left turn then, asking his dad what his next art project would be. The three of them chatted as they enjoyed breakfast. But it wasn't long before a scowl clouded Tom's face.

"Sorry, I can't sit any longer. Gotta take a pill and do a few laps around the living room before I do my morning PT exercises."

"No problem." Ian began stacking the dishes, depositing them onto the tray like an experienced bus boy.

It was with a good deal of effort that Tom got to his feet.

"I'll clean up in the kitchen," Ian said. "Katie, can you wipe the table?"

"Sure thing." She followed him into the kitchen to get a dish cloth and headed back to the living room. While wiping the table, she watched out of the corner of her eye as Tom took a few unsteady steps, holding firmly onto his cane. His features were twisted with pain as he sucked air in through gritted teeth.

"Dad, would you mind if I borrowed some of your cardboard boxes?" Ian called out, reappearing in the kitchen door.

"Are you moving?"

"I'm cooking up a little joke on our resident tattletale. Don't worry, I'll bring them back in good condition. I know you need to have two dozen large boxes in your closet at all times."

"You should be a sit-down comedian."

Ian laughed. It took Carly a minute to get it.

~

"So Natalie tells your dad she should look him up while she's on vacation," Carly said the minute they got in the car. "What does that suggest?"

"Can't possibly mean what you're thinking."

"Can't possibly? I think we're way past *can't possibly.* Sounds like she was planning on going back in time and looking him up when he was a lot younger than he is now."

"But how?"

"My guess: through the same door that brought me here. I definitely need to get inside her apartment."

They were quiet for a moment before Carly asked about his father.

"I don't mean to be a busybody, but what's with the ice pack slippers?"

"He's got terrible burning in his feet. So he has to cool them down. He has burning in his legs and torso too, but not usually as bad as the feet."

"Caused by the surgery?"

"Right."

"Why did he have the surgery?"

"Scoliosis and spinal stenosis. He had major spinal fusion surgery with a thirteen-inch incision down his back. Then, a couple of years later, he underwent another major surgery to remove the two long rods and all the screws they implanted because they caused more pain than he started out with. Unfortunately, all that slicing and dicing caused tons of nerve damage and scar tissue. Which turned his body into a hibachi packed with hot coals. But unlike the hibachi on your balcony, his coals keep getting hotter and hotter instead of gradually cooling down."

"My God. Your poor dad."

"He needs all that sunshine coming through the windows to help keep his spirits up."

"What about your mother?"

"He discovered she was cheating on him when I was in high school. After they split up, she married the guy she was two-timing with. After he divorced his wife, that is. Then they moved to California."

She shook her head, feeling bad for Tom. And for Ian.

The apartment smelled like bacon and eggs when they got home. Pop music was playing that had a counterfeit sound to it. Cruz and Mona were in the kitchen chowing down.

"What the hell!" Ian called as they arrived at the kitchen door.

"Welcome, buddy!" Cruz replied. "Join us! Plenty of food!"

Funny, Carly thought, anyone would think they lived here and Ian was the visitor.

They looked like they'd coordinated their outfits for a photo shoot, Cruz wearing a bright chartreuse sleeveless T-shirt and tangerine shorts and Mona decked out in a neon pink sundress.

"Katie, you're still here!" Mona said as Carly and Ian eased into the kitchen. "I wondered if you might stay a while, the way you and Ian were looking at each other yesterday."

Holding her phone away from her body, Mona leaned over to give Cruz a kiss to demonstrate what she meant, snapping a couple of selfies. Meantime, Carly did her best not to look in Ian's direction.

"Where'd you guys disappear to?" Mona asked, glancing down at her phone as she posted a picture on social media.

"We visited Ian's dad."

"He's cool for an old guy," Mona said. "In fact, subtract a couple of decades and he'd be hot."

"Any word yet from Natalie?" Cruz asked, as if Mona had finally embarrassed him talking about his friend's old man that way.

"Not yet," Carly said.

It didn't take long for the always-hungry duo to finish eating. Mona loaded their dishes into the dishwasher, leaving it for Ian to start later. They were on their way out the door when Cruz noticed the stack of flattened cardboard boxes leaning against the wall.

"Hey, man! Don't tell me you're moving out!"

Ian shook his head dismissively.

"I'm serious, man," Cruz said. "Katie, did you tell him this place isn't big enough or something?"

"I'm not moving," Ian said. "Needed a few boxes to store some things."

"That's a relief. It would seriously screw up my life if you moved away."

"You can breathe easy."

Once they left, Ian turned the volume down on the music and got to work taping boxes together.

"I give up," Carly said. "What are the boxes for?"

"They'll make a nice screen so nobody can see you breaking and entering."

5

"First, we stack them in the hallway." Ian lifted the largest box and headed for the door.

Carly followed, carrying another box. They piled them in two stacks between his door and Natalie's door. Stacked three high, they were tall enough so nobody could see someone standing behind them.

"Next, I've gotta twist Raj's arm," he said. "Your job is to be ready. When I give you the signal, you push both stacks of boxes to the far side of Natalie's door to block the view from Raj's apartment. When the power is off, the door should be unlocked so you can enter her apartment. I don't know how much time you'll have so you need to move fast. When you've got what you came for, slide those boxes back to where they were when you started beside my door. Then go back inside and stash whatever you *borrowed* out of sight. If anyone sees you and asks what you're doing, you can tell them you're moving."

With that, he placed a call.

"Hey, Raj. I need a few minutes of your time. It's about the building security system. Something's gotta give."

There was a brief back and forth, then Ian hung up.

"He's coming over. You can make like you're working on your laptop."

Raj arrived before she had time to get comfortable on the sofa.

"What's with all the boxes?" was the first thing out of Raj's mouth.

"Katie's getting ready to move," Ian said. "Borrowed the boxes from my dad."

Raj glanced at Carly, who gave a small wave of acknowledgement.

"All right, what's with?" Raj said, focused on Ian again.

"The situation with the security system is not acceptable, Raj. Everyone knows what happens during a power outage. Management needs to stop dragging its feet and fix it. Next time the power's out, I don't want someone busting into my apartment and helping themselves to my computer stuff."

"I've reported it three times. They say a fix is in the works."

"You've been saying that since I moved in last fall. I don't think they realize the gravity of the situation."

"What else am I supposed to do?"

"What if we can prove how real the threat is?"

"How do we do that?"

"We turn the power off and shoot footage of how long it takes for the security system to reboot while we also shoot footage of how long it takes someone to walk into one of the darkened apartments and make off with something valuable. Then you present the videos to management."

"I don't know."

"I'll bet Mona would be willing to help."

Carly watched and listened from her spot on the sofa.

"How do you propose we turn the power off?" Raj asked.

"I don't know. That's your department. Possibly the circuit breaker?"

Raj stared at Ian, hands on his waist.

"The lights would be off for a minute or two," Ian said.

"Yes, but—"

"Don't you think it would be better to convince management to fix the problem than wait till someone's apartment is broken into? I'm no expert but I'm guessing if you wait until a theft occurs, there could be a lawsuit. The owners and the management company won't look good. There are plenty of tenants who would say this has been going on since the security software update last summer and that despite repeated complaints, nothing's been done.

"Why now?" Raj demanded.

"I bought a keyboard the other day," he said, pointing it out for Raj to see. "I also bought a new laptop. If someone breaks in while the power's off and my stuff is stolen, I'm gonna be seriously pissed."

Raj shifted from one foot to the other.

"Keep in mind," Ian added, "everyone who lives here knows about this security failure. So if the power goes off, I wouldn't be surprised if some residents with fewer scruples than you and me, are tempted to covet their neighbors' belongings."

"Okay. I'll call Mona and see if she's available. I'd like to get it over with."

He stepped into the hallway to make the call and returned a few minutes later.

"Mona says she'll be the thief. She'll break into my apartment. Priya is there with Veda. She'll shoot video to include in my report and take notes about the thief breaking in, how long the power is out, and how long the security system is down."

"You ready now?" Ian asked.

"First I'm sending a mass text to residents of the building letting them know we're conducting a brief test and not to be alarmed."

He took care of that chore, then announced he was all set.

Ian gave Carly a thumbs up behind Raj's back as the two of them left the apartment headed for the locked circuit breaker box on the outside of the building.

Without a moment's delay, Carly retrieved the flashlight from the kitchen and grabbed her rolling suitcase. She was ready. When the building went dark a few minutes later, she turned on the flashlight and tucked it in the waistband of her pants. Its muted light was directed at the floor when she moved into the darkened hallway. She started by sliding the cardboard boxes to the far side of Natalie's door. Once they were in place, she pulled her suitcase beside her as she walked to Natalie's apartment. With the security system disabled, she opened the door with ease.

Unlike the dark hallway, there was ambient light inside the apartment from the windows. Heart pounding, she scurried into the living room, making a beeline for the stereo table. She grabbed the portable pocket recorder, depositing it in her suitcase. She also took the record album she'd seen earlier. A magazine that had been hidden behind the album caught her eye as she turned to leave. On the cover was a sepia-tone photograph of the Vandermeer mansion in its heyday. Curious that Natalie would've been reading about that before she left, she dropped it in with the other things and cleared out. As she closed the door, a voice said something. It was a woman's voice, her words indistinct. Carly froze for an instant, convinced that someone was close by. But there was no one there. She wished she could stay and listen but there was no time.

She hurried along the dark hallway toward Ian's apartment, pushing her suitcase inside. Next, she started dragging the boxes back to Ian's door. She'd moved one stack and was in the process of pulling the second stack into place when she heard a noise, this time from further down the hallway. She was in near complete darkness.

"Who's there?" a woman called out, followed by the sound of a baby babbling. It was Raj's wife Priya and their little daughter. Priya was still in her blue nurse's scrubs.

Carly held her breath. Then she heard Mona's voice from inside Raj and Priya's apartment.

"Everything okay?"

"I don't like this," Priya replied.

"Come on!" Mona said, giggling. "This is fun. I'm ready to steal your jewelry box."

Priya retreated into her apartment and closed the door, leaving the hallway quiet again.

Carly moved the second stack of boxes into place. As she retreated into Ian's apartment she was screened from view by the boxes.

She didn't waste any time hiding her loot, carrying her suitcase into the bedroom. As she closed the door behind her, the power came back on. She breathed a sigh of relief.

Now that the lights were on, she was anxious to examine the contents of her suitcase. She pulled the magazine out first. It was called *Big Apple Burbs*. Flipping through its pages, she was looking for the article on the mansion when three big sheets of paper fell onto the bed. They were large format sheets of graph paper with grid lines in blue ink, folded in half to fit within the pages of the magazine.

The first sheet was a detailed diagram of the old mansion and the land it sat on. Measurements were marked in pencil, including distances from the main street to the house, from the side street to the house and from the oak tree to the house. The diagram included more than the exterior walls. It also specified interior walls with doors marked for each of the first floor apartments.

The second sheet was a similar diagram of the new apartment building that now occupied the lot. All the same distances were marked, with interior walls and doorways meticulously drawn.

The third sheet was a close-up diagram of the door to Carly's apartment in the mansion overlaying a similar diagram of Natalie's doorway in the new apartment building. The dimensions and measurements for the mansion were drawn in red and the dimensions and measurements of the new apartment building were drawn in green. A quick glance was all it took to see that the door to her mansion apartment in 2024 and the door to Natalie's apartment in 2054 occupied the same space. Which is what she suspected. Her experience leaving Natalie's apartment a few minutes ago – hearing a muffled voice behind her when no one was there – served as further evidence of her theory.

Why or how a time portal existed, she had no way of knowing. But looking at these diagrams, it was obvious Natalie somehow discovered the portal and made use of it to travel to the past. It was no accident. She planned her departure. A big part of her preparation included moving into the apartment where the portal existed. What was not clear however, was why Carly was transported simultaneously from 2024 to this time period.

Setting the diagrams aside, she found the magazine feature on the mansion. She skimmed through the article detailing construction of the home in 1889 and the wealthy Vandermeer family that occupied it for decades. The last heir turned the home into an apartment building in the 1990s to generate income.

The mansion had developed a reputation for ghosts over the years. The article said that reputation continued after it was divvied up into apartments. From time to time people were reported missing and there were also occasions when people would mysteriously show up inside the house. A real estate agent who sold property in the area said it seemed as though the reputation attracted oddballs whose presence in turn magnified the bad reputation.

An incident at the mansion was described that nobody put any stock in. A middle-aged woman who everyone called the crazy lady, showed up in the mansion claiming to be a time traveler. That woman, Vera Miller, told the reporter she'd been living in an apartment building on the same property in the year 2049 and found herself in the hallway of the old mansion in 2019 after walking out her door. She said a man saw her arrive and said the woman he was with – Daria Jenkins – disappeared at the same time, as they walked into her apartment in the mansion. Ms. Miller said management didn't believe their stories and assumed Daria Jenkins skipped out on the rent. She was apparently two months behind and facing eviction. Ms. Miller said management didn't believe her story either, or the claims made by the man, and had both of them thrown off the property.

The article said Vera Miller stayed at a homeless shelter for some time before she found a job and was able to support herself. She described a number of things about 2049, including that the mansion had been torn down and an apartment complex had been built on the property, saying the one thing still there was the big oak tree out front. She described how most cars were autonomous electric vehicles in the future. She said she lived in apartment 113 in the building, the apartment that overlooked the oak tree. She said Daria Jenkins had lived in the mansion apartment that was also directly behind the tree in 2019.

Carly imagined Natalie studying this article, then making her diagrams after measuring inside and outside. That's what she was doing when Mona and Cruz saw her – preparing diagrams that confirmed her suspicions that the door to apartment 113 was a time portal. She likely heard voices too.

When Ian got back he was amazed when Carly showed him the article and the diagrams.

"How many people's lives have been screwed up by this portal?" he said.

"Unlike the others, Natalie used it on purpose."

Eager to hear Natalie's recordings, he hooked the small recording device up to his speakers and they sat in the living room to listen.

The recordings were of Natalie singing along with every song on the Hawke & Carly album. Sometimes she sang lead vocals over Carly's voice, sometimes she sang harmony behind Carly and Hawke. For some songs, there were multiple takes where Natalie tried different stylings.

Sometimes she also played tambourine. These were not tentative practice sessions by any means. She was comfortable with the lyrics, melodies and arrangements. There was no doubt she had sung these songs over and over. There were times when she would say thank you, as if addressing an audience.

"She targeted me. She gave herself a makeover so she would look like me and learned our music. There's no doubt in my mind that she purposely traveled back in time to replace me in my band."

"As you arrived here, she arrived in the old mansion. Mind-boggling."

"That bloodsucker is trying to steal my life!" Her hands balled into fists. "But she can't waltz in and take my place. I won't let her get away with it."

It was easy to talk big but how was she supposed to undo what had been done? Natalie had finagled her way into the very apartment that would allow her access to the portal. Carly couldn't do that. The apartment was still rented to Natalie. Management assumed she'd be back soon. The apartment could sit empty for a long time before any action was taken to rent it out again. There would likely be an obligatory missing person report and subsequent investigation. Who knew how long that could drag on? She'd already learned that passing through the door on her own didn't accomplish anything. It seemed obvious now that for Carly to go home, it would require walking through the time portal at the same moment Natalie passed through from the other side.

She leapt from the couch, pacing the small living room.

"Don't despair," Ian said.

Maybe it was his gentle tone, or the sudden feeling of helplessness. Whatever it was, that's the moment her emotions nearly got the best of her. She was trapped. And no amount of self-confidence would free her.

"I thought once I discovered how I got here, I could find my way home," she said, her voice quivering. "But it's not that simple."

"We need food," he said, guiding her into the kitchen. "You sit here," he said, pulling a stool out from the counter. "I'll fix grilled cheese sandwiches."

She gave in to his ministrations, accepting the glass of tea he offered.

"I have to walk through the door at the same time she does. That's gotta be it. Ever since I moved in, I've been hearing distant voices when I was near the door. I kept turning around and finding no one there. When I was leaving my apartment Friday night, once again I heard someone behind me. It had to be her. She must've been waiting. She must've done a lot of waiting and listening for me to walk through the door."

"But what if you pass through the door when someone else besides Natalie comes through on the other end?"

That was a sobering thought. What if, in trying to get her own life back, she screwed up someone else's life? She moaned under her breath.

"As wily as she is, I wouldn't be surprised if she's staying in my apartment for a while. It's possible she convinced the manager she's my sister or something."

He set two plates on the bar and took the stool beside her.

"Do you mind if I use your laptop to do some research on the band?" she said. "It might give me some useful information."

"I'll set you up with your own login."

He jumped up to retrieve one of his laptops, setting it on the bar between them so he could create a login for her. They ate their sandwiches and sipped their tea. He sat beside her, guiding her as she searched for articles and posts.

It took a while, but with his assistance, she found a post on a rock music blog that slammed the album launch show that night at the Triple Vee. It was tough reading.

"After receiving a copy of the band's debut album, I was impressed enough to venture out to the Triple Vee last night. I was expecting a high-energy show, but it was hard to believe the band that took the stage was the same group that recorded the album. Lead vocalist and songwriter Carly Munro was a no-show. Which was a colossal fuckup. Performing in her place was a bland, older imitation named Nelly Carleton, whose voice was fine, in the 'ho-hum' definition of that word. But her vocals lacked the power and heart of the woman whose onstage flair has been a big part of the band's draw. For his part, Hawke looked and sounded like he didn't know the music. All in all, a major bust not lost on the crowd that thinned out noticeably halfway through the set."

Beside the blog post was an image of the band on stage. She recognized Hawke, Shawn and Owen. And there, center stage, holding a mike to her mouth, was a woman with a gauzy shawl and long blonde hair who might've passed for Carly to people who didn't follow the band. But it wasn't Carly.

"That's Natalie!" Ian said, as though even now, he didn't quite believe Carly's story.

Enraged, she almost knocked her stool over getting up. Dashing from the kitchen, she sprinted through the living room, into the hallway and out the front door. She stopped when she reached the bench, a short distance from where she sat not so long ago with Hawke. She'd been filled with hope that night and excited about the future. Now it was all she could do to contain her fury.

Unable to sit, she stalked back and forth on the sidewalk, cars whizzing by on the busy street out front. She had known her absence would be a blow. She had imagined Hawke cussing behind her back for leaving him in the lurch. But she was stunned at how fast Natalie took over. After listening to her recordings and seeing those measurements, she knew what Natalie had in mind. But it was shocking that she was ready to jump right in the minute she arrived in the past. She must've known when she got there that it was the day of the album launch. She must've spent weeks doing research and preparing for her big move. Then she rushed over to the Triple Vee and muscled her way in to see Hawke as he struggled to come up with a plan. Learning that Natalie conned him into letting her be a sub for that show was a gut punch. How could he have let a nobody do that to him?

A moment later she found herself feeling sorry for Hawke. What a nightmare he faced. He would've been breathing fire when she didn't show up. And then, when this interloper turned up and offered herself as a sub, saying she knew all the songs, he would've grasped at what must've seemed like a life vest, hoping to salvage the album launch. She imagined him having Natalie sing for him backstage, asking her about her experience and making a decision to let the show go on. That's what they were used to doing, putting on a show even when the shit hit the fan – absent band members, equipment failures, flat tires, venue screwups. You name it, they'd made lemon ice box pie out of lemons plenty of times.

Like the night Owen threw his back out changing a flat tire while they were on tour. There was no way he could play drums for the show in Philly. He could hardly move, for one thing. And for another thing, he was drunk on muscle relaxants. So Carly used the drum setting on her keyboard to play percussion in addition to piano for the songs Hawke sang lead on. And when she sang lead, Hawke used a backup keyboard beside him to provide basic percussion, slipping up once when he used a reggae beat by mistake. Everyone rose to the occasion, though, and it was a good show. Ever since then, it was an ongoing inside joke when they launched into "Main Squeeze," Hawke would shout out mid-song, "reggae one drop, baby!" Owen would switch from a rock groove to a reggae rhythm and the audience would hoot its approval.

She smiled to herself at the memory. Hawke was a pro. She shouldn't blame him. The blame lay squarely on Natalie's shoulders.

She sat down on the bench, eyeing the blue Rose of Sharon bushes planted along the sidewalk. Their blue flowers were lovely. So, okay, the oak wasn't the only nice thing about this corner lot here in the future. Gazing at the bushes, she did some breathing exercises and rolled her shoulders to loosen her muscles.

"You all right?" Ian called out behind her.

"I had to vent my spleen."

"Is it vented?"

"Mostly. But I've got to confront her. There's so much I want to say. Like, how dare you steal my life?"

He sat down beside her, handing her one of two paper bowls. "Homemade mango ice cream."

Taking a small bite, her taste buds were overwhelmed with the flavor of fresh mango mixed with the sweetness of ice cream.

"Did you make this?" she asked.

"Followed along with a video."

"I'm lucky you were the first person I met when I got here. It's been a nightmare trying to wrap my head around what happened. But it would be so much worse if I didn't have you on my side. Wish there was some way I could repay you."

"No need. Like I said, how many people get to host a time traveler?"

When the bowls were empty, they headed back inside.

Taking her laptop to the couch, she resumed her search. Ian left her there while he moved to his bedroom to catch up on some of his own work. She'd been at it for a while when she ran across a post by another local music blogger dated several months after Natalie first performed with the band. He expressed disappointment that the band fizzled when they were about to break through.

"The loss of Carly Munro relegated Hawke & Carly to the lower rungs of the music ladder. Nelly Carleton doesn't have the chops to pull off being lead singer. Fans have noticed. Attendance at their shows has dwindled. Band leader Hawke tells me he's working on some new material and hopes to return to the recording studio soon to produce a second album. For her part, Carleton says she's also been writing songs. So far, none of them has made the set list. Her last name might fool some people into thinking she's the Carly in Hawke & Carly. But not the band's fan base."

It pained Carly to learn how the band went downhill after she and Hawke and the guys worked so hard. They'd paid their dues at hole-in-the-wall bars while developing their skills. Then, with a hit song and a successful album – just as they gained some traction – to have Natalie single-handedly torpedo their act made her want to scream!

She closed her eyes for a moment, massaging her temples.

Her next find was a post about a band doing a show at a bar she'd never heard of. Nelly Carleton was listed as vocalist. No further details. In fact, she couldn't find another post or article with the name Nelly Carleton. Was that the end of her music career? Or did she leave town for greener pastures?

Continuing to search in the 2020s , she looked for Hawke's name, finding him listed as bass player with Casey Newman's band. The post was dated about a year after Natalie showed up. Carly had worked briefly with Casey. He was talented but unreliable, in large part because of his never-ending romance with cocaine. It was not a good sign that Hawke was working with him. Did Hawke survive? And what about Natalie?

She realized she needed to change her search filters for more recent posts. But then an idea dawned on her.

"Ian!" she called out.

He emerged from his bedroom door.

"I don't know why I didn't think of it before," she said. "I believe I *can* confront her. How old is she?"

"She's always been coy about her age. I'd guess early forties."

"So she arrived in twenty twenty-four as a forty something year-old woman. Thirty years after she arrived – now – she'd be seventy something. All I have to do is track her down."

<u>6</u>

"As we say down south, breakfast is served, y'all!"

After a toss and turn night, Carly forced her eyes open, squinting as Mona crossed the living room carrying a basket of freshly baked biscuits, a jar of preserves and a bowl of strawberries. There was also a bag on her arm. Mona was much too loud and way too perky for so early on a Monday morning. She was dressed in an African style wrap dress, big soft braids touching her bare shoulders.

Ian came out of his bedroom as Carly sat up in the rumpled T-shirt he loaned her. He was already dressed and ready for the day in shorts and a classy Hawaiian shirt with his hair in a playful spiky style, a few strands trailing over his forehead. He gave Carly an amused smile that said everything she needed to know about what she must look like. Not good.

She hurried to the bathroom, washed up, tamed her bedhead and added a touch of lipstick before joining her new friends in the kitchen. Pouring herself a cup of coffee from a brand new full-size coffee maker that had magically showed up beside his single-cup machine, she sat on a stool across from them.

"I enjoyed playing *To Catch a Thief* yesterday," Mona said. "I got to practice my mommy skills with that plumpy-wumpy babykins. Her mother wasn't much fun. Priya didn't order me to put my hands up or anything."

Ian chuckled.

"But cutie-tootie little Veda laughed when I gave her my goo-goo-googly eyes," she went on. "Did you guys accomplish your mission?"

"Yeah, I think I lit a fire under Raj's butt so he'll make a case for fixing the security system."

"Ouch!" Mona shot back.

Carly spread blackberry preserves on a biscuit and added several strawberries to her plate.

"Cruz is gonna be jealous he missed all the fun," Mona said. "By the way, Katie, I was thinking about Natalie asking me to swap apartments. The oak tree wasn't all she was interested in. She also wanted my apartment because I told her it was haunted and I was hearing voices. She thought that was so cool! I think she wanted to live in a haunted apartment. So I was like, whatever. I mean, I wasn't scared of having ghosts exactly. Although sometimes it was a little unnerving. But who would turn down two months' rent and an all-expenses-paid moving crew?"

"You heard voices?" Carly said.

"Yeah, it was a little spooky. But they weren't talking to me. It was like I was overhearing a conversation, you know?"

"Where were you when you heard it?"

"In the living room, near the front door. It sounded like voices from the apartment across the hall. But sometimes nobody was home across the hall when I heard a voice."

Carly glanced at Ian.

"Because she was so into it, I told her about this girl named Jess who lives on the third floor whose mother used to live in the old mansion they tore down to build these apartments. They had ghost stories back then too. Her mom was a writer for a local magazine – *Big Apple Burbs*. She did a lot of research and interviewed people for an article about those ghost stories. Natalie made friends with Jess and I think she got a copy of the magazine. I asked if I could see it but she kept forgetting to show it to me."

"Wow," said Carly. "Do you know if her mom is still writing articles?"

"Her mom died last year of something."

Carly nodded.

"Oh, before I forget," Mona continued, reaching down to get the bag she had set on the floor. "I brought you a few things. A drone delivered the package this morning." She handed the bag to Carly, then wiped her mouth with a napkin and hopped down from the stool. "I've gotta go. I have a nine o'clock with a guy suffering lumbar pain."

Peeking in the bag, Carly saw several pairs of undies, a couple pairs of spandex shorts and a couple of T-shirts.

"Thanks a zillion, Mona. This is so generous of you."

"No biggie. I had a credit for a collection of high-tech sex toys I returned last week because they didn't turn me on." She let loose with a loud guffaw, giving Ian a wink.

He laughed like she was incorrigible. "Thanks for breakfast, Mona."

She sashayed out, basking in the limelight. Carly immediately turned to Ian.

"So that's how Natalie came across the magazine article. And that's how she knew apartment one-thirteen was the place to be. She must've done research to find out who was living in my apartment in the mansion. Once she knew my name, she would've learned I was in a rock band. She may have already known about my band, being such a music geek."

"Man!" Ian said.

"It definitely crossed my mind – why she chose me to switch places with. I see now it was a crime of opportunity. Once she found out I was on the other end of the time gate, then she came up with the idea to take my place."

Ian shook his head over and over.

Because he was under deadline pressure on a project he was supposed to spend time on over the weekend, she continued researching on her own, staying out of his way. She was acutely aware that he hadn't gotten much work done because of his unexpected guest.

One of her priorities was to identify bars and restaurants where cover bands played retro rock, specifically cover bands made up of older musicians. She found a place that had a Monday oldies show that wasn't too far afield.

She interrupted Ian long enough to ask if he could accompany her that evening since she didn't have a car, a driver's license, a transit card or any money. He agreed. She hoped to find people who had known Natalie. She also hoped to find someone who could tell her about Hawke and the guys.

She found an address for Hawke. But it wasn't like she could drop in and shoot the breeze. He was in his sixties now. One look at her and he'd be thinking *The Picture of Dorian Gray*. She couldn't tell him the truth. He wouldn't believe her anyway.

After having a bite of supper, she and Ian drove over to Tom's condo. He had asked them to stop by on their way to the subway station. Ian thought his dad needed help with something, but when they arrived, Tom looked like something fishy was going on.

He motioned them toward the couch. Using his cane, he made his way to a chair, sitting down in slow motion, jaw clenched.

"I was streaming some music last night – rock from the twenties when I was young – and I heard a great song by a band I saw in person one time. I liked their music so much that I bought the album after the show. I couldn't remember the name of the band, though. Not until I rummaged through my record collection and found the album. This album."

He reached for an album on the lamp table beside him, holding it up for them to see. It was the Hawke & Carly album.

"The song I heard last night was 'Happenstance.' And the band was Hawke & Carly. When I looked at the cover, I thought, wow, that singer looks exactly like Ian's new friend."

He paused to study the album cover, then focused on Carly.

"You don't just resemble Carly Munro. You could be identical twins! And that's no exaggeration."

Carly looked from Tom to Ian. She hadn't made up a cover story. She should have. This was bound to happen sooner or later. But she had expected to be gone before the sooner or the later arrived.

She was trying to think of a reply when Tom went on.

"I saw them perform a week before the official album launch. They were selling copies at the merch table. I bought it and Carly Munro autographed it for me." He pointed to the bold signature on the front cover. "I didn't know what happened to the band. They faded away. Never saw them perform again. Which surprised me, they were so good. Carly had a dynamite voice."

Carly wrestled with how to respond as Tom continued.

"Later, I read that she disappeared and was presumed dead. Which made me so sad. She was a beautiful, talented young woman. It hit me hard, partly because she was about my age, you know. Also because I was starstruck. I had hoped to see her in concert again." He paused for a moment like he had to compose himself. "When I saw you yesterday, you looked so familiar, but I couldn't place you. Then I heard the song last night, and it started coming back to me. The resemblance is so strong, you *have* to be her daughter."

Carly fixed a smile on her face. "You're right. Not many people remember her, but if they do, they always comment on the resemblance. It makes me happy that you liked her music, and it's touching that you have an autographed album."

"What happened to her? How did she die?"

"Well, it's a complicated story. Can I save it for another time?"

"Of course."

"We're headed out to a restaurant that has live music," Ian said, getting to his feet. "You need anything before we go?"

"No, you guys run along. Have a good time. I'm doing some painting tonight. Then tomorrow, Asher is bringing lunch over."

After saying their goodbyes they went on their way, Carly with mixed feelings. She hated lying to him but didn't have much choice. They drove to the Wakefield Station, New York City's northernmost subway station, south of the Westchester County line. From there, it was one easy train ride.

Falcon Head Grill was a neighborhood restaurant in the Bronx that featured live music several evenings a week. Monday was Classic Rock Night. Carly and Ian sat at the bar and ordered beers. After Tom went on about how much she looked like Carly, she used the train ride to braid her hair into one thick braid that fell down her back. Keeping it off her shoulders altered her look. Hopefully, no one else would notice the resemblance.

A four-piece band played a decent rendition of a Shaboozey song about needing some good news. Carly could relate. With long grey hair pulled back into a low ponytail, the frontman sang with feeling and strummed an acoustic guitar. Backing him were three other grey-hairs, a guy on upright bass, a drummer and a keyboardist who sang harmony. They called themselves Hair of the Hound Dog. Living up to their name, they threw in an Elvis song now and then.

When the band took a break, Carly staked out a spot at the stage steps, catching the eye of the lead singer as he descended.

"Good show!" she said.

His eyes brightened. "Thanks for coming out!"

"I like oldies. Do you guys play any Hawke & Carly songs? 'Happenstance,' for instance?"

"I think we could do that one. I'll pull it up on my tablet." He kept moving.

"Whatever became of that band?"

"They were hot for a minute, then lost their mojo after the girl singer dropped out of sight. Hawke plays some of the same venues we play. Last time I saw him, he was doing covers with a loop pedal at a neighborhood festival. Still good, but nothing like the old days."

"How about the guitarist and drummer?"

"Saw 'em a few times with other bands, but that's been years ago." He edged away.

"And the woman singer?"

"Died, I think. They never found her body. I gotta visit the facilities. Thanks for coming out."

She called out to him as he walked away. "And the woman singer who took her place?"

"Don't remember her," he answered over his shoulder and kept walking.

Two of the other musicians had already left the stage, but she caught the drummer coming down the stairs, asking him the same questions. He hadn't worked with any of her bandmates except for Hawke.

"Always complaining how he almost hit the big time till his partner bailed on him. I don't think dying is bailing on somebody, though. Not a fun guy to work with."

"He still plays around the city?"

"Yeah, he has a retro band like ours. Does a little session guitar work with a small record label."

Then he moved on.

When they launched into the second set, she could tell Ian was ready to go. But he knew she wanted to talk with the keyboardist and bassist, which meant hanging out till after the show. When the last song ended, she dashed on stage and helped the keyboard player pack up. Because she knew what she was doing, he acted like she was a hired hand, taking her assistance for granted.

"I've been trying to find a member of a band that was popular back in the twenties – Hawke & Carly. Did you know the woman singer in that band?"

"Yeah, Carly Munro. She was cool. But she vanished. Then Hawke hired a no-talent singer whose name I don't remember. Big mistake. No idea what became of her. You work for the restaurant?"

"No, I came to see the show. I like oldies."

"A bit young to be an oldies fan."

She laughed and saluted him, then hurried to follow the bassist as he lugged his stuff out the door. But he didn't know anything about Hawke & Carly. Or pretended not to. He was in a hurry to leave.

On the train ride home she told Ian she'd learned.

"If there was a way I could ask Hawke about Natalie, it would help. But there's no disguise that would fool him. He'd recognize me in a heartbeat."

"*I* could talk with him. I could say I'm writing a blog post or something and need a short interview."

She looked over at him, taking in his profile as the elevated train zoomed northward in the darkness. She'd already pegged him as kind-hearted, but, jeez, the guy didn't seem to have a selfish bone in his body.

"I already feel like I'm taking advantage of you," she said.

"I wouldn't offer if I didn't want to do it."

She didn't know how she could ever pay him back. But she couldn't pass up the offer.

~

It was easy finding Hawke's website. There, on the home page was a photo of him playing what appeared to be the same bright red Fender Stratocaster guitar he had the last time they performed together. She was thunderstruck. He looked so much older. He also looked harder, the characteristic twinkle in his eye snuffed out. A wave of guilt swept over her, as if she had caused the bitterness in his face as well as the extra years.

Scrolling down, she saw that his decades in music were featured, including the *Happenstance* album and the song that made it big. There were links to online retailers where the album could be purchased as well as streaming services where it could be heard. Recent videos of Hawke performing solo and with a band were also there. She clicked on one where he was playing with a band. He was the lead singer. Another guy sang harmony. They sounded decent, but Hawke didn't have the powerful voice she knew so well. As lead guitarist, he was competent, but not flashy. She clicked off the video. He was still cobbling together a living.

That's what she did too, supporting herself as best she could. Performing in a wedding band was how she paid the rent. She did a wedding or two a month through an agency. She also played keys and sang backup vocals with a pop music band that had a couple of gigs a month around town. Every once in a while, she even subbed in a country band. And once a week she was a music teacher at a school for young children. All this was on top of gigs and rehearsals with her own band. It could be tiring keeping up with her commitments, but she felt lucky to make a living doing what she loved. All those side gigs allowed her to produce her own songs and have her own band, which made it all worthwhile.

She clicked on another page that included a calendar of Hawke's upcoming gigs. Among the listings was a solo show at an upscale hotel restaurant, playing retro songs as part of a trio at a Brooklyn club and doing his own music at a small festival across the river in New Jersey the following Saturday.

It was good to know he was still performing. But she didn't want to watch any more of the recent videos. Better to wait until she was back home where she could see him on stage beside her.

Looking at his website reminded her that there was no one to take care of the Hawke & Carly website while she was gone. She was the one who kept it updated. Hawke didn't even have the password anymore. After he went online and screwed up the home page a few months ago, she was forced to take sole responsibility. It was bound to be forgotten in her absence. Not to mention their social media pages. She shook her head.

Ian was already typing up notes for the fictional backstory he would use to persuade Hawke to do an interview. He couldn't make up the name of a music blog that didn't exist. Hawke could easily verify that. Instead, Ian decided to tell him he was writing a story on spec and would pitch it to several websites that relied on freelancers for content. Once he had his story straight, he sent a message to the address on Hawke's website, requesting an interview about Hawke & Carly. She was impressed by his professionalism.

There was a lot about Ian that impressed her. As anxious as she had been since all of this began, and as hyper as she'd felt about finding her way home, his presence had a calming effect. He supported her, no questions asked, repeatedly joking that he was lucky to have a time traveler in his apartment. She knew for a fact that if she'd run into someone else in those first moments after arriving here, things would have been much more challenging.

She didn't realize she was staring until he caught her looking.

"A ten dollar bill for your thoughts," he said.

"You must think I'm awfully self-centered. All I talk about – all I think about – is myself."

"Anyone in your shoes would be focused on finding their way home."

"I take advantage of you every hour of the day."

"It's okay, Carly. I agree with you. There's no time to waste. Don't feel guilty."

"It's almost like you adopted a child in need. You feed me, pay my way, drive me, help me every time I have an idea. You're a saint."

"Wrong. I ain't no saint." He laughed, then turned serious. "And I definitely don't think of you as a child in need. I think of you as a woman."

The heat in her cheeks made her realize she was feeling attraction. Which was awkward. She didn't need that kind of complication. The thought hovered for a moment in her mind. She felt that weird itch again to write it down. Another hook for a song. But for the present, she had nowhere to store ideas for later.

To tell the truth, this wasn't the first time she'd felt chemistry between them. Being involved with Hawke, she was used to dismissing such fleeting feelings. But here, so far from her own time, she was enjoying Ian's company. She liked his voice, his sense of humor, his adventurous spirit. He made her question her feelings for Hawke. Of course, that made her feel guilty, as though she were cheating. Right now she needed to keep any feelings of attraction for Ian in check. She had to focus on finding a way to reverse the time travel exchange.

His phone dinged. "Hawke says he's available tomorrow morning at ten."

<u>7</u>

Sitting at his desk, Ian had his notes and questions ready. He would ring Hawke through his computer for a video phone meeting while Carly sat on the couch out of sight. She could monitor the call, seeing the live picture and hearing the audio through earbuds Ian gave her. But since there was no camera and no mike on her laptop, Hawke wouldn't see or hear her.

Her emotions were all over the place. She hoped he had information that would help her locate Natalie. She felt sure that was how she'd be able to find her way home. But it was unreal contemplating this conversation with sixty-something Hawke. He was a stranger to her. He would've gotten over his initial anger that night when she didn't show up, now believing she had died tragically. Ugh. Why did she feel like she was to blame? Natalie was to blame.

"Do you have a little notebook I can use?" she said.

"By all means," Ian replied. "And consider that laptop yours for the duration. I don't need it."

He found a small notebook and pen for her. She wrote down her idea for a song – "I don't need that kind of complication," then wrote down another phrase – "Who's to blame?" She was reminded of something her dad used to say when she was younger. After she would break up with her latest boyfriend, he would chuckle and remind her there was a silver lining to that cloud, that every time she broke up with a guy, it was good for another six or eight songs.

At precisely ten o'clock, Ian placed the call. Hawke answered promptly and Ian explained he was recording the conversation for possible use of video or audio clips in the article. Hawke agreed.

It was disturbing looking at him on her screen. She felt like he was looking directly at her as he spoke. In many ways his face was the same, but there were wrinkles now and crow's feet at the corners of his eyes, a couple of age spots and looser skin on his neck. He still had a full head of hair but it was mostly grey. His eyebrows were greying too. As before, he wore a single earring in his left ear. He sounded like himself, but with gravel in his throat.

Ian started off by asking how Hawke & Carly came to exist. Hawke relaxed and shared the story of how he and Carly met as their previous bands took the stage for back-to-back gigs. Later, when they were both playing the same venue and his keyboardist didn't show, he asked Carly to fill in.

"It was amazing!" he said. "It's like we'd been playing together for years. A natural fit. For the cover tunes, she sang harmony while I sang lead. For my originals, she caught on like a real pro. She sang some of her songs too and I sang harmony. The crowd loved it. She was a natural on stage. Of course, because she was a good-looking young filly, the guys ate it up. And the women, well, the women imagined themselves being cool and talented like Carly Munro. I knew right away we had to throw in together. It took some convincing because she was crazy independent. Acted like she didn't need me. But I wore her down. Man, those were good times."

Carly remembered it well. Back then she and Hawke did seem like a match made in rock 'n' roll heaven.

Hawke talked about how they wrote their songs, with the two of them often working together to develop an idea, then building on each other's input.

"That's how we wrote 'Happenstance.' She brought me this cool idea and we worked on it together over a period of a few days, coming up with lyrics together. It was the peak of our songwriting partnership, which is why it was copyrighted under our joint names – Carly Munro and Marcus 'Hawke' Williams. I'm very proud of that song and the album we put out."

Carly jumped up from the couch, waving both arms at Ian to get his attention, shaking her head emphatically. "He's lying!" she mouthed. "I wrote that song!" She pointed at herself.

He understood.

"I read that 'Happenstance' was Carly's song entirely," Ian said, "and that you did not contribute."

"That was a misunderstanding in the early days. It was definitely a partnership song. I mean, we called it Carly's because she sang it and she had the original idea, but the two of us molded her idea into lyrics and a melody."

"My father attended the show a week before the album's official release. He told me Carly introduced 'Happenstance,' saying she wrote it."

"She didn't mean it literally. Yeah, she came up with the hook, but we developed it together."

As he continued talking, it was all Carly could do to keep her mouth shut. She wanted to rush over, push Ian aside and give Hawke an earful. He didn't contribute one note, one word, not even a single syllable! It was *her* song and her song alone. She registered the copyright in *her* name. Joint copyright? Is that what he'd been saying all these years? That the two of them co-wrote it? Asshole!

Then Ian asked a question that surprised her.

"Fans always wanted to know if you and Carly were in a relationship. Were you?"

"Yeah, we were having an affair. You work closely with a beautiful, talented woman, it's hard to resist. But the music and the band came first. For both of us. That's part of rock band life. And if those rumors helped us get more attention, fine by me."

Carly didn't know how she felt when Hawke put it that way. It sounded like their relationship was an enjoyable pastime, nothing more. A byproduct of the music scene. Nothing that involved love.

Ian asked about the album launch concert when Carly was missing in action.

"At first I went fucking ballistic. But I knew she was as fired up as I was about the gig that night. If she wasn't there, something was wrong. It was heartbreaking. We went ahead and did our soundcheck, hoping she would show up at the last minute, you know. I called her, like, a dozen times but she never answered. About fifteen minutes before we were supposed to take the stage, I was getting desperate. We invited a lot of important people. A record company rep was supposed to be there. An agent promised to come, you know, to consider representing us. All kinds of people were coming.

"Then this woman finds her way backstage and offers her services. Nelly Carleton, she said her name was. She was dressed like Carly and her hair was a lot like Carly's. She knew all our songs from the new album, which was hard to believe since we'd basically done a few warm-up shows and hadn't officially released the album yet, except for the one single. She didn't play the keys, but she could bang a tambourine. I asked her to sing 'Happenstance' and she nailed it. Not as good as Carly, of course, but beggars can't be choosers. I was thinking maybe Carly would show up after we got going. So I let Nelly take the stage with us. We started with my songs and she did an okay job singing harmony. Not real strong, but okay. I kept hoping Carly would come dancing onto the stage in the middle of a number, but she never did. So I let Nelly sing 'Happenstance,' since it was the title cut. I sang harmony and we all did our best. And that was the beginning of the end. The agent walked out. The record company guy walked out. And we never knew what happened to Carly. Breaks my heart even now to think about it."

Shifting gears then, Ian asked what became of the other band members. He started with Nelly Carleton.

"I let her perform with us a few more times but she didn't have what it takes. Owen and Shawn said she sucked. When we stopped getting the good gigs, I had to admit they were right. Of course, Carly's the one who mostly got bookings for us. Owen and Shawn drifted off to other bands. As for Nelly, she sang with a couple of other bands. But not for long. Within a year, she vanished from the music scene. She used to call me from time to time. She confessed one time that she'd never been onstage before that first night with us except for karaoke nights at her favorite bar. Man, did I feel like a sucker. After a while, she stopped calling."

"I tried looking her up," Ian said, "hoping to interview her too. But I couldn't find her listed."

"I heard she changed her name to Emily something. Don't know where she lives now. You can ask Owen. I think the two of them were a thing for a while."

"I guess I can find Owen and Shawn online?" Ian said.

"Yeah. Owen lives in Brooklyn last I heard. Plays drums with different bands at a lot of corporate gigs, private events and weddings. Shawn lives in Washington Heights, I think. He mostly does jazz these days. Tours Europe every year with a jazz trio called Harbinger. They should be easy to find."

"And what about yourself? Married? Partnered? Kids?"

"Married to a good woman named Sheena. We have two teenagers."

Carly was floored. It was impossible to imagine Hawke as a loyal husband. It was also beyond belief that he was a father. He was most definitely not the dad type. Was it jealousy churning inside her? A few nights ago he shared her bed. Now he had a wife and teenage children.

After a few more questions, Ian wrapped up the call, telling Hawke he'd keep him posted as to when the story might be published. The soft tap-tap-tap of his typing was the only sound in the room. Then she felt his eyes upon her as she continued staring at the blank screen of her laptop. She felt like she'd been slapped in the face. Hawke could never bring himself to commit to *her*, even though he swore he loved her. But he had committed to Sheena. No doubt he was talking about Sheena Christie who sang with them from time to time.

Carly felt like she was split into two different people – the "before" Carly who was in a tangled relationship with Hawke and the "after" Carly who was sitting here in Ian's living room trying to work out how to get back to 2024. The "after" Carly knew Hawke wasn't right for her, but the "before" Carly hadn't accepted the truth yet.

"I think I'll get some air," she said.

She hid in the deep shade beneath the great spreading branches of the oak tree to shield herself from the blazing sun. Leaning against the trunk, she breathed, eyes closed, reaching deep inside herself, trying to find a calmness of spirit that eluded her. The tree was like an old friend, the one thing that survived the decades she skipped over, the sole remnant of her own time on this entire plot of land.

Normally, she thrived on creativity and ambition. Now she craved tranquility as she tried to pull herself together. Known by family, friends and music colleagues as Take-Action Carly, she found herself stuck in neutral. It was stupid to be angry with Hawke for making a home with someone else years after she left him hanging. Still, she couldn't help feeling abandoned and forgotten. For her, it was a few days since they'd lain in each other's arms. For him, it had been decades.

There was also the business of him stealing her song. That was unforgiveable. When she made it home, there would be no "forgive and forget." One thing was certain, she'd be contacting a lawyer. It was important to prove the song was copyrighted in her name. She had proof of the song's provenance – voice memos recorded on her phone from the idea stage and early performance recordings in a file on her laptop at home. The song would be copyrighted in *her* name alone and she would forge her musical path with her eyes wide open. She would make business decisions – and personal decisions – more cautiously going forward.

Lingering a few minutes more, she listened as birds called out secret messages to each other in the branches above her while music wafted from the open window of a passing car. When her heart rate slowed, she made her way back inside to find Ian in the middle of another video interview. This time with their bass player. Recognizing his voice, she sat down on the couch so she could see him on her screen.

Like Hawke, Shawn looked a lot older. He was a good-looking sixty-something Black man with salt and pepper braids. Unlike Hawke, Shawn still had a playful glint in his eye and his voice was as smooth as ever.

"When I understood Carly was probably dead, I shifted from rock to jazz, which is my real passion. I teamed up with some of my jazz buddies to form our own band and never looked back."

"Would you say Carly's departure killed the band?" Ian asked.

"Oh yeah. Without her it was an average band, nothing special. She was the spark that made it work. She was on her way up and taking us with her. Sometimes I try to imagine what it would've been like filling stadiums. But once she was gone, it was over. Me and Owen saw the writing on the wall. Hawke was in serious denial, thinking he was the driving force behind Hawke & Carly. For a while there, he fooled himself into believing he could train Nelly to fill Carly's shoes."

"Did Hawke and Carly have a romantic relationship?"

Why was Ian asking that question again?

"Yeah, although it was kinda stormy. They usually worked well together musically. As long as Hawke could control his… uh… appetites."

Carly glanced over at Ian, who seemed to struggle with what to ask next.

"Do you stay in touch with your former bandmates?" he said, opting not to follow up on Shawn's comment.

"Not much anymore. Hawke texts me now and then. Owen makes a good living drumming for event bands. We keep saying one day we'll get together, but we're both too busy."

"What about Nelly?"

"I don't consider her a former bandmate. She wasn't a musician. She was like a little girl who wants to grow up to be a princess. Except in her case, she was a little girl wishing she could be a rock diva. I never understood why Hawke let her take the stage with us that night. We should've cancelled the show rather than deliver a shitty performance."

"You don't have any idea what happened to her?"

"Hawke would know if anyone does. He kept saying she was talented and would improve with mentoring. Me and Owen always took that to mean talented in bed because we never saw any indication that she was talented musically."

Carly removed herself to the kitchen where she found a container of watermelon chunks in the fridge. She loaded a few onto a paper plate and sat down at the bar, remembering that sometimes Hawke was nowhere to be found after a show, and it wasn't to have drinks with the guys. She saw the girls flirting with him while he was on stage. And she saw the sexy smile he threw their way in reply. She knew what was going on but let it slide, preferring not to force a confrontation. She never wanted to deal with it. Too messy. Too distracting.

When Ian joined her a few minutes later he sat on the stool across from her, raising his eyebrows in question.

She thought for a moment before speaking, refusing to address Shawn's comment about Hawke's "appetites."

"They talk about me like I'm dead," she said. "I have this feeling of displacement." She took another bite, a troubled expression on her face. "And I'm outraged! How dare he claim he co-wrote my song? That song was written by me, myself and I! He's always been prone to exaggeration, but this time he's gone too far. Saying he co-wrote it with me? That's a lie the size of Manhattan! I uploaded the file to the US Copyright Office website last week. And the indie record label we worked with to produce the album registered the copyright of the recorded version of all the songs on the album. Hawke and I were both guaranteed a respectable take of album sales.

"We can look up the copyright history," Ian said. "I asked Shawn who wrote the song. He said 'Happenstance' was all yours. He said he heard Hawke compliment you more than once."

"Maddening. And I can't challenge him. I'm dead!"

When her voice caught in her throat, Ian reached across the bar and took her hand.

She stared into space, struggling with her emotions.

"By the way, just curious, why isn't the band name Carly & Hawke?" Ian said. "Why is Hawke's name first?"

She thought back to the conversations she and Hawke had about forming a band. They met at a bar a couple of times. There were a few phone calls. At first, he joked a lot, coming up with some names that made her laugh, making her think he was fun to be around. He suggested The What.

"It's no stupider than The Who," he had said.

After a dozen goofy band names, including Fig Preserves and Flush Twice, he got serious, suggesting Hawke and Carly. "We hire other musicians to play with us, but you and me, we're the band."

She liked his idea but immediately thought of suggesting Carly & Hawke instead. It had haunted her ever since that she sat there nodding her head.

She deferred to him. She did that a lot early on, treating him like he was more experienced even though he wasn't. Thinking back on it now, it was clear she allowed herself to be charmed. He's the one who asked her to form a band with him. When they were first getting started together, she treated him like he was the leader. It took her a few months to step up, demanding full partner status. By then, the band name was established. She never told him, but it was true, having his name first – Hawke – had a vibe that audiences seemed to like.

"Earth to Carly," Ian said.

"Oh, sorry. Thinking back to—"

His phone dinged.

"It's Owen Keeler," he said, moving to the living room where he could take the video call.

She left her perch in the kitchen to settle on the couch again so she could see Owen on her laptop. Unlike Hawke, Owen had been open about being a ladies' man in his youth. Now, although his blond hair was turning white, he was still handsome but acted like he'd gotten over his good looks.

Thankfully, he seemed like the same nice guy he'd always been.

His story was much the same as Shawn's. He denied having an affair with Natalie, who he knew as Nelly, saying she was not his type. But he had an old friend who moved in with her after the band's breakup. He agreed to give his buddy a call to see if he knew what name she adopted when she gave up on being a singer.

Afterwards, Ian fixed chef salads for lunch. They sat across from each other at the bar.

"I ordered you a phone," he said. "It'll be delivered in the next hour or so."

"Ian! You were already in Good Samaritan Territory. Now you're moving up to the Martyr Zone."

"Stop your fretting. It's not like it's a real phone. It's a model people get for the elderly. No internet connection. Calls, texts and a clock, that's all."

"Still!"

"You know what you need right now? You need to take your mind off all of this stuff. How about watching a movie? I've got access to lots of films."

She was about to shrug him off, but she could see in his eyes how much he cared. He was trying so hard. He didn't hesitate to give of himself at every turn, from interviewing her former bandmates, to fixing her lunch, to being a sympathetic ear for her tirades, to driving her wherever she wanted to go. She gave him nothing in return other than a quick "thank you" or "I owe you."

"Rather than a movie," she said, "how about telling me something about yourself."

That surprised him. Pleasantly, she thought.

"Well, I'm not nearly as interesting as you are."

"I've become a drama queen. Nothing good about that."

He shook his head. "You're no drama queen."

"What's the most fun you've ever had?"

"Hm. Well, if you had said the most excitement, I would've said the last few days have been the most exciting of my life. It's also been fun. For me, that is. But since it hasn't been fun for you, I can't call it the most fun I've ever had. I'd have to say the most fun I've had was playing Monopoly when I was growing up – with my dad, my brother Zack, my cousin Joey and my Uncle Hwan."

"Monopoly," she said, incredulous.

"A lot of times, it's not *what* you're doing, it's *who* you're doing it with. I've never laughed more than when the five of us played Monopoly, bending the rules, giving each other grief. Uncle Hwan was a riot. So was Dad when he was in his ruthless Monopoly mode. Me and Zack and Joey learned from the masters."

"That does sound like fun," she said.

"I also had a blast when Dad took Zack and me on trips as graduation gifts when we finished college. When I graduated we visited Korea. That's where my American grandfather met my Korean grandmother while he was teaching English in Seoul for a couple of years. It was a very meaningful visit. Then two years later when Zack finished, the three of us went to Ireland, Scotland and England, home to our other ancestors. Really fascinating and all the more special because the three of us were together."

She didn't know what she expected, but to hear him describe those family times as the most fun he'd ever had was inspiring. She'd asked that question of other friends. Their responses were usually along the lines of getting to surf in Hawaii or meeting a celebrity. It made her wish she had an Uncle Hwan and a cousin Joey. She and her sister and brother weren't awfully close, in part because of the age difference. She was five years older than Mia and seven years older than Brian.

The door chime interrupted them. It was Cruz.

Ian took his salad with him to his desk so the two of them could noodle about the project they were working on. Carly retrieved her laptop from the couch and returned to the kitchen to finish eating while poking around on the internet. She had resisted searching for her family, but gave in to curiosity now. The search didn't take long.

Although she shouldn't have been, she was stunned to learn her brother and sister were both with partners and had children. Brian and his girlfriend Alicia had a seven-year-old daughter. Mia and her husband Paul had teenagers, a boy and a girl. She needed to reconnect when she returned to her own time. It was a shame they'd drifted apart.

Ian and Cruz were busy for about an hour before Cruz took his leave. Ian arrived in the kitchen a moment later with her new phone. He plugged it into the charger before taking another call, this time from Owen's friend Miguel Perez who lived with Natalie for a while. Ian sat down again at his desk to do the interview.

"Owen Keeler told me you might know what name Nelly Carleton used after she stopped singing," he said.

"He says you're writing an article on the band they were in?"

"That's right. Hoping to find Nelly so I can interview her too."

"Yeah, well, we moved in together for a while. She said she used the name Nelly Carleton as her professional name. But then she went back to using her real name, Emily Smith."

"I don't suppose she mentioned a middle name?"

"No, but one time when she was about two and a half sheets to the wind, she mentioned that her mother called her Natalie. But she was drunk. Who knows."

"Any idea where she lives now?"

"No. She used to call me every few years but I asked her to stop when I got married."

"Finding a woman named Emily Smith is gonna be tough if I don't at least know what city she's living in. Is there somewhere she talked about wanting to live?"

"Yeah, as a matter of fact. San Francisco."

8

"San Francisco, here we come!" Ian flashed two thumbs up as he walked into the kitchen.

"A needle in a slightly smaller haystack," Carly replied.

"A needle in an astronomically smaller haystack! A big city is much better than having to search the entire country." He put his empty salad bowl in the sink and sat down across from her. "Think positive!"

"I keep trying. But I feel like I'm deluding myself. *If* I can find her and *if* she's willing to talk, and *if* she can tell me something about her first couple of weeks in the mansion to help me catch her in the doorway, and *if* I can figure out a way to put *myself* in the doorway at the same time *she's* in the doorway. Every last one of those *ifs* is the size of the Empire State Building!"

"Listen, considering how bad things turned out for her, she might like the idea of reversing the swap as much as you do."

"Even if that's true, how am I supposed to get access to her apartment so I can walk through the door when the time comes? They're not going to rent me the apartment. They're not going to rent *anyone* the apartment. And we can't trigger a power outage night after night."

"I tell you what – let's deal with one *if* at a time."

She heaved a big sigh. "Believe it or not, I didn't used to be the princess of pessimism."

"I believe it."

That evening while Ian was on a business call, Carly left the apartment. She went as far as Natalie's door. She didn't touch the knob or the keypad. She just stood there, inches from the door and listened. Hoping to hear a voice, she waited a good fifteen minutes, on alert for the slightest sound. As she was about to give up, she thought she heard a small noise that could've been someone speaking or breathing.

Because she traveled from the past to the future by stepping from her apartment in the old mansion to the hallway in the new apartment building, her theory was that it was a directional portal. If so, a person would always move from 2024 to the future by passing from inside the mansion apartment to the hallway, and would travel from 2054 to the past by stepping from the hallway of the new apartment building into apartment 113, which led to the old mansion apartment. If she was correct, then to reach her own time, she would have to pass through the door from the hallway into the apartment at the same time that Natalie walked from the old apartment through the door to the hallway. She imagined it in her mind as a small wormhole. A wormhole that, for some inexplicable reason, required two people to cross paths simultaneously.

Hearing a door open further down the hallway, she pivoted away, as though she was arriving home. It wouldn't do for Raj to become suspicious of her behavior. Then she slipped back into Ian's apartment.

When he finished his call, she told him she was ready to get to work diving into the San Francisco haystack. He gave her his login for telephone listings. Then she was left with the mind-numbing task of searching through the abundance of listings for Emily Smiths in the San Francisco area. She used her new phone to call the likely prospects.

Three interminable hours later, she was nauseated from all the scrolling and clicking. Her call list had been whittled down to a dozen names. A couple of them had the middle initial N. Of course, no one answered when she dialed. She left a brief message explaining she was trying to reach the Emily Smith who had once lived in New York. Carly identified herself by her real first name. Natalie would know who she was.

She was eating an apple, trying to banish the queasiness in her stomach, when her new phone chimed. It was so unexpected, she dropped it trying to answer. When she said, "hello, this is Carly," an older woman responded.

"I used to live in New York."

"Where in New York?"

"On the northside."

If it was Natalie, she was being awfully coy.

"The Emily Smith I'm searching for used to sing for a band. Do you remember the name of the band?"

"Have I inherited some money?"

"Thank you for calling, Ms. Smith."

That's all she needed – fortune hunters.

"I overheard," Ian said as he strolled into the kitchen. "Let's go out somewhere for supper. We need a change of scenery."

He had a point. She wasn't used to being cooped up like this. Then again, there was work to do and time wasn't on her side. Literally.

"I'm getting tiny apartment fever," he said. "You know, cabin fever but without the scenery. That's how you can repay me, by going to dinner with me and rescuing us from these four walls."

"You've made it impossible for me to refuse."

"Exactly my intention."

~

They parked the car at the transit station and took the train. Once they exited the train, it was a couple of blocks to the restaurant.

They were seated at a table on a charming patio with small trees, stands of bamboo and potted ferns. The patio was inside a large glass enclosure with a hint of a breeze that made it feel like you were outside but without the heat or bugs.

"Welcome to The Veranda," their waiter said. "Would you like to start with cocktails?"

He gestured at menu screens embedded in the table.

Ian ordered a Negroni. She selected a glass of wine.

"I'll bring your drinks. Order your food when you're ready. If you have questions, press the 'help' button." He pointed at the menu screen and a small intercom button beside it. Then he was gone.

They had ordered their food by the time the drinks were served. It was a pleasant environment, much like dining at an open-air café. And the sky was a sight to behold this evening – the setting sun making the clouds look like orange sherbet.

"Now it's your turn to tell me about the most fun you've ever had," he said.

She didn't know how to answer.

"Whatever pops into your head," he suggested.

"When I was fourteen, my family vacationed in the Adirondacks. Gorgeous views, the hiking was fun, and we stayed at a cool log cabin with a sauna. The à la mode on the pie though, was a visit to one of those sliding rocks. My sister, brother and I wore cut-off jeans and shirts and slid down this huge slab of rock covered by a fast-flowing stream. Dad slid down with Brian. Mom was Mia's partner. I was old enough to go by myself. It was the middle of summer but the water was freezing! When we plunged into the pool at the bottom, it was like we were landing in the Arctic Ocean. We did it over and over till our lips turned blue and our toes were about to fall off."

They laughed together.

"What about more recently?" he asked.

"I've been consumed with music since I was a teenager. Peak fun for me are the shows that turn out awesome. Like when audiences love the music, when the chemistry on stage approaches the metaphysical and I'm totally in the zone. Like when we played a show in Boston last week. I couldn't believe it! The crowd knew every word of my big song! It was the first time I've ever had my own lyrics sung to me! It was pure nirvana!"

A wistful look washed over her face.

"You miss it," he said.

"Yeah. Music can make people happy and make them forget their troubles. And a song can make a difference in a person's life. Take my grandmother. She said when she was depressed after her divorce, she heard 'I Can See Clearly Now' by Johnny Nash and she knew she was going to be all right. It was like a salve for her soul. Some songs genuinely mean a lot, like Bob Dylan's 'Blowin' in the Wind,' which resonated with millions of people."

He was quiet for a beat before responding. "Wow."

After their food was delivered, they were engrossed in conversation when Carly sensed someone staring at her. She didn't turn to investigate right away, instead glancing one way and another as if taking in the terrace environment. She caught sight of a man who looked vaguely familiar. As they continued eating, she realized he was a guy she dated several years back. He was a game developer she met through friends. They went out a couple of times, but she broke it off because there were no sparks. He was much older now, early sixties. She wouldn't have recognized him if he hadn't been staring at her. No doubt, he was thinking there was no way it was the same girl he went out with, but her daughter instead. She didn't want to have that conversation and turned her chair so he couldn't see her face.

She and Ian shared stories of growing up, both of them animated by the restaurant atmosphere. Not once did either of them bring up her predicament.

"I've gotta ask," he said when they finished their entrees, "are you by any chance named for Carly Simon?"

"Yes – by any chance – I am. The grandmother I was telling you about was a big Carly Simon fan. She played her albums when my mother was growing up, so Mom liked her too. When I was born, that's the name she chose."

"Like she had some notion you'd be a singer."

She wagged her head uncertainly. "How about you? Where did your name come from?"

"From a variation of a tradition in a lot of families around the world. I'm named after two of my great-grandfathers."

"So Ian is from your dad's grandfather?"

"Right. And Jeong is from my grandmother Bo-min's father. So it's Ian Jeong Stewart.

"What does Jeong mean?"

"Loyal."

"Naturally."

On the train afterwards, she realized she was having fun. There was something about riding the train with a guy you enjoyed talking with. And she couldn't help noticing his vibe tonight, dressed in jeans and a casual shirt. He had definitely attracted admiring looks while they were dining.

They picked up his car at the transit station and drove home with the windows down. The temperature had dropped nicely after sunset. Carly felt more peaceful than she had in days. Ian was everything Hawke was not. And he hung on her every word.

When they arrived at his apartment, they were stunned to find Tom waiting for them in the living room, his eyebrows in a knot. He rarely ventured out alone and never visited his son uninvited. Now though, he was seated at Ian's big desk, the Hawke & Carly record album lying in front of him along with the magazine and the audio unit from Natalie's apartment.

Carly thought Ian might be angry, but there was no scolding. In fact, he seemed upset with *himself*. But it was her fault for not storing the items out of sight. She gave Ian an apologetic look. He responded with a smile.

Tom glanced from one to the other. "I know you're asking yourselves why I'm sitting here uninvited. I acted on impulse, thinking it would be a good idea to drop in. I don't know what came over me. I invaded your privacy. My bad." There was an uncomfortable silence. "But once I got here, I couldn't help noticing this stuff." He glanced at the album, the pocket recorder and the magazine. "I've been trying to fathom what it all means."

Ian sat down in a chair, motioning for Carly to do the same.

"From what I gather," Tom continued, "Natalie left town after learning all the songs on the Hawke & Carly album. Curiously, it was almost as if she planned to join the band. That magazine article suggests there was something odd about the apartment that overlooked the oak tree. The story about the crazy lady who claimed to be from the future and the other woman from the past who disappeared, made it sound like something strange was going on." He fixed his eyes on Carly. "You showed up the night Natalie left. And you don't just look like Carly Munro. You're her identical twin. You told me she was your mother. But after examining all this stuff, I have this uncanny feeling that you might *be* Carly Munro. Of course that's ludicrous."

There was another uncomfortable glance between Carly and Ian.

"Admittedly, it's none of my business," Tom said. "I should never have let myself in tonight. But now that I've seen these things and heard the recording, I'm dying to know."

Carly locked eyes with Ian, giving him a look that said *what do you think?* His eyes responded with *I don't know.* She turned toward Tom again.

"As far-fetched as it sounds, you're right, Tom. My real name *is* Carly Munro. I was born in nineteen ninety-three.

Which would make me sixty-one years old if I'd gotten here like you did – living one day at a time until the years piled up. But I'm thirty-one. As for what happened – although I didn't know it at the time – my life was stolen from me this past Friday night as I was leaving home to go to my band's album launch show. When I walked through the door of my apartment into the hallway of the old mansion I live in, I arrived in *this* apartment building, outside the door of a woman whose name I learned was Natalie. When I left my apartment, the year was twenty *twenty*-four. When I arrived here, it was twenty *fifty*-four. The first thing I noticed was a man I'd never seen before standing outside a door that wasn't supposed to exist. Lucky for me, it was Ian. I was confused and ticked off. But your son kept me from going over the deep end during my first few hours here. He's been helping me keep my sanity ever since while I try to find a way to return to my own time."

She looked at Ian then.

"I thought she was Natalie at first," Ian said, his eyes on Carly. "You know, with the long blonde hair, although yours has that strawberry thing going on." He turned to his dad. "But she was definitely not Natalie. She kept saying she was in a hurry to get to her gig at the Triple Vee. I didn't know what she was talking about. In fact, I thought she was a little unhinged at first. Then I drove her to the address she gave me, but it wasn't there. Which made her even madder."

"I remember the Triple Vee," Tom said.

"I understand why you're skeptical," Carly said. "It took me a while to accept what happened. It's so unbelievable."

It was clear he remained dubious.

"Ever since I got here, Ian's been helping me find a way to undo what Natalie did. We're trying to track her down, hoping she can give me some information that would allow us both to return to our own time with another time travel swap. Ian thinks because she didn't make it as a rock star in my time, she might be keen to get back to her own time."

"A time travel swap?"

"My theory is that the time portal is like a wormhole. But for it to work, two people have to cross through at the same moment, one traveling from the past to the future and one traveling from the future to the past. I think that's how she arrived in my time and I ended up here in her time. If I'm right, I need to pass through the doorway from the outside to the inside of the apartment at the same moment she walks through the door from inside to the outside of her apartment. To do that, I have to find out when she's passing through the door so I can walk through from the other end."

"What sort of information would she have that could help you?"

"She may remember when she exited the apartment during the first couple of weeks after she got to twenty twenty-four. I had no inkling what happened until I saw how fixated she was on my band and listened to her recordings. The magazine article helped me understand how she became aware of the portal."

"Assuming you truly are Carly Munro, and assuming you did, in fact, travel through time, isn't it possible you could simply walk back through that door to return to your time?"

"I thought so at first. But I've already tried that twice."

Tom shook his head.

"I know it's a lot to swallow," she said.

"Particularly in this era of hoaxes," he replied, "when anything can be faked."

"Let me drive you home, Dad," Ian said.

"Before you go, Tom," Carly said, "please don't tell anyone about this. Of course, most people would think you're a nutcase. But if by chance someone did believe you, it could cause trouble for me."

"Believe me, I won't repeat a word of this to anyone. Not even Asher. The last thing I need is a reputation as a demented old man."

While Ian was gone, she ventured into the hallway again, standing outside Natalie's apartment. Shoulder against the doorframe, she bowed her head in concentration. There were small noises. Sounds from the street out front wafting in through the window? Then she thought she heard a voice saying 'no.' She held her breath, waiting, listening. She was still in that position when she heard a door open down the hallway. It was Ian returning.

"I think I heard someone say 'no,'" she whispered.

Another door opened on the other end of the hallway, prompting Ian to wrap his arm around Carly's waist to guide her into his apartment.

"Whoever saw us just now likely assumed we were a man and a woman slipping into his apartment for a tryst," he teased.

"Quick thinking."

Once inside, he closed the door. But rather than let go, he pulled her close, his eyes searching hers.

"My apologies for what I'm about to do," he whispered. "But I've fallen under your spell."

Then he kissed her like she'd never been kissed before. She responded instinctively, her body leaning in even though she didn't belong here with this man from the future. She had imagined what it would be like to kiss the guy who met her when she was at her worst and accepted her anyway. He was, without a doubt, the only man she'd ever met who checked every box on her list of desirable qualities. Although it was more than those desirable qualities that made it so difficult to put the brakes on now. There was also the physical allure of his body pressing against hers.

But she was on the precipice of success in her own time. That's where she came of age, where she wrote songs that held meaning. Here, she was a visitor, out of her depth. She knew no one in the music world where popular music had a plastic sound to it. Where songs sounded a little too perfect, a little too bland. She needed to go home where she belonged.

She gently pulled away, avoiding his eyes. She didn't want to hurt him, not after all he'd done. But she couldn't take this any further, knowing she was going home at the first opportunity.

"I'm sorry, Ian. It's not you. I don't belong here."

He withdrew his arms like he had embraced a mannequin by mistake. He crossed the living room, his shoulders sagging, and fled into his bedroom. That's where he stayed for the rest of the evening. She hadn't meant to encourage him. Now she had wounded him.

9

For a second when she woke up the next morning, she didn't remember hurting Ian. Then it hit her. She ached for him. And for herself. While he hadn't actually spoken the words, his kiss had been so much more than a sensual come-on. There was love in that kiss. Which left her with warring emotions.

After showering and dressing, she found a text on her phone saying he'd be home later in the day, that he had to visit the office. She hoped he wasn't in trouble for getting behind in his work because of her.

She spent the morning on the tedious chore of searching listings for Natalie in San Francisco. There was no evidence she moved there. But since she didn't have a better idea, Carly kept at it. She left a dozen more messages, hoping to get a callback.

Hunger caught up with her by midday. She was having soup when Ian got home. From the noise he was making, it sounded like he was setting something up in the living room. She was curious but stayed put, uneasy about facing him.

There was even more pressure on her now to go home. She didn't want to torment him by staying. But when he waved at her from the kitchen doorway, he acted as though nothing had happened, giving her his usual warm smile.

"I found something for you," he said, gesturing for her to join him in the living room.

She was stunned. There in the center of the room was a full-sized Yamaha keyboard.

"Ian, seriously?"

"Don't worry, it's secondhand. I found it online and looked at it this morning. The guy played a quick medley for me. It sounds decent. I know it's not the quality you're used to but I could tell you miss playing your music."

Her eyes teared up. "What if I go home tomorrow?"

"I'll sell it." Said with a tinge of regret. "Don't worry. I didn't pay a fortune. Try it out!"

With that hopeful look on his face, there was no way she could refuse since her presence here was making it hard on him. At least he acknowledged that their living arrangement was temporary.

She sat down on the stool and adjusted the settings as she contemplated which song to do. When he took a seat on the couch, she launched into a new ballad from the album, a song she wrote during the pandemic when she was reeling in the wake of her mom and dad's deaths. That's when she began to feel that life was a lot more tenuous than she thought. Their deaths caused her to throw herself into her work more than ever as she tried to accomplish her goals.

Here in Ian's living room, she felt a self-consciousness she didn't normally experience. But with a quick glance in his direction, she could see he was drinking in the private concert. She hadn't sung a note in five days and had started to feel something akin to withdrawal. Performing for this very special audience of one was cathartic. When she sang the last note, she found herself feeling less anxious.

He gave her a standing ovation, topping it off with a loud wolf whistle. His enthusiasm made her happy. Once again, with his help, she had found another way to pay him back for his many kindnesses.

Deciding to continue, she started into her big song. Playing and singing with confidence, her voice filled the room. There was a piano solo in the middle and she nailed it. It was exhilarating to perform her music again after fearing she might be stuck in a time and place where she didn't fit in.

"Wow," he said when she lifted her fingers from the keys. "I'm in awe."

Besides the admiration in his gaze, there was also yearning. She couldn't tear her eyes from his. She was rescued by a chime on his phone.

"Cruz and Mona are here," he said, reluctantly clicking the app to unlock the door.

"Hey man!" Cruz bellowed, walking in, his arms and Mona's arms entangled like climbing clematis attached to each other's bodies. "You don't usually jack the volume up like..." They stopped in their tracks when they saw Carly at the keyboard.

"Was that you?" Mona cried.

"Ian bought it. I was trying it out. Pretty cool, huh?"

"I'll say! Was that you singing?"

"Yes, it was her," Ian said. "Phenomenal, right?"

"I'll say!" Cruz replied. "You could be a star with that voice!"

Ian shot Carly a secret smile.

"Yeah," Mona agreed. "So different from all the female rock wannabes out there who sound like they came off the AI production line! Not to mention the *singers* created by artificial intelligence."

Carly was dumbfounded that some songs didn't at least have a real person singing. So depressing.

"You should be singing in the big nightclubs," Cruz went on. "You're light-years ahead of those copycats with their fake eyelashes and auto-tune voices! I should give notice on my job and become your manager. If I knew the first thing about the music business, that would be a smart move."

"Ooh! Wouldn't it be a blast to be in the music business?" Mona said.

"Yeah, too bad I didn't study that in college," Cruz said. "I could have a cool job now promoting musicians. But no! I worked my butt off putting myself through college. Never had time to party. All work and no play. Now I've got a boring job battling deepfakes."

"Hey, man," Ian said, "we do important work. And it's more important with each passing year as AI gets better and better."

"Right. The Deepfake Police. The Fraud Squad."

"Poor wittle Cruzie Woozie," Mona teased, holding his chin in her hand and giving it an affectionate shake.

Carly headed back into the kitchen, remembering her laptop and notes lying open on the counter for anyone to see. She didn't want to make that mistake again. Not with Cruz and Mona.

"What brings you two over in the middle of a Wednesday?" Ian asked. "You come to bum a free lunch?"

"Hey, man!" Cruz said. "When do we *ever* bum anything offa you?"

"Uh, three, four, five times a week."

They all laughed.

"We came to ask if you guys want to go out with us tonight," Mona said. "The Blue Light Bar & Grill does Retro Rock Night every Wednesday. Since Katie likes the old stuff, she'd probably get a kick out of seeing this oldies band called The Vultures. They get great reviews online."

"Katie?" Ian called out.

It took Carly a second to respond, momentarily forgetting her alias. Then she popped back into the living room, her things safely hidden.

"They're inviting us out tonight," he said.

"I heard."

"Because you guys are old fogeys before your time," Cruz said, "we can get there about eight and you can be home by eleven. That way you'll be home before you change back into mice or lizards or whatever the hell you change back into when your EV morphs into a pumpkin."

Ian mock punched his friend on the shoulder.

"Might be fun," Ian said, giving Carly a nod of encouragement.

"You say an oldies band is playing?" she asked.

"The Vultures," Mona said. "The website shows three grey-haired guys who look old enough to be my granddaddy long legs. But I think they play *this* century retro stuff, not the old-as-dirt stuff."

"I'm game, old fogey that I am," Carly said.

She was hoping to speak with the musicians like she did before, to see if they knew something about Natalie. Ian understood what she was up to.

When Cruz and Mona didn't make a move to go, Ian spoke up.

"You guys have time for a quick sandwich?"

They traded a surprised look as if they hadn't considered staying for lunch.

Ian chuckled as he led the way to the kitchen, rattling off all the sandwich makings he had on hand.

~

It was a bit cramped with the four of them riding cheek by jowl in Ian's little car. But located in the Bronx, the Blue Light Bar & Grill wasn't too long a drive. The venue was in the middle of a small retail area on the edge of a gentrified older neighborhood of rowhouses now owned by professionals who could afford the exorbitant prices.

Concerned about being recognized, Carly wore a pair of glasses they picked up at a drug store, pulling her hair into a loose chignon on the back of her head.

They took a table in the back of the dimly lit restaurant. Recorded oldies from the early 2000s were playing as the band finished setting up on the small stage. A waiter stopped by, taking their drink orders. They placed their dinner order on the menu screen while trading barbs and funny stories.

When the guitarist played a riff, signaling it was time for the live music to begin, Carly turned in her chair to get a better view. It felt like her heart skipped a beat. There, standing at the microphone, hands resting on his red guitar, was Hawke. If she hadn't seen him on the video call, it would've taken a minute to recognize him. The experience of seeing him in person was much more visceral than seeing him on her laptop. She slouched down in her chair so he wouldn't notice her as he counted down their first song – a pared down rendition of a tune from the *Happenstance* album.

Ian touched her knee under the table. She glanced his way, giving a tiny shake of the head. Her plan to pump the band for information was toast. That's all she needed was for Hawke to recognize her.

Her phone vibrated with a text from Ian. "We'll leave before they take a break."

With Hawke on lead guitar, backed by a drummer and a guy on keys, the three of them managed a big sound. They were veterans who knew what they were doing. Hawke's voice wasn't what it used to be, but he had transposed some of the songs to a lower key so his older voice could handle them. Cruz and Mona were impressed, and after a couple of drinks they were hooting and whistling after each song, and taking selfies to post. Carly turned her chair so she was mostly facing the back, hoping Hawke wouldn't notice her.

It hurt listening to him play her songs. Especially his performance of "Happenstance." She was ready to leave long before the set ended but stuck it out so Ian's friends wouldn't get their feelings hurt. She was also afraid Hawke would spot her if she got up to leave.

When she and Ian finished their dinners, she gestured with her eyes that she was ready to go. He tapped Cruz on the arm and told him they were heading home. Carly leaned over and thanked them for the invitation. Cruz and Mona hadn't planned on returning home with them in the first place. They were meeting other friends at another bar after the "old fogeys" called it a night.

As Carly and Ian were about to leave, the band wrapped up the song they were playing and Hawke announced they were taking a break.

She looked at Ian, whose eyes widened as he checked the stage. "He's coming this way," he whispered.

Without delay, she rose and walked out the door to the small parking lot. Realizing belatedly that she didn't have a way to get into Ian's car, she took a sharp right around the corner of the building. Unfortunately, the rear exit of the restaurant was on that side. The drummer came through the door, heading outside for a smoke. She did an about-face and retraced her steps to the parking lot. Hopefully, Hawke was busy talking with Ian. She weaved her way between cars until she reached the street, then followed the sidewalk past some of the well-maintained rowhouses. She found a spot where she could hide behind a large bush at the bottom of one unit's front steps. She sat on the ground so the bush blocked her from being seen. She sighed in frustration about the close call. It would be a bad move coming face to face with Hawke.

But what if they did run into each other? What if Hawke recognized her and believed it was her? She could easily convince him. She could tell him things about their time together that nobody else would know. And then? She wouldn't be able to hold back her rage at what he had done in her absence. She would accuse him of lying when he laid claim to her music. She would demand he give up his copyright to her songs. Of course, it's not like she could threaten to sue. Even if *he* believed she was Carly Munro, no one else would. They'd think she was psychotic. She could imagine trying to engage the services of an attorney. First, she had no money to pay one. Second, she had no identification. Third, Hawke presumably registered those songs as joint copyright years ago. She would be asked why she waited until now to object. She would also be accused of being a phony. Plainly, she wasn't old enough to be Carly Munro. On top of that, once he knew she was coming for him, he might take further action to strengthen his case.

So what good would it do to confront him? It would feel good in the moment to scream in his face. Then the moment would pass and she'd be left with nothing.

No, she didn't want to come face to face with Hawke. When she made it home to her own time, that would be the best time to tell Hawke a thing or two. Or three. Or four. That would be the time to protect her rights to her own music. It would also be the time to end their rocky relationship. She should've recognized already they weren't a good match and he didn't have it in him to be true to her. And, very importantly, that she was not willing to settle for less. Which is what Hawke was. Less. She'd been in a state of lazy denial. But she would no longer bend her will to his.

It took about fifteen minutes for her phone to vibrate with a text from Ian. "Where are you?"

"Hiding down the street. Will return to the parking lot."

Keeping her eyes peeled, she walked back to the bar and texted him. "Pick me up as you exit the lot."

His car started toward her immediately. She watched it approach, keeping her eye on the restaurant door. Ian pulled up beside her and she hopped in.

"He talked my ear off," he said.

Not in the mood to hear about it, she stared out the window as the car accelerated onto the street. He sensed her mood and remained quiet. She liked a man who could sense her emotional state. They drove home in silence. As they entered the apartment building, he patted her shoulder. It was not a romantic touch. It was a friend lending support. She appreciated the gesture.

After a shower, she donned a pair of shorts and a T-shirt that Mona had given her. Perfect for relaxing in the living room. Ian asked if she'd like to watch a movie but she thought reading would be better. Using his account, she downloaded a book of poetry onto her laptop and made up her bed on the sofa. She stretched out, leaning against a couple of pillows.

It was a book she had on a shelf in her own apartment. She revisited it often, choosing poems at random. She admired the music of the words that were harnessed so beautifully by gifted poets. She liked to think of herself as a poet. Songs were poetry after all. She had no illusions that her songs measured up to truly great poetry. Still, it was food for the soul.

Ian spent the evening in his bedroom, giving her plenty of space. She didn't hear any music or voices. If he was watching something, he was using earbuds. Ever the considerate roommate.

Eventually, she drifted off to sleep, unaware of Ian tip-toeing through the room to check on her, pausing to move her laptop to the lamp table.

~

The smell of bacon awakened her the following morning. It carried her back to Sunday mornings when she was a little girl and her mother made bacon, eggs and biscuits. She could almost hear her mom's voice as she poked her head into the bedroom, singing out, "rise and shine!"

But this was not her family's home and she was not a little girl. She opened her eyes to find Ian peeking into the living room.

"You were mumbling about eggs and bacon in your sleep."

"I was?" she said, her voice soft and husky.

"No." He laughed. "I was in the mood."

She sat up on the side of the couch, hugging the pillow to her chest.

"Scrambled?" he said.

"Mm."

"Ready in a shake, rattle and roll."

She mustered a smile.

He ducked into the kitchen while she washed up and tamed her tousled hair, pulling it through a scrunchy to make a loose ponytail.

He poured her coffee as she planted herself on the stool that had become hers.

"Five star service," she said.

"We aim to please."

He set a bowl of scrambled eggs and a small plate of bacon on the bar, then retrieved two halves of a toasted baguette smeared with butter. It was nothing like her mother used to make.

As they ate, she asked him about his conversation with Hawke.

"As soon as he set his guitar down, he headed straight for me. Luckily, Cruz and Mona wandered off to the bar before he reached our table. He was surprised to see me there. I told him that after the interview I poked around searching for some of his local gigs and found the Blue Light listing. I gave him some good strokes and he ate it up. He watched for you, then asked what happened to you. I shrugged. He said he noticed you during the set, that you reminded him of Carly. I asked if that happens often. He said it makes him feel like a fool when he thinks a woman might be you because it's always a young woman who catches his eye, even though he knows you'd be in your sixties now."

"If I'd known he was performing, I never would've agreed to go. As usual, keeping his website up to date isn't one of his top priorities. Sorry you had to talk with him."

"Yeah, he got under my skin. He told me he loved you but couldn't say that in the interview because he didn't want his wife and kids to hear. He says she gets jealous when something comes up about you."

She sighed, not knowing what to say.

"I wasn't going to tell you that part," he went on. "But it *is* your life after all. Naturally I hate his guts."

"When I knew him, Hawke didn't know the meaning of true love," she said. "He was a fair weather lover."

"Now there's a song for you, right there." He wagged his finger at her.

Her new phone chimed. Since Ian was the only person who had her number besides the women she'd left messages with, she answered it.

"Hello?"

"Is this Carly?" a woman asked.

"Yes it is."

"My name is Sutton. I'm Emily Smith's friend. Why are you trying to reach her?"

"I want to find the woman who lived in an apartment building on Crescent Avenue in the New York suburbs to ask if she'd like to reverse her journey. If so, I can help."

"Reverse her journey?"

"I'll text my message to your number and you can forward it to her. She'll know what it means."

The woman hung up and Carly immediately sent the message.

A minute later she received a reply. "Emily is dead."

10

Carly covered her face with her hands. The possibility that Natalie might be dead had not once occurred to her. She would be in her early seventies, which wasn't that old. Of course, there were all kinds of potential scenarios – disease, accident, even violent crime. Regardless, if her theory about how the portal worked was correct, and Natalie was dead, the only way to get back to 2024 was to entrap someone else in the doorway and steal their life from them. No way she could do that.

"Text her back," Ian suggested. "Ask when and how she died."

She hastily dictated another text: "So very sorry. When? How?"

Waiting for a reply, she paced the living room. She'd been pacing a few minutes when her phone vibrated again. The text read, "Five years ago. Don't bother me again."

Returning to the kitchen, she showed Ian the message.

"We don't know if that's really Natalie," he said.

"Time will tell. On the other hand, maybe time will never tell."

Although deeply disheartened, she resumed her search, leaving more messages while Ian got busy at his desk in the living room.

A few moments later, he called out to her. "Dad is here."

She walked into the living room as he opened the door.

"Philadelphia," Tom announced, skipping "hello" entirely. "That's where Natalie went."

"She's not dead?" Carly said.

"That, I don't know. But Philadelphia is where she moved."

"How'd you track her down?" she asked as Ian waved his dad in.

"First, I pressed sonny boy here for information." His cane thumped step by deliberate step as he made his way inside. "I found out that when she left the mansion apartment – your apartment – she moved to the old Tempo Sheridan Apartments. I located the resident manager, pretending to be with a law firm handling a class action settlement. I told him she was entitled to a share of the payout but the law firm didn't have her current address. His mother had been resident manager before him and she remembered Natalie. She said when Natalie moved out, she said she was moving to Philadelphia and already had a couple of shows lined up there."

"I guess we can start calling you Sherlock," Ian said.

Which made Tom smile.

"I figured you were convinced I was a fraud," Carly said.

"Well, after everything Ian told me, and what you said, I concluded your story might be true. When I started digging, I was stunned to find her trail in twenty twenty-four corroborating your story."

He stared at her in wonderment.

"Thanks so much, Tom. I need to shift gears and start researching Emily Smiths in Philadelphia."

Tom turned toward the door again. "I'll get out of your way."

"Stay for lunch," Ian said.

"I already barged in. I don't want to wear out my welcome."

"Carly can sing you a song while I make sandwiches."

That got Tom's attention. "Carly," he repeated. There was awe in his voice like it was still hard for him to believe the young woman in front of him was the real Carly Munro.

"Avocado, tomato, cucumbers, chickpeas, onion, arugula and feta cheese on toasted French bread okay with everyone?" Ian asked.

Carly laughed. "My sister would make a sandwich like that."

As Tom settled on the couch, she sat down at the keyboard which had been moved from the middle of the room to where one of the overstuffed chairs used to be. She started off with a light run, then sang an up-tempo song from the album. Tom was captivated. Ian showed up in the kitchen doorway toward the end. Both applauded when she finished.

"Sensational," Tom said, starry-eyed. "You really are Carly Munro."

She smiled.

"Okay, lunch is served," Ian said.

They gathered at the kitchen bar, each with a gourmet sandwich, baby carrots and fresh peach slices. There were also glasses of iced tea, Tom's in a colorful insulated glass.

"You should hang out your shingle," Tom said, giving his son a thumbs up. "Far superior to a sandwich at a fancy restaurant that would charge you an arm and a leg and a big toe."

"Yeah, jackrabbits would love it here," Carly said.

Ian responded with a smirk.

Carly was impressed with his talent in the kitchen. Although she knew guys who cooked, she wasn't accustomed to being on the receiving end of such talent."

"So, tell us what it's like performing in front of a crowd." Tom said.

"When they're dancing and singing along and they're into the music, I feel like a millionaire. It makes me feel good to bring happiness into peoples' lives. Or help them deal with tough times. And when people come up afterwards telling me a particular song resonated with them, I feel like I'm making a difference in the world. Of course, sometimes it's a challenge."

Recollections of crap nights on stage popped into her mind. She'd worked when she had cramps so bad, it was hell to perform. She'd worked when there was no air conditioning in the hot summertime, nearly passing out from the heat. She'd performed in front of an audience of four apathetic people without earning a dime. But no need to share those memories.

They were all ears as she told them what it was like playing a bar in a college town.

"As you know, drunk people think they're God's gift to humanity. And when it comes to drunk men, they believe in their groin that a woman will fall for their charms if they come on to her with a clever line like, 'what's a hot babe like you doing in a place like Bob's Barbecue?' Take those laws of drunken behavior and multiply them by a factor of ten, and you get an idea of what college kids are like when they're wasted."

The men laughed.

"It also depends on whether you're performing before a paying audience or a non-paying audience. They're much more likely to listen and show their appreciation if they buy a ticket to see you. If they're hanging out at a bar and your band happens to be on stage, they may not listen at all." She paused to eat a peach slice. "I've played before all kinds of audiences. Mostly, it's a blast. But sometimes not so much. You can have a drunk guy puke all over your keyboard trying to convince you to meet him at the door when the set is over for the best time of your life."

Which elicited uncomfortable chuckles and a quick glance between father and son.

"Yeah," she continued, "there are times you'd like to tell a guy making an asshole of himself to take a dumpster dive from the fifth floor."

She could see both men were a little surprised by the peek behind the curtain. And maybe by her language. But she didn't mind if they got to know her a little better. When she started out as a musician, a lot of guys labeled her a goody two shoes. Dispelling that notion helped her cause. Other musicians and club managers were less likely to take advantage of her if she sounded more like one of them, meaning she knew her way around.

"I dusted off my turntable last night and put your album on," Tom said. "It took me back to when I saw your band perform. As you were talking, it occurred to me that you and I are of the same generation. You said you were born in nineteen ninety-three. I was born in nineteen ninety-one.

Two years before you." He paused as if this was important. "Ian was born in twenty twenty-five," he continued, giving his son a meaningful look.

A brief flash of annoyance crossed Ian's face.

"Thanks for the trendy cuisine," Tom said, clapping Ian on the shoulder. "I need to go home. I've got my virtual class to teach." With his cane to steady him, he got to his feet.

"I'll drive you," Ian said.

"I ordered a ride hail." Tom lifted his phone for emphasis.

"Cancel and let me take you. It's the least I can do considering you found Natalie."

"I wish I could drive you," Carly said. "But my driver's license expired twenty-eight years ago."

They laughed and Tom relented.

Carly cleaned up the kitchen while Ian was gone, taking special care with the insulated glass Tom used.

Because it was so hot outside, she was walking up and down the hallway to exercise when Ian returned. He caught up with her, matching his steps to hers.

"Dad had a fantastic time thanks to you."

"He's a great guy."

"I can't believe he's been going out on his own lately. It's not like him to call a ride hail and show up at my apartment." He was quiet for a moment as they walked. "It's almost as if..." he said, but stopped mid-sentence.

"As if?" she said.

He sneaked a glance in her direction out of the corner of his eye. "Oh, I don't know. It reminds me of what they say about endorphins, that they help reduce pain. I mean, he wanted to share that information about Natalie *in person*. And singing that song for him? That was worth, I don't know, at least a couple of days' worth of pain pills. So thank you."

~

The afternoon was Drudge City all over again as Carly started her research from scratch focusing on the Philadelphia area. There were a lot of phone numbers to call, even after winnowing the list down by age. She'd placed five calls before hunger pains forced her to take a supper break. Of course, her search would be futile if Natalie was dead. She tried to kick that thought to the curb.

She checked the refrigerator and cabinets to see if there was something she could cook so Ian didn't have to do all the work. There were veggie crumbles in the freezer, a can of spaghetti sauce and noodles in the cabinet, an onion and a few other things she could use for a spaghetti dinner. He was such a good cook, she knew anything she made wouldn't measure up. But this would be a small gesture of appreciation.

When she stepped into the living room, he turned from the wall screen, giving her his attention.

"Mind if I fix spaghetti for dinner?"

"You know how to cook?" he said, eyebrows sky high.

"I may not be a gourmet chef like some people I know, but my skill set extends well beyond bellowing in front of an audience for tips." She shot the bird at him and smiled.

He laughed. "Well, have at! Give me a bellow if you need help."

They both grinned.

It was a challenge, not knowing his kitchen like she knew hers. When the sauce, noodles, garlic toast and salad were ready, she called him to dinner. He swooped in, declaring the meal too fancy for the kitchen bar.

Instead, he unfolded an antique wooden table by the window at the far end of the living room. Covering it with a tablecloth, he opened a bottle of red wine and set wine glasses out. The two of them transferred the food and silverware to the table and sat down across from each other.

"This is nice," she said.

"This is better than nice," he said, pouring the wine.

He gave her a smile that was so inviting, she was afraid she'd blush. Which caused her to get flustered. She dove into the first topic of conversation that popped into her head.

"I've been thinking that when I make it home I can try to warn your dad about having that surgery."

His reaction wasn't at all what she expected.

"You're joking, right?"

"Well, I haven't given it a great deal of thought, but if we do some research ahead of time, I—"

"Although I appreciate where you're coming from, that is one god-awful idea."

The romantic vibe of a moment before wilted like a thirsty rose bush during a heat wave.

"You could make things worse if you interfere," he continued. "A ton worse."

"I was hoping I could help him avoid all that pain."

The dinner was forgotten as they stared at each other across the table.

"First off," he said, "if Dad never had the surgery, there's no telling what would've happened. He could've ended up having a different surgery, a surgery that – who knows – could've had a worse outcome. Or if he chose not to have surgery at all, he'd be like the little old ladies who show up at the pain clinic with such advanced scoliosis, their internal organs are squashed as their body folds over on itself. And if you try to convince him the surgery is a bad thing, he'd still have several doctors recommend it. Who do you think he would believe?"

"Well, I guess I'd tell him—"

"That you're a time traveler? Tom Stewart has always been a rational man. He's never been prone to believing tall tales, even if the tall tale teller is a good-looking musician." His dry laugh had a scoffing quality to it.

"*You* believed me."

"That's because you had proof. But if you go back, how will you convince him you visited the *future* and met him as a disabled sixty-three year old man?"

She felt like she was under attack.

"And besides," he went on, "what if your interference causes him not to marry my mom? If you show up in my dad's life at that moment in time, would I be born?"

"I wouldn't—"

"My dad already has a crush on you."

"He doesn't have a—"

"You don't know him like I do. It hit me this afternoon when he showed up here unannounced *again* bringing you his research. Unlike before, he's leaving his apartment without me cajoling him, badgering him and dragging him out the door. He definitely has a crush on you."

She was embarrassed. Usually she could tell when a man was interested. But she hadn't been paying attention to Tom's behavior. Her radar had been focused on Ian and the growing realization that she was falling for him against her will.

Staring at her plate, she knew he was right. Interfering in Tom's life – interfering in anyone's life – could screw things up. And yet, was there a way she could help Tom without him knowing it? She wasn't going to say another word about it to Ian though. He had never spoken to her like this before. She found herself biting her lip. But there was no way she was going to boohoo in front of him.

He sighed. "I'm sorry. I didn't mean to be hostile. I know your heart's in the right place."

She touched the stem of her wine glass, twirling it from side to side.

"You know what I think?" he said. "I think I experienced an attack of jealousy."

Unsure what to say, she held her tongue.

"You heard him say the two of you are members of the same generation," he went on. "Then he said I wasn't born till twenty twenty-five, like I'm a baby. Thus, reminding you I wasn't born yet when your album came out. It all came together in my head as I was driving home that he's infatuated. So when you started talking about looking him up so you could help him, well, I imagined him asking for your number."

"My fault."

"Not your fault. I shouldn't have growled like that." He slid his hand across the table and touched hers. "Forgive me?"

She bobbed her head but didn't take his hand.

"The spaghetti is cold," she said.

"Let's heat it up."

He grabbed both plates and started for the kitchen. She followed. He warmed his food first, then put her plate in the microwave. As it was heating, he placed his hands on her arms and leaned in to kiss her forehead. Much too close. He gave her an amorous look that made her long for a real kiss. But the last thing she should do was stir the pot. When she returned home, she didn't want to leave behind a man with a broken heart. She also didn't want to arrive home pining for a man she couldn't have.

He moved closer.

"Please…" she said. She was going to say, 'please don't do this.' But another part of her *wanted* him to kiss her, consequences be damned. "Let's eat our dinner," she said, moving around him to get her plate.

They returned to the table, struggling to make small talk as they ate. She hoped against hope that Natalie was still alive and that she could find her as soon as possible. The time travel swap needed to happen on the double.

11

As if in answer to her prayer, Ian received a message the next morning from the drummer's friend, Miguel Perez, who lived with Natalie when she went by the name Emily Smith. In his message he said he remembered something else. He said he got a text from her after she moved away mentioning she lived in an old neighborhood where all the streets were named for something to do with Christmas. "Like Christmas Lane, Santa Avenue, and Reindeer Drive. She lived on Mistletoe Avenue a couple of houses from the intersection with Rudolph Road."

After Ian shared the message with her, Carly began strategizing her next step. Needless to say, she had to make a trip to Philadelphia. Another big favor to ask of Ian, making her feel guilty all over again. But she had to confront Natalie. Perhaps "confront" was too strong a word. She didn't want to alienate her. She wanted to offer her a chance to reverse the time travel exchange. She hoped Ian was right, that Natalie would be interested.

Before she could ask him, Ian offered to drive her. She closed her eyes for a second, trying to think of an alternative.

"It's not an imposition," he said. "I'm all in. It's a lot easier than traveling to San Francisco!"

She screwed up her mouth.

"I want to help," he said. "Luckily, I have a lot of flexibility in my job. I can work anywhere, anytime."

"As long as you meet your deadlines."

"I always do. Don't worry."

"You're a lifesaver."

He winked at her.

Back in her spot at the kitchen bar, she was perusing images online of houses on Mistletoe Avenue when her phone chimed. She remembered what to say if it was one of the Emily Smiths, then answered.

"Are you Carly?" a woman said.

"Yes."

"Why do you want to talk with Emily Smith?"

"I'm trying to reach the Emily Smith who lived in an apartment building on Crescent Avenue in the New York suburbs so I can ask if she'd like to reverse her journey. If so, I can help."

"Sounds like a scam to me."

"Then you're not the Emily I'm searching for. Sorry."

Carly hung up, disappointed.

Turning her attention once again to her laptop, she studied the brick bungalows on Mistletoe, choosing several addresses to approach. They were all within a few houses of the intersection with Rudolph Road. She hoped Miguel's information wasn't out of date. If Natalie had moved since she communicated with him, it would mean further delay. And delay was Carly's enemy. Of course, if she had died, his information would be useless.

Researching all the houses on her list, she learned that none of them listed Emily Smith as owner. The listings didn't mention the names Nelly Carleton or Natalie Maynor either. So if she lived there, she was a renter. Not surprising.

Now that she was preparing for a face-to-face meeting, it occurred to her she needed to know what Natalie looked like. The few pictures of the band that included her had been taken from a distance and were not high resolution photos easily enlarged. She needed some close-ups. She asked Ian if he could show her some pictures and videos on social media.

"I don't do anti-social media."

"Anti-social media?"

"Think about it. It kills in-person friendships, makes people see each other less, not more. What's it full of? Ads, BS, preaching and braggity braggity braggity. They're all owned by giant companies that want you to loiter online to see all the ads, not your friends' posts. Ask Mona. She can help you."

Turned out even a super considerate guy like Ian had a touch of the Grinch in him. She smiled to herself.

~

Like Natalie's apartment, Mona's place was a mirror image of Ian's. It was decorated in green, pink and yellow. On the walls was a variety of framed art straight out of superhero movies and video games – lots of characters in bright skintight body suits, many engaged in battle with a bad guy.

Mona welcomed her with a big smile, dressed in white short shorts and a pink crop top.

"Let's see here." She sat on the yellow couch, patting the seat beside her. Opening her laptop, she scrolled through a couple of screens, landing on one of her social media pages.

"Now here's a picture from earlier this summer when Natalie stopped by to bring some of her homemade brownies. Dee-lish, by the way. Of course Cruz was disappointed they weren't magic brownies."

She laughed, pointing at a woman in a dark caftan. She had brown hair with blonde streaks that fell on her shoulders. While not beautiful in the beauty pageant way, she oozed sex appeal. She had large brown eyes and full, sensuous lips. In the photo, she playfully pointed at the photographer.

Moving on, Mona next showed her a video.

"I took this video in the spring when we were at a party. You can tell she's had a couple of drinkie-poos by how glassy her eyes look."

In the video, Natalie danced, mugging for the camera, singing along with loud music. She had a smoky voice. Her hair wasn't as long as in the more recent photo and, without the blonde highlights, it was a rich brown.

"Brown is her natural color," Mona said. "She had the blonde highlights added a few weeks ago. Interesting how her hair looks more like yours in the later picture."

They looked at several more photos and a couple more videos so that Carly had a better feel for what Natalie looked and sounded like. Of course, they were taken when she was thirty years younger than she was now. Still, it would be helpful.

"Can you text a few to me? I like to have pictures of friends as keepsakes. In fact, I should take a selfie of you and me!" Carly pulled her phone out, motioning Mona to scoot over beside her. "Oh, I forgot. This is a dumb phone. No camera."

"I'll use mine," Mona said, grabbing hers and holding it like she'd done it a million times. "Say tee-tee!"

When Carly got back to Ian's place, she pulled up the pictures Mona shared by email on the laptop. Then she used an aging app to predict how Natalie would look in her early seventies. The app showed an attractive older woman with long silver hair, the same big eyes, the same nose and mouth, but with wrinkles and crow's feet. If she looked like this, there would be no problem recognizing her. Still, she was glad Ian would be with her. He knew Natalie. He would recognize her even if she'd aged thirty years.

~

Carly was stressed as she climbed into Ian's car the next morning even though he had reassured her that everything would work out. He believed Natalie would be motivated to cooperate since reversing the swap would bail her out of a disappointing life. As they headed onto the freeway, he let the autonomous car do the driving while he tried again to ease her anxiety.

"I'll be with you every step of the way. No reason to be uncalm, uncool and uncollected."

He gave her a teasing sidelong glance. She responded with a weak smile.

"I've gotten used to thinking of her as the enemy," she said. "I'm trying to make the shift to thinking of her as an ally. But it doesn't feel right."

"Understandable."

"I hope she's home."

"If she's not there, we'll come back later."

"I wish I had your confidence."

Including the time it took to get out of the city, it was a three hour drive to reach their destination. She didn't spot any police cars along the way. Instead, the freeway was patrolled by drones and monitored by an abundance of cameras.

After checking into a hotel, they drove to the Christmas neighborhood in the older suburbs, where they hoped to find Natalie alive and well.

The brick houses were built in the 1940s, many of them with a shady front porch. Some were still the original dark red brick. Others had been painted grey or cream or white. They all had small lawns, some with grass, others were covered with English Ivy, decorative gravel or wild flowers. They parked at the corner of Mistletoe and Rudolph and walked to the first house on Mistletoe. An older man answered, telling them what they wanted to know, that Emily Smith lived two doors down on the other side of the street at 1319. Carly thanked him, relieved beyond measure that they were in the right place and that Natalie was alive.

She'd been incensed after learning her trip through time wasn't an accident, that Natalie engineered the whole thing with the intention of stealing her place in the band. Now she had to let go of at least some of that fury if she hoped to convince her to help both of them get back to *when* they belonged. But forgiving wasn't easy.

They crossed the street and followed a stone walkway to the front porch of a grey house with black shutters. Climbing the steps, they reached a heavy wooden door with a summer wreath on it. Carly looked at Ian who gave her a thumbs up. She touched the electronic doorbell and stepped back, trying to compose herself. A minute went by. Then another. There was no sound from within.

She touched the doorbell again.

"What if she's out of town?" she whispered.

"Don't worry. We'll cross that bridge when we come to it."

"If she's out of town, I'll bet she's watching us on the security video right now."

Ian trotted down the steps and walked to the driveway, peering toward the back yard.

"I'll check around back to see if she's working in the garden." He was gone for a moment.

That's when a slight movement drew her attention to the front window. She was startled when an orange tabby jumped onto a table beyond the glass. He stared at her with green eyes as though he knew what she was up to and would defend his mistress to the death.

Ian reappeared with a shake of the head. As they walked back to the car, discouragement weighed her down.

They stopped for lunch at a restaurant on their way back to the hotel. Sitting in the air conditioned dining room, her mission was all Carly could think about. She asked to go back to Natalie's place after they ate.

This time, they parked in front of the house. Once again, no one answered, leaving Carly even more dispirited.

"She's intentionally avoiding me," she said as they drove away.

"It's possible she's out with friends."

"It's also possible she's inside the house, eyes glued to the camera feed."

They went to their separate hotel rooms for a couple of hours. But Carly wanted to try again. Their third trip to Mistletoe Avenue was as unproductive as the first two. Which left her cranky.

Returning to the hotel, she said she preferred to spend the evening in her room. But Ian had other ideas. He suggested they have supper at a place recommended by one the hotel clerk.

"She said they have live music and the food is good."

"I don't think I'd be good company. Besides, you've already spent way too much on me. Plus I don't have anything to wear."

"You're wrong on all three counts. You're good company even when you're bad company. That's the name of an old rock band, isn't it?"

She smiled.

"Second, because I work from home and don't go out much, I don't spend much money. So I'm loaded."

"You're lying."

"I kid you not! I'm rolling in the dough. Is that an old rock song?"

"In the deep."

He responded with a confused look.

"The rock song – 'Rolling in the Deep' by Adele."

"Right, right."

"You've still spent too much on me."

"Third… what was third? Oh yeah, you don't have anything to wear. There's two clothing stores down the street from the hotel. We can make quick work of buying an outfit. You can add it to the running total of all the expenses you're going to reimburse me for."

She sighed.

"Going to dinner tonight would make me happy," he said.

She relented. After all, he had driven her to Philadelphia and granted her every request, visiting Natalie's house three times. So they walked to one of the nearby stores and bought her a pair of black evening pants, a jazzy blue blouse and a pair of dressy black sandals. She winced at the prices. He argued that she was out of touch.

After showering, dressing, applying makeup and fixing her hair, it was worth it when she met him in the lobby.

"You could pass for a glamorous songstress of the nineteen sixties," he said. "Or the seventies. Or the nineties. I get all those decades mixed up."

She smiled. "You could pass for a Hollywood heartthrob of the twenties," she said, taking in his cool blue slacks and silky shirt.

He responded with a little faux preening.

They walked into The Ten Spot expecting a band to be on stage, but recorded music was being piped into the dining room. The lighting was muted and most of the tables were filled. Which was a good sign. After they were seated, a waiter took their drink order. They had placed their food orders via the menu app by the time their cocktails arrived. That's when a man seated a couple of tables over walked to the stage and sat down at the grand piano. He began playing jazz tunes, greatly improving the ambience.

He was still playing when their food was served, making Carly and Ian think he was the paid entertainment for the evening. But after several tunes, he stood and bowed to appreciative applause. Then he called out to the diners, "The live entertainment was a no show tonight. I'm a volunteer. Are there any other musicians in the house who could play for a while?" He retired to his table, rejoining a woman who greeted him with a loving smile.

"Your turn," Ian said, eyes on Carly.

"My food will get cold."

"Eat first, then you can take a turn."

Her face betrayed her reluctance.

"It would be the perfect way to reimburse me for travel expenses," he said. "Much better than filthy lucre."

When they finished eating, he reminded her that no one had taken a seat at the piano. She glanced around the dining room, checking for familiar faces. Unlike in New York, here in Philadelphia the chances that someone would recognize her were minimal. She checked her teeth in her compact and applied a fresh coat of lipstick before making her way to the small stage.

It wasn't often she had the opportunity to play a grand piano. She was used to electronic keyboards. But she was accustomed to weighted keys, so she was comfortable. Choosing to do some hits from the nineteen seventies rather than her own tunes, she started with a familiar piano intro, then sang "You've Got a Friend" by Carole King.

She didn't want to gauge audience reaction tonight. This was for Ian. She mostly closed her eyes and sang from the heart, enjoying playing a rock 'n' roll classic. An appropriate song to sing for a true friend she cared about more than she dared admit. When she played the final note, she held the chord until the strings stopped vibrating.

Her second song was by Fleetwood Mac's Christine McVie – "Songbird." It was a quiet message to Ian letting him know she loved him even if she couldn't tell him so.

Before she started on her third and final song, Ian called out, "Long Long Time." That was a hard one. A Linda Ronstadt hit written by a guy whose name she couldn't recall, it was a sad lament about pining for the one love she could never have, confessing that she would love him for a long, long time. Carly didn't want to sing it but since it was one of the many songs in her repertoire, she couldn't bring herself to refuse Ian's request. She avoided looking at him as she sang.

When it was over, she was surprised at the applause. Ian stood and clapped, looking as though he was deeply moved. She was about to return to their table when a well-dressed Black man arrived at the bottom of the steps. He was applauding too. He was too young to be someone she'd known in the past. And if she'd ever met him, she would remember his striking face.

"I'm Caleb Barlowe, manager of The Ten Spot. I'm always on the lookout for singers and musicians. Wondered if you might be interested in making this a regular gig."

She was flattered. She'd never thought of herself as a chanteuse of the sort who sang at dinner clubs.

"I normally perform with a rock band," she said.

"Oh? What band?"

"It's a New York band. I'm sure you haven't heard of us."

She should've said "no, but thank you for the offer" and left it at that.

"Even so, we could come up with a schedule to suit you."

"Thanks but I'm just visiting the city."

He glanced at Ian who was on his way over, wearing a concerned expression.

"Well, here's my card," Barlowe said, handing her a glossy business card with a QR code on it. "We love a good voice and a talented pianist. Especially when they come in an attractive package."

He inclined his head at Ian, then walked away.

"A job offer?" Ian guessed.

"Yeah."

"At first I thought he was a pest. I'm guessing you attract them now and then."

"Very chivalrous of you."

"Gallant too," he joked.

As they walked back to the hotel, Ian told her he was surprised by her impromptu performance.

"I had you pigeonholed as a rocker. But you play the piano like you've had years of formal training. Either that or it's tons of talent. Then there's your voice! On your album, you have that rock 'n' roll voice going on. But tonight was different. Your voice was like velvet."

She felt like she'd experienced verbal foreplay.

~

They returned to Mistletoe Avenue the next morning. Carly was just as nervous and Natalie was just as absent. This time, she left a note.

"Natalie, I want to get back to my time and I'm hoping you're keen to do that too considering your dreams of rock stardom didn't pan out. I think I know how we can both return to our own time. But I need your help. I had hoped we could sit down and talk about it. But now I have to return to New York. So maybe we can discuss it over the phone."

She signed her name and wrote her phone number below it. Stuffing the note in an envelope she brought from the hotel, she left it at the foot of Natalie's front door.

They drove away without looking back. Once they were out of the neighborhood, Ian turned onto a side street, pulling to the curb.

"You ready?" he said.

"Ready."

He turned back on the road heading toward Natalie's house. This time he made a right a couple of blocks before Mistletoe. He drove to the second cross street, Merry Lane, and parked under a tree. Carly peeled off the outer layers of her clothing, revealing stretch shorts and a T-shirt. She fixed her hair in a messy twist on top of her head, then added a cheap visor to further alter her appearance. Last, she switched the large sunglasses she'd been wearing to a smaller pair. Leaving Ian in the car, she walked south on Merry Lane for two blocks, then turned left on Mistletoe Avenue.

12

When she was a few houses away, she shifted into jogging mode, looking for all the world like a neighbor out for a morning run. As she neared her destination she saw a woman in a summer dress, with shoulder-length grey hair, step through the front door, locking it behind her. It had to be Natalie. She walked across the porch and down the front steps, a purse hanging from her shoulder.

Carly called out in a friendly tone.

"Hey, Emily!"

Natalie turned in her direction, using her hand to shield her eyes from the sun.

Carly jogged toward her, slowing as she approached.

The two women locked eyes. The contrast between them was pronounced. Though still an attractive woman, Natalie looked every bit of her seventy-four years, with wrinkles, crepey skin and a couple of age spots. The heavy makeup she used to wear was gone, replaced by a more natural look. Carly, on the other hand, had the firm flesh, smooth skin and radiance of youth. One thing they did have in common was a wary look of distrust.

Despite admonishing herself not to be confrontational, Carly couldn't stop the words that leapt from her mouth.

"You absconded with my life." There was no anger in her voice, but her frustration and hurt were unmistakable.

"If it's any consolation, mine hasn't exactly been a bed of begonias."

On the verge of responding in anger, Carly reined in the contempt that welled up. "Then you may like my idea for reversing the time travel swap."

"What's done is done. I'm too old to go back."

"The exchange would take place a few days after you arrived at the Vandermeer mansion. You'd be the same age you were when you walked through the portal."

Natalie responded with a look of disbelief.

"Can we sit down so I can explain?" Carly asked.

Natalie led the way into her modest home. The living room was done in muted shades of green, a much gentler feel than the living room of her apartment in New York with its stainless steel lamps and red sofa. After Natalie brought them both ice water, they sat facing each other in matching chairs.

Carly explained how it would work.

"If I walk into apartment one-thirteen in the apartment building that now exists while at the same time the younger you walks out of my old apartment in the mansion, we would once again pass each other as we cross through the portal. Which means I would return to twenty twenty-four and the younger version of you would return to twenty fifty-four. But it has to happen during the early days after you arrived. Once you move out of that apartment, a swap can't take place because you won't be there for me to exchange places with. It goes without saying that time is of the essence."

Carly was confident Natalie knew how the exchange worked. But it apparently hadn't occurred to her that another switch was possible with the younger Natalie.

"If it works," Carly continued, "and I believe it *will* work, your life since then will never have happened."

Natalie's eyes drifted downward.

"When you return to your own time, it'll be like you've been away on vacation," Carly added.

Natalie remained silent.

"Of course I need your buy-in," Carly went on. "Right now I don't have access to your apartment. Management thinks you'll be back soon from wherever you went. It could take a very long time for the apartment to be made available to rent again. By that time, you will have moved out of the mansion. Which means there would be no way to engineer the switch. Here's the critical piece – for me to walk into your apartment, you'll need to sublet it to me. Which you can do over the phone by calling Raj. He won't have any idea he's not talking with the younger Natalie."

This seemed to surprise her. Still, no reply.

"That's the first step. I can arrange to pay you that rent money so you'll get it as soon as you return."

After a moment lost in thought, Natalie responded.

"I need to think. I'm feeling overwhelmed right now and I don't like that feeling."

"I understand. I could come back later today?"

"I need more time than that."

"Tomorrow then?"

"I don't know."

"Well, we can't delay too long. It could take multiple tries before we get it right. I'll need guidance from you about the best times of day and the best days of the week."

Natalie looked distracted.

"Why don't we trade phone numbers," Carly said. "Then I can call you tomorrow after you've had time to mull things over?"

They swapped numbers and Carly called Natalie's number as a test, in case she was trying to ditch her.

"Please help me," Carly said. "I think this swap would be good for both of us."

A non-committal lift of the chin was Natalie's reply.

"Oh, and I'm using an alias rather than my real name – Katie Gambill. I told Mona and Cruz that you and I are friends."

On her walk back to Ian's car under the broiling sun, she hoped Natalie would recognize how it would benefit her. It seemed logical to want to undo a trip to the past that delivered on none of her dreams. Surely, she would see that. When she rounded the corner where Ian was parked, he cranked the engine and turned up the AC.

She climbed into the passenger seat, adjusting the vents so the cool air blew directly at her.

"Well?" he said.

"I made my pitch. She's gotta think about it. Fingers crossed she'll sign on."

"What now?"

"I'm supposed to call her tomorrow."

"Should we stay another night?"

"Staying longer would cost you more."

"Not to worry. I've got a sugar mama who says she's going to send me money in the future to pay all my expenses." He grinned.

"Well then, since it would cost *me* more, I vote for driving back to New York."

~

She was glad to get home. Ironic that walking into Ian's apartment felt like home considering she slept every night on his uncomfortable couch and spent her days at his kitchen bar using a borrowed laptop. She shook her head.

Her tête-à-tête with Natalie had taken more out of her than she realized. She slouched down on the sofa, pillows around her, closing her eyes when Ian left for the market. When the door chimed, she was awakened from an unsettling dream where she was performing on a bare stage in front of an empty room.

She rubbed her eyes as she checked the monitor. It was Mona and Cruz.

"Hola, mi amiga!" Mona said as they walked in, her skin glowing, big soft braids wrapped around her head like a crown. "You're the mysterious girl I was looking for."

"Is Ian here?" Cruz asked.

"Gone to the store."

"Mind if we get a snack?"

Carly shrugged, which Cruz took as her consent, and proceeded into the kitchen. Using an app on his phone, he launched a classic rock playlist on the ceiling speakers.

"You'll never guess who called me a while ago," Mona said, eyes wide.

Carly waited.

"Natalie Maynor! She called to ask about *you!*" She plopped down in a chair.

"I said to her, 'I thought you and Katie knew each other.' And she says, 'We do, but not all that well.' And I said to her, 'How are you guys acquainted?' And she says, 'Well, we met through friends of friends.' And I said, 'I thought you and Katie had retro music in common.' And she says, 'We do.' And then she says 'I wanted to ask you what you think of her. Is she trustworthy?' And I told her, 'I think so but I don't know her all that well.' I told her you've been sleeping on Ian's couch and he's been paying your way, but that I don't know anything bad about you. I explained how you asked to see pictures of her and how I showed you some."

"Interesting," Carly said.

"Yeah. I wondered if she's investing money in a start-up company you're launching. So I asked her. She said she might sublet her apartment to you for a while and she wanted to talk with people who know you. By the way, it would be great if you moved in. Anyway, I told her you're not a wildcat like some women I know."

They heard Cruz's phone ring. He answered in the kitchen but they could hear him talking. It sounded like he was being asked similar questions.

"I don't know much about her but I can tell you she's decent people," he said. "Ian must think so too, otherwise he wouldn't let her stay at his apartment."

There was a pause for another question.

"If you want to know the truth, I think he's in love with her. He hasn't said anything to me but it's as plain as the sand stuck in my crack after a day at Rockaway Beach."

Mona struggled to stifle a giggle.

"So when are you coming back?" he said.

He was quiet for a moment.

"When you get home we'll have a party. It's been Dull City around here lately."

Mona stared at Carly who tried to act like they both hadn't overheard the part about Ian being in love with her.

Cruz sauntered in, eating from a bag of baby carrots as another song began.

"Doesn't Ian ever buy any snacks? Man cannot live on raw vegetables alone!"

Mona laughed and snatched one of the carrots.

"Cool song," Cruz said, gesturing at the ceiling speaker above him as "Mary Jane's Last Dance" played. "No wonder Bob Dylan was so popular."

"I don't think that's Dylan," Mona said.

"Yeah it is," Cruz said.

Mona shot Carly a questioning glance.

"That's Tom Petty," said Carly. "But sometimes he does sound like Bob Dylan."

Cruz grunted under his breath, then glanced at Mona. "Let's head over to Casa Maria and get a nacho something or other for supper."

"We could fix nachos at home."

"It's way more fun at Casa Maria."

He left the bag of carrots on a lamp table, then pulled Mona up from her chair. They started for the door, his hand squeezing her left butt cheek. She responded in kind, causing him to laugh.

"See you later, Katie!" Mona called out as they closed the door behind them.

When Ian returned with groceries, she followed him into the kitchen, filling him in on Mona's news about Natalie doing a background check before agreeing to sublet the apartment.

"I guess that's a good sign," he said with a distinct lack of enthusiasm.

She wandered back into the living room, leaving him to finish putting away groceries. A moment later, she heard him speaking to someone, an urgent tone in his voice. Then he hurried into the living room.

"Dad fell! I'm meeting the ambulance at the hospital!"

He sprinted out the door.

She was sound asleep when he got home in the wee hours of the morning, tip-toeing through the living room to avoid waking her.

~

Ian looked like a zombie the next morning. He said his dad fractured his hip and would undergo surgery immediately. After a few hours' sleep, he was headed back to the hospital.

"He was trying to get his autoharp down from the top of the closet. I can't believe he climbed up on that step stool! As unsteady as he is, he always asks me or Asher or a neighbor for help with stuff like that. Last night when I got there and learned what happened, I wanted to shake him!"

The normally unflappable Ian was furious with his father. And, no doubt, furious that his dad was in such bad shape to begin with that he couldn't use a stool to get something down from the closet.

"I'm so sorry, Ian. What can I do to help?"

"If you know where there's an old lamp tucked away that you could rub your hand over and summon a genie who would grant me three wishes, that would be much appreciated." There was no smile. "Naturally, it comes at a bad time. I've got to get a move on with the Underwood project. We've fallen behind somehow. I'll have to work on it while I'm in the waiting room."

He put his laptop in his backpack and hurried out the door.

Later that day he called saying Tom's surgery went off without a hitch. He said the prognosis was good for recovery, although rehab would be difficult given his pre-existing condition.

"Let me come over and relieve you," she said. "I noticed your transit card on the shelf by the door. I can take a bus."

"He's my dad. It's my responsibility."

"I owe you, Ian. Let me help while I can. It would make me feel better."

Silence.

"I promise, no flirting," she added.

There was a muffled sound like a swallowed chuckle. "All right. Once he wakes up and I have a chance to talk with him."

He told her which bus to take and how to get there.

~

When she arrived in Tom's room, he greeted her with an attempted smile that looked more like he had gas. Before she had time to speak, a nurse walked in.

"Well, Mr. Stewart, you ready to do the tango?" Said with a friendly grin.

She was an attractive Asian-American woman, early fifties, with shiny black hair styled in a page boy.

Tom groaned.

That's when the nurse stopped and looked more closely at her patient.

"Oh my God, you're Dr. Stewart from NYU!" She couldn't hide the hero worship on her face. "I took two history classes from you when I was in college. Multiculturalism in America and the Global History of International Migration. Coming from a Chinese immigrant family, your classes meant a lot to me."

"That's one of the reasons I taught them, being a living, breathing example of multiculturalism myself."

There was an uncomfortable pause before she went on.

"Is this your daughter?" She waved a hand in Carly's direction, seemingly embarrassed by her fangirl outburst.

He groaned again.

"Family friend," Carly answered for him. "The name is Katie Gambill."

The nurse's smile faded a bit.

"I'm friends with his son," Carly explained, sensing disapproval, probably because she assumed Carly was Tom's much younger girlfriend.

"I'm Naomi Xu." She checked Tom's blood pressure, oxygen level, temperature and his I-V. "How you feeling?" she asked.

He muttered something under his breath.

"This afternoon you'll start your rehab."

Carly and Tom were clearly taken aback that physical therapy would start right away.

"Call if you need anything," she said before walking out the door.

Following what Tom complained was a tasteless soft lunch, a physical therapist showed up as promised. The first exercise was to sit up on the side of the bed. It was a struggle but Tom managed. The therapist helped him transfer from the bed to a chair where he did a range of strength and flexibility exercises, including some leg lifts and ankle rotations. Then she assisted him as he stood up and returned to the bed. Thankfully, that was the extent of the first session because Tom was shaky and a little green around the gills.

"Just what I need is even more exercises to do every day," he mumbled before falling asleep.

Carly made her way outside the building to call Natalie. Sitting on a bench in the shade, she was jumpy, afraid her plan would be deep-sixed. Natalie answered on the first ring, which Carly hoped was a good sign.

"Listen, I'm a different person now than I was when I first got here," Natalie said. "I know now that I wasn't ready. I should've worked with some bands when I was preparing. I could've polished my voice, developed more skills. I see that now. But in the days and weeks after I first got here, I was positive things would work out. I thought Hawke would teach me, show me the ropes, you know. But he didn't. He strung me along for a while, then cut me loose. It was painful. I moved out of the mansion two weeks after I arrived, the night I went to the Stevie Nicks concert. When I left the mansion, I was all about making a name for myself. You see what I'm saying?"

"Now you know it wasn't such a good idea."

"I don't think you're hearing me. The Natalie who stayed in your old apartment would be irate if she found herself back in her own time. She would feel like she'd been robbed. She would want to undo it. She was determined to make it in the music business."

It was a strain for Carly not to raise her voice since that's how she, herself, had been feeling every minute since she'd been commandeered in a time travel exchange against her will.

"We could make sure she couldn't turn around and swap places again," Carly said.

"How?"

"Close off that doorway in twenty twenty-four so nobody could go through it again. Cut a new door on the other side of the room."

"That would take days, if not weeks."

"True, but the minute I get back to my own time, I'll be moving out of the Vandermeer mansion for good. There will be no swapping places with *me* again. I could keep the apartment in my name for a while so nobody else can use it until renovations could be done."

"You understand what I'm saying, though, right? It's taken me three decades to realize my mistake. Back then – when I had recently arrived – if I'd been forced against my will to return to my own time, I would've been infuriated. If I'd been tricked into returning to twenty fifty-four, I would've fought tooth and nail to turn right around and go through the time portal again to get back to the past."

It was galling to hear Natalie make out like *she* was the injured party.

"Does that sound familiar or what?" Carly said. "I was forced against *my* will to travel from my own time to your time. I'm the one who was wronged!"

Silence. Then the phone connection dropped.

Carly leaned over until her head touched her knees. She had let her temper reach a rolling boil despite telling herself repeatedly to treat Natalie like she was a reasonable woman.

She was supposed to act like Natalie's feelings were equally as valid as her own. She muffed it.

13

Claustrophobia overcame her as she walked back inside. She needed to get out of this hospital. While she didn't have a bank card or a mobile payment app on her cheap phone, she still had that twenty-seven dollars in her wallet. Surely that would buy her a coffee slushy or something.

She did a quick braiding trick, twisting her hair up on top of her head, then slung her pocketbook over her shoulder. On her way out of the building she slipped her sunglasses on. She trudged toward a strip of shops she'd noticed down the road. On foot, it was a lot further than she expected. By the time she reached it, she was wet with sweat.

There was an ice cream shop, a drug store, a hair salon, a coffee shop and a store called Tootsie's Used Records & Movies. That's where Natalie worked and where she found the Hawke & Carly album. That was her first stop.

It was a store only devoted fans could love. Dusty and cluttered, it smelled like someone's attic. But it had a friendly vibe.

A tall guy re-arranging items on the shelves gave her a casual glance as she entered.

"Let me know if I can help you."

"I'm looking for Natalie. Can't remember her last name."

"She's on vacation. Can I do anything for you?"

"Someone told me she's a good person to ask for recommendations."

"Well, we all have our specialties. Her areas are twentieth century rock music and time travel movies and shows. Me, I'm an R&B kind of guy. I know a good bit about soul and jazz too. As for movies, I'm into thrillers and spy movies. We have a couple of other—"

"Time travel. That's what I wanted to ask her about. Does she have any movies she recommends, in particular?"

"Oh yeah. Of course she goes for the oldies. Believe it or not, she created a *paper* handout!" He moved to a glass counter to get one, handing it to her. "I can find whatever we've got on the shelf if you see something you want."

"This is quite a list!"

"Yeah, Natalie is, like, the president of the Wish-I-Could-Time-Travel Club." He grinned. "She's all about time travel. Won't shut up about it. She joked that she wished she could travel back to her childhood and tell her parents to let her take music lessons so she could grow up to be a rock star. She begged them but they told her it was too expensive. Of course, they could afford going out on the town every weekend. Great parents, huh?"

Carly was intrigued by this little nugget. More proof, as if she needed any, that Natalie fully intended to travel to the past by swapping places with a rock musician on her way up.

"I'll take this with me and look up some reviews," she said. "Thanks!"

She made a quick exit, heading for the coffee shop as she perused the long list of time travel flicks.

Inside the coffee shop, she examined the menu app, discovering her twenty-seven dollars would indeed buy a mocha frappé with a few bucks left over. She pushed the corresponding button on the menu screen, waited for her drink, then sat at a tiny bistro table on the sidewalk outside. Her coffee milkshake, coupled with shade from an awning and the breeze from a couple of fans, was enough to keep her from melting.

Gazing out toward the street, it was impossible to tell she wasn't in her own time. Granted, the cars looked different and they were quieter, but most everything was familiar. Except the prices. After her latest conversation with Natalie, she was concerned she might have to get used to living here. She shuddered at the thought. She had to find a way to convince Natalie the reverse swap was in her best interest.

On her walk back to the hospital, she thought back to Natalie's comment about moving out of the mansion the night of the Stevie Nicks concert. Carly's the one who bought those tickets and couldn't wait to see one of her idols in person. The concert was scheduled for Friday night, the first of August, which was two weeks to the day after her unexpected departure through the time portal. She had now been in this future time for a week and two days. That meant this coming Friday would be her last chance to trade places. After that, Natalie would no longer live in the mansion. She needed access to Natalie's apartment pronto.

When she knocked on Tom's door, his 'come in' sounded weak.

"How's it going?" she said.

"Frankly, I feel like a barf bag with a quart of vomit in it."

"Song lyrics if I ever try grunge music."

No smile. He shook his head. That little bit of movement made him wince.

Noticing a tall cup of ice water on his tray was nearly empty, she pushed the call button.

"Do you need a snack?" she asked.

"Crackers."

A staffer arrived, refilling the cup and setting out some crackers and applesauce. Then he took Tom's blood pressure and checked his heart rate and oxygen level.

When the nursing aide left, Carly pushed the rolling bed tray closer so Tom could reach everything.

"No doubt, Ian is exasperated," he said. "I don't blame him. Trying to avoid calling him like a helpless old man, I succeeded in making his life even more miserable. Now he'll have to help me with every last thing under the sun. And the moon. Other than wiping my ass. Who knows, he might have to help me with that too!" He grunted. "I had the urge to play my old autoharp. I don't know. Guess I was inspired being around a real musician like you."

That was the last thing she wanted to hear. She had inspired him to be more independent? Damn. But she definitely understood where he was coming from.

"I'm so tired of calling Ian day in and day out," he said. "Zack – my younger son – never has to worry about Old Dad because he knows Ian's close by. And Ian would never pressure Zack into moving back here to help out. I didn't have the faintest idea when I chose to have the surgery that it would not only ruin *my* life, it would drag Ian down too."

"I haven't known him very long, but I've never felt like he was an angry or bitter man," she said, tidying his tray. "You could be blowing this a little out of proportion."

"He doesn't let on. But believe me, he's given up a lot for me. He passed on a great job he wanted a couple of years ago because it would've required him to relocate. I'm the reason he turned it down."

"Did Ian say that?"

"Of course not. But I know it hurt him to say no. He lies to me as much as I lie to him, both of us hiding what we don't want the other to worry about. His commitment to me has also wrecked a couple of relationships."

"Why?"

"Well, there was the tall one. She dumped him when he explained he had to be available when I called."

"Did he tell you that?"

"*She* told me. And there was the teacher who bailed on him when he asked if she minded inviting me along to an afternoon concert by a jazz group I liked. She was nice about it, but I guess she wanted someone who didn't have to babysit his disabled old man."

"He was lucky to find out they were that selfish before he got in too deep. But he's got time! He's not even thirty yet!"

"You know how often he goes on a date? Last time he had a date was, I don't know, nearly a year ago. His sole longtime relationship is with solitude. That's not good. I'm a burden to him. Now, I'll be even more of a burden."

It was true – Ian always took Tom into consideration when making decisions.

"He told me you did get to speak with Natalie," Tom said.

"I ambushed her after she pretended not to be home. I'm hoping she'll go along with my plan."

She didn't tell him about the discouraging phone call.

He paused before changing gears in a surprising direction.

"You know, it occurred to me that if you do manage to get back to your time, you might be able to help me out with something."

She moved to the foot of the bed, giving him her full attention.

"I'm hoping you'll be able to warn me about the terrible pain I suffer now because of that back surgery. You could tell me how disabled I become. It's possible a warning from the future could save me – and Ian – a lot of misery."

"Warn you?" she asked, feigning innocence.

"In twenty twenty-four I was thirty-three years old. My back was the furthest thing from my mind. If you could convince the younger me how much pain I'll suffer when I'm in my sixties, it's conceivable I'll make a different decision when the time comes. That way I can save myself – and Ian – from having to deal with this steaming pile of bullshit."

Before she could answer, he plowed ahead.

"I know it's not likely I'd believe you. I get that. But if I tell you something now that I've never told anybody else, then you can tell the younger me to prove you spoke with me in the future."

If she hadn't already thought of it, she'd be thinking it was a decent idea right now. But Ian had opened her eyes to the havoc she might wreak trying to do a good deed. She laid it out for Tom like Ian had for her.

"I think if I intervened like that, you could end up just as bad off in your sixties as you are now. What if you still decided to have the same surgery after several surgeons recommend it? Or you could end up having a different surgery that also leaves you disabled. And if you choose not to have surgery at all, you could still end up in terrible pain."

"But—"

"And there's something else to consider. In the short time I've known you, Tom, there have been moments when I was aware that you were attracted to me." This was Ian's impression, not hers. She fibbed about that part of it to make it more dramatic. From his blushing reaction now, she could see that Ian was right. "If I visited you in your thirties, it's possible you'd also be attracted to me then. In fact, you said you were starstruck after coming to my band's show. As I recall, Ian was born a year later. My interference could cause your life to change in a big way. What if you didn't marry Ian's mother?"

He released a long sigh, staring up at the ceiling. "Then Ian and Zack wouldn't be born."

"If I do make it home, I can't butt in and try to save you from the pain, as much as I wish I could. There's a very real chance I would screw things up big time."

Without warning, Tom grabbed his cup of ice water and hurled it across the room. It crashed against the wall, splattering to the floor as he grunted in pain.

He stared at the wet spot, water dripping down the wall, and took some deep breaths.

"Three different surgeons said it was the best route to take. That it would keep me mobile and reduce my pain. How was I to know it would rob me of my life? The surgeon who did the deed gave me a sympathetic look when I told him those two long rods and all those screws were killing me, that I could feel them with every breath. He was baffled when I told him the screws he put in my sacrum hurt like he'd hammered a couple of six-inch nails into my back. After the second surgery when they removed all that hardware, I didn't feel it anymore, but it didn't remove the pain. I might as well have jumped out of an airplane without a parachute. I'm like a pain bomb. It hurts to walk, to stand, to sit, to lie in bed. It's not fair!"

His eyes brimmed with tears.

"So when it dawned on me that you really are from the past and you might make it back, I thought you could help prevent this medical travesty from happening. But I understand what you're saying. And I get it – there are some things we can't fix. We have to learn to live with them. Learn to cope. Learn how to avoid letting them drag us so far down we can't function anymore."

He turned away.

"My own dad was a lot smarter than me," he continued. "One day he climbed up on the roof to adjust the cable dish and keeled over and died of a heart attack. Boom! He was gone. Sixty-seven years old. Dad used to quote a Brian Setzer song – 'we've only got sixty years and if we get more than that, we might wish we hadn't.'"

She wanted to say something but couldn't think of words that would provide any solace. So she gave him a hug instead.

"Sorry I'm in asshole mode," he said.

"You're tired and hurting. I understand."

"That's the problem. I'm always tired and hurting. Guess you could say I've passed my sell-by date."

Talk about being robbed of your life – he was a poster boy for broken medical promises. If there was anyone who deserved a do-over, it was Tom.

~

Stepping off the bus at the corner, she wasn't ready to go inside. She sat on a bench out front, filling her lungs with warm air, shaded from the sun's relentless rays by her friend, the giant oak. With time slipping away, she needed to speak with Natalie again.

"Please give me five more minutes. I have an idea I think you'd be interested in."

That was the text she sent.

"Five minutes," was Natalie's reply.

Carly tapped her number.

"I get the feeling you'd like to come back to your own time," Carly said. "The you who has lived thirty years in the past and had a lot of challenges to overcome."

"You have no idea."

"You explained that the Natalie who showed up in the past thirty years ago would be teed off being forced to return to her own time. What if I could help pave the way for her, I mean for *you* to have success as a singer in *this* time? What if I put together a manual with contact info to shortcut the process of learning the ropes and honing your skills? I could have a document ready for you as soon as you walk through the door. You're a product of this era with a feel for the culture and the music. I think you would stand a better chance of being successful *here* rather than in the past."

"How can you do all that in such a short time? I mean, you don't know anybody."

"I have enough experience to know who to approach. And I've been listening to music since I got here. I've also visited some bars that hire live bands. I even have the number of the manager at a Philadelphia restaurant that has live music, if you're willing to travel a little."

There was no reply. Only the sound of breathing.

"It must've been hard using an alias," Carly said.

"It was always complicated. Things have improved since last Friday, now that there's only one of me."

"I hadn't thought of that." She paused for a second letting that sink in. When Natalie arrived in 2024, her younger self was thirteen years old, living in Pittsburgh. The time-traveling Natalie had to avoid her younger self for thirty years. Which would've become more challenging once her younger self moved to New York. Surreal.

"So if you want to proceed," Carly continued, "the next step is to sublet your apartment to me. But time is running out."

"Let me sleep on it."

After they hung up, Carly texted her Raj's number.

~

Ian was fixing supper when she walked in. She wouldn't breathe a word to him about the emotional conversation she'd had with Tom. If he knew his dad came up with the very same idea she had about warning the younger Tom not to go through with the surgery, she could imagine him blowing his stack.

"How's Dad?" he asked, brandishing a spatula.

The aroma of garlic and onions teased her taste buds as he stirred vegetables in a frying pan.

"He started rehab this afternoon. Sat up on the side of the bed, did a few strength and flexibility exercises."

Ian shook his head. "Thanks for sitting with him. I got a ton of work done, which erases any debt you *think* you owe me."

It did not even come close. But now was not the time to argue. Instead, she gathered napkins, silverware and plates and arranged them on the kitchen bar.

He plated up his stir fry along with a couple of spring rolls. Without asking, he poured them both a glass of white wine and sat down across from her. His body language told her he was out of sorts. She tried to think of something innocuous to talk about but nothing was innocuous enough.

They ate in silence until she couldn't take it anymore.

"Are you okay?" she said.

"Yeah. Sure. Just, you know."

He took another bite, avoiding her eyes. After a moment, he came clean.

"It was way too quiet around here today. Empty. I was used to that before, except for when Cruz and Mona busted in filling the place with noise. It was a relief when they came. Then it was a relief when they left. But now, it's changed. I'm feeling…"

He let his words float in the air for a minute.

"I've gotten used to having you around," he went on. "Even when we're not in the same space, even when I'm working on my project and you're working on your project, I can feel you in the next room. I can stop what I'm doing and see you, talk with you, hear your voice. On our trip to Philly, we were together almost the whole time. It felt good. Very good. Then today, while you were at the hospital and I was here working, it hit me, this is what it's going to be like when you leave. Like it was before you arrived."

The longing was obvious in his gaze.

"Carly," he said, reaching across the bar to take her hand. "I love you."

He'd gone and done it now, saying the words out loud.

"My heart tells me you love me too," he said.

No, no, no. If she lost control now, he would suffer even more when she left. But she wanted him. And she wanted her life back too.

Moving around the bar, he sat on the stool beside her and leaned close to kiss her. She couldn't bring herself to push him away.

"Sometimes," he murmured in her ear, "you're like a hard-driving rock song with a pounding rhythm and a wild guitar, but sometimes you're like a heartfelt ballad with lyrics that stay in my head forever."

She was mesmerized.

"I want to make love to you," he whispered, touching her cheek.

She shouldn't have allowed that kiss. She was walking on ice so thin, it was about to crack, plunging her into the depths.

"I need to visit a couple of clubs tonight," she said, forcing herself to ignore the impulse to slide her hands under his shirt.

He stiffened.

"If Natalie agrees to the swap," she continued, "I promised I'd help her get started when she comes back. So I have to do more field research."

He got to his feet, waves of rejection radiating from his body.

"And you need me to drive you," he said.

Although his back was to her, his disappointment was palpable. There was a hint of irritation as well.

She did need him to drive her. Which was unfair. He'd been her right-hand man since she careened into his world, continually at her beck and call. He'd been accommodating and generous. She didn't want to hurt him. But going to bed with him would be selfish since there was no chance she'd give up her life to stay here.

Watching him load the dishwasher, she couldn't help but be reminded how much she enjoyed looking at him, the shape of him, the set of his shoulders. No phony bulges from hours every day at the gym. She liked the way he moved, his natural masculinity, not an exaggerated swagger.

He glanced at her then, catching her avid gaze. His expression softened.

"Obviously, you need a chauffeur and escort," he said. "I'm all yours."

14

First stop was the hospital so Ian could check on his dad. He knocked and walked in, all in one motion, taking his dad and the chatty nurse by surprise. She was taking Tom's vitals, her joking patter bringing a smile to his face. Tom flushed a little but the friendly nurse wasn't bothered in the least.

"You must be the son," she said, greeting Ian. "I'm Naomi Xu."

"Right. I'm Ian. This is Car—"

"Katie," Carly said before Ian let her real name slip. "We met earlier today."

"Glad to see you're in good spirits," Ian said to his dad.

"Tom and I were discussing awful concerts we've been to," Naomi said. "Like the one I went to a few years ago where Arlo Saluda's auto-tune shorted out in the middle of his big hit. Talk about torture on the ears! I don't know who was more embarrassed, him or the audience."

She and Tom laughed.

"I went to a show once that was delayed over an hour because it took that long to get the AI music app working," Tom said. "Pathetic that some bands aren't really musicians who play an instrument. They manipulate AI pre-sets on stage."

"Speaking of concerts," Ian said, "We're headed out to see a live band. Wanted to stop by."

Tom seemed relieved the visit was a short one. And Ian was grateful his dad was doing better than he expected.

"I thought he'd be in pain," he said as they walked to the car.

"Nurse Naomi seems to be a good analgesic," Carly replied.

She had lined up bars to visit that were within reasonable driving distance. They headed for The Blue Light Bar & Grill first. It was the place where they'd been surprised by Hawke and his band the night they went out with Cruz and Mona. Carly wanted to talk with the manager in hopes of setting something up for Natalie.

When she asked the bartender where she could find the manager, he said she'd found him.

"Dan Foster at your service."

"Katie Gambill," she said, shaking his hand across the bar. "I'm doing legwork for my sister. Looking for bars that have live music. She's coming in from out of town next week. She's interested in developing some regular gigs. Wondered—"

"She can stop by in person so I can see what she's got, whether she's a good fit. If that works, then a Monday night opening slot would be her audition. It helps if she can bring an audience. Bands earn tips and a percentage of the bar. Then we go from there."

He wiped the bar with a rag, bored with yet another rock star wannabe trying to find a stage.

"Can I send you a video?"

He handed her a business card with a digital address and a scannable code on it. "Scan this and upload the videos. Send me a message with contact info."

She sighed on the way out to the car.

"Some things haven't changed," she said. "You have to pay your dues and prove your worth."

"So you're trying to whittle some of those dues down to size?"

"Trying to get her pointed in the right direction when she comes back. But she has to be willing to put in the time and effort."

"Seems to me the reason she traded places with you in the first place was so she could skip putting in the time and effort and bypass paying those dues. She was fine letting you pay them for her."

"I hope she realizes she has a lot to learn. The Natalie I talked with in Philadelphia knows that. I'm not sure the younger Natalie will be willing to work her way up. But I promised I'd do my best."

"You don't believe she has what it takes, do you?"

"I don't know. It involves talent, drive, persistence and luck."

They swung by another bar that booked performers on Monday nights. They earned tips and a percentage of the bar, like the Blue Light. Carly got the code for uploading videos and the manager's contact info.

At the third bar, a police drone hovered above the parking lot. She didn't know if that was a good sign or a bad sign. A band was already on stage, blasting away. The volume was excessive. They obviously had a sound guy who didn't know what he was doing. The mix stank. You couldn't hear the bass and the guitar was too loud. A man was singing lead with a woman doing backup harmony but the overall effect was hard on the ears. Amazingly, the place was half full. Friends and family? Who else would stay under the circumstances?

Once again Ian took a spot at the bar. She found the manager seated at the other end, a whiskey glass in front of him. He gave her an unapologetic once-over as she approached.

"The name's Katie Gambill." She had to practically shout to be heard. "I'm doing some legwork for my sister."

"Don't I know you?" he said, his eyes boring into her.

"I don't—"

"I never forget the face of a good singer. What band are you with?"

"I'm not—"

"It'll come to me, it'll come." He seemed to enjoy the game, certain his memory would click any second now. "Let me think."

His eyes narrowed as he studied her. "I remember your voice is a little husky, a rockin' good voice."

"I think you're confusing me with—"

"You said your name is Katie Gambill?"

"That's right. But I'm here to talk about my sister."

"The name doesn't ring a bell."

He drained his glass.

"My sister's name is Natalie. She's coming into town—"

"I know!" he blurted. "You remind me of a first-rate singer I knew back in the day. Her name was Carly Munro. You look like a young Carly Munro." He smiled in triumph, proud of himself. "But it's like the song says, 'only the good die young.' Damn shame too."

Even if she knew it wasn't true, it was disquieting to hear herself talked about like she was dead.

"I'm sorry, I forgot to ask your name," she said.

"Everyone calls me Dragon. As in Puff the Magic." He chuckled like the joke never got old.

Then she remembered. Kenny Dragon. He was the drummer for a hard-driving rock band called U-Turn. They were like a local version of The Grateful Dead, throwing all kinds of music together to create a sound that audiences either loved or hated. Before she joined forces with Hawke, Carly's former band opened for U-Turn a couple of times. The musicians were well known for drug use. They started to come apart at the seams shortly before the Hawke & Carly album came out.

It was hard to believe he'd ever been a fine young buck. Now he looked his age and then some. Amazing that he remembered her, all things considered.

"U-Turn," she said. "My dad was a fan," she lied.

"So, does your sister look as good as you do?" Said with the same leer that used to look cool.

"Yeah. Can I give her your name and info?"

"Send me links to some videos." He handed her the same type of succinct business card the other managers gave her.

"Great. Thanks, Mister Dragon."

"Lose the 'mister.' Call me Dragon."

She gave him a thumbs up and took his card.

Back in the car, she told Ian she was done for the night.

"It's been a while since I was inside bars like that. I don't miss 'em."

"You've gotten used to a better class of drunks?"

She shot him a mock evil eye.

Her phone pinged. It was a message from Natalie: "I called Raj. He'll check with management in the morning to confirm that it's okay to sublet the apartment."

Carly told Ian. He said nothing in reply.

If building management gave the go-ahead, she could start trying for the exchange tomorrow. Oddly, she wasn't quite ready.

First off, she hadn't finished preparing her cheat sheet for Natalie. She needed to visit a few more venues and get all her notes and contact information organized. She had to shift into high gear. Second, she wasn't emotionally prepared to leave Ian behind. Or ahead. Whatever. She wished she'd been able to undo the swap right after it happened. The longer she was here, the harder it would be to say goodbye. She hadn't meant to lead him on. She never wanted him to fall in love with her. And she certainly hadn't meant to fall for him. Her goal had always been to find her way home. This was not her time. Ian wasn't even born the year her album came out. She would've been thirty-two the year he was born, easily old enough to be his mother. A shiver ran through her.

"You all right?" he asked.

"Yes," she whispered, lying again.

Back in the apartment, she set herself up in the kitchen with her laptop, searching for possible bars for Natalie. She had to speak with the manager of each one in person, not over the phone, and not through their online application process. Which meant another round of visits. If it wasn't half an hour's drive to the nearest subway station, she'd take the train. Realistically though, it would take an eternity to make it to four venues in different parts of the city on the subway. She needed a car.

She couldn't ask Ian to drive her again. Instead, she knocked on his bedroom door to ask a different favor.

Although he had put on pajama shorts and a tee, he looked anything but relaxed. A wave of guilt slammed into her. The words "never mind" were on the tip of her tongue, but she had to keep her promise to Natalie and time was running out.

He raised his eyebrows in question.

"I have to go to a few more venues. I've identified two restaurants and two more bars."

"Tonight?" His voice was louder than she expected.

"Besides using your time and your gas, I know they ding you for the congestion toll every time you drive into the city. So I'm not asking you to drive me."

"You're not?"

"Can you loan me money so I can get a cash card? That way I can order a ride share myself."

Anger showed in his eyes.

"As soon as I get home, I'll repay you," she said. "Which means you'll have your money back by the end of this week."

"Carly—"

"I'll repay you for all the money you've spent on me, not just for the cash card. Every penny. I promise."

"Seriously? You think that's what I'm concerned about?" He raised his hands in frustration. "You can't go to those places late at night by yourself."

"I'm used to it. It's part of the job."

"You're with your band when you go to your gigs."

"I usually go alone and meet the guys there."

"But you have them there to protect you."

"I know how to handle myself," she said, a little huffy. "I'm a grown woman and I've been doing this quite a while now. I know what to look out for, situations to avoid."

"I can't let you do this solo," he said, his voice rising another notch. "No way!"

"I know you don't want to go. You've got that project—"

"I'd rather you leaned on me than risk your life going to some low-class bar in the middle of the night! It's fucking dangerous!" he shouted.

She stepped back as though dodging a speeding car.

"Sorry," he said, lowering his voice. "I don't want you to get hurt. I know you're used to being independent. I know you don't like to impose. I'll get my project done. But you'll only be here a few more days, possibly less than that. Let me help. I could never live with myself if you were..." But he trailed off, refusing to say the words.

~

First, they drove to a restaurant in the East Village called The Side Door. It didn't have live bands on Monday nights but Carly could make her pitch anyway. The manager referred her to a woman named Celia who handled bookings. She was a Black woman with long braids and expressive eyes. She greeted Carly with a seen-it-all look.

"Your sister?" Her tone implied Carly was lying.

"She's getting into town next week. I'm doing some legwork for her."

"We book bands for Friday night, Saturday night and Sunday night. Tuesday through Thursday we book solo performers. We already have a roster of regulars. If she wants to try out for an on-call spot on the roster, she should send me a link to her press kit."

Natalie wasn't far enough along to qualify for this place. She thanked Celia and headed for restaurant number two. But it used a booking agency that supplied bands and singers to venues. So much for the possibility of finding that type of gig. Back to the low-class bars, as Ian put it.

The first one had the same set-up as the places she'd already visited. Carly took the manager's card so she could submit videos and Natalie's contact info. By the time they walked into a joint called The Salty Saloon, it was almost midnight. Of course, the later the hour, the rowdier the crowd. Her usually reliable antenna should've told her to turn around and walk back out of there as soon as she spotted a nearly topless woman dancing with a drunk guy intent on feeling her up. Ian stood behind her as Carly asked the bartender, a plump blonde woman with heavy eye makeup, if she could speak with the manager.

"If you're gonna complain, you're in the wrong bar," she said, retrieving a couple of empty glasses.

"I want to ask him about booking my sister's band."

"He's kinda busy."

"Since I'm here, you think he could spare me two minutes?"

The woman studied her closely. "I'll check. Have a seat. What can I get you and lover boy?"

Carly didn't want anything to drink but had a feeling she better show support so she ordered two beers. She and Ian sat at the bar to wait.

The bartender clicked a button on her phone, then poured two draft beers, setting the steins in front of them.

Ian waved his phone over the code on the screen to pay, then touched Carly's elbow. He gestured with his eyes toward the exit.

A moment later the man she assumed was the manager showed up, taking the stool next to her.

"We like whiskey music," he said, not bothering with introductions or small talk. "A lot of rockabilly, hard rock, anthem rock. We like whiskey lyrics. Songs you can sing along to and dance to, music you can fornicate to, if you know what I mean. If your *sister*," said as though he figured she was asking for herself, "can do that, tell her to go to our website and upload links to some of her stuff."

With that, he headed for a group of young guys who looked like they were a band in search of their big break.

"Let's go," Ian said, getting to his feet.

As they made their way through the front of the room, he slipped his arm around her protectively. She breathed a sigh of relief when he pushed the door open and they made it outside.

With only the light emanating from the front of the bar, the sidewalk was dark. They'd taken a couple of steps when two large men materialized out of nowhere, blocking their path. Sunglasses, dark shoulder-length hair, mustaches and beards hid their faces. The hair didn't look real.

Carly froze as Ian moved forward a half step as if to shield her.

"We're in need of some cold hard cash," the larger one said. "Need you to send some to this number." He handed Ian a slip of paper with a phone number on it. "A thousand bucks."

Ian didn't argue, focusing on making the transaction on his phone.

"You too," the thug said, directing his gaze at Carly.

"She doesn't have a bank account," Ian said.

"Then use a cash app."

"She doesn't have any apps on her phone."

"Yeah, right. Unlock your phone and hand it over," he said to Carly.

She did as she was told.

"What is this? A baby phone?"

"Sort of," Ian replied. "She doesn't have internet."

"I thought—" the second robber began.

"Zip it," the leader said, then turned his attention back to Ian. "By my reckoning, it's two minutes till midnight. So in two minutes you can transfer another thousand to that number."

They obviously knew about daily limits on cash transfers.

"Can I have my baby phone back?" Carly said.

The thief in chief tossed it in her direction.

Someone exited the bar behind them, the blaring music louder until the door closed again.

The four of them stood motionless, watching the countdown to midnight on their phones. Ian didn't have to be told what to do when midnight arrived, immediately transferring the additional cash. Then he wrapped his arm around Carly, sidestepping the bandits.

She held her breath as they hurried along the sidewalk to where Ian's car was parked. Using his phone, he unlocked the car as they ran the last few yards. They leapt inside, the doors locking automatically as he started the engine and put it in drive, bypassing self-driving mode. She had expected to be tackled from behind every step of the way.

Ian was right to worry. She put him through hell. If she'd been alone, it could've been much worse than robbery. Even with the two of them together, they were still at the mercy of those creeps. How cocksure she'd been.

She should've known better. Even though she was used to being at bars and clubs late at night, she normally took precautions and kept her radar on. She'd gotten in the habit of offering one of the guys a ride home from a gig. That way she'd have a man with her as she left a venue. She saved him the cost of a ride share, taxi or a long trip home on the subway and he saved her from being vulnerable. A fair trade-off. But tonight? She screwed up tonight.

"You were right," she said. "I was wrong. I'm so sorry."

He could've said I told you so, but held his tongue. He still hadn't said a word when they reached his apartment.

Of course, now she owed him another two thousand dollars. She would reimburse him, but he deserved a lot more than that.

"Thank you," she whispered. "I know that's not enough but..."

He walked through the living room without answering.

"Ian?"

She stood silently as he retreated into his bedroom. Unthinkingly, she followed him, stopping outside his door. If she knocked and he opened it, she would tell him she loved him. Not good. Not good at all.

15

Ian ate breakfast at his desk the next morning leaving Carly to her own devices. She set up at the kitchen bar to continue preparing the document for Natalie, having toast and coffee as she worked. She listed the managers of the venues she'd visited. She would leave their business cards in an envelope in Natalie's apartment. She listed online bulletin boards where gigs and musician jobs were advertised. She was adding contact info for a handful of booking agents when she heard Ian on the phone. A moment later he called out to her that he'd given Raj her number. Her phone chimed right away.

"Natalie Maynor called me saying she wants to rent her apartment to you for the rest of this week," Raj said. "She told me you two are working on a project together." He sounded suspicious. "I contacted management and they said since it was for such a short time, they were okay with it as long as I can vouch for you. I had to think about it for a minute since I don't know you. But because Ian is an honest, reliable tenant and he says you're okay, I told my superiors they could trust you."

"I appreciate that."

"Please don't do anything that would get me in trouble."

"Got it."

"Yes, well, the rental is good through Saturday. You pay Natalie directly. She asked me to have you sign a sublease agreement since she's out of town. I've got time right now if you can come to my apartment."

Carly put on her shoes and walked down the hallway to his door. With his baby daughter in a high chair by his desk, Raj sat down, handing Carly an e-tablet with a form to sign. Once she signed it, he signed it too as a witness, then uploaded it to the company portal and texted a copy to Natalie. He sounded like he was still uneasy about the whole thing.

"If you don't mind my asking, what are you and Natalie working on?"

"Well, it's Natalie's project so I'll let her fill you in. Do I get a code to open the door?"

"I'll transmit it to your phone."

The code was delivered instantaneously.

"Are the two of you good friends?" he asked.

"No." She shook her head more vigorously than she intended.

She thought he would say something else but little Veda began pounding the tray on her high chair.

"Is it time for a little snack?" he said to her brightly, thus drawing their brief meeting to a close.

She thanked him, giving the baby a small wave as she left.

It was ironic she had what she'd wanted since she first arrived – access to the apartment – yet now she was a case of nerves. She shook her head. What a sissy she'd become.

She texted Natalie, thanking her for making it happen. She asked about the likeliest times for a successful swap during her last few days in the mansion. There was no reply.

Returning to Ian's apartment, she resumed working, hoping he would stop by the kitchen like he often did to get a snack or a drink and engage in small talk. Not today. He didn't want to speak to her. He didn't want to look at her. Getting the cold shoulder hurt.

As lunchtime approached, he poked his head in the door. But it was to tell her he was off to the hospital to spend time with his dad.

With him gone, she went for a little walk. When she reached the hallway, she paused by Natalie's apartment and listened. Moving closer, she tilted her head to hear better. She thought she heard a woman's voice. She leaned even closer until her ear was almost touching the door. Yes, it was a woman's voice. Natalie's voice.

Afraid to accidentally trigger an exchange, she stepped away. She wasn't ready. Which sparked a wave of guilt. But it was the truth. She wasn't ready yet. She had a promise to keep.

She returned to Ian's kitchen and ate a sandwich as she added more information and suggestions to her document. One of her suggestions was to be willing to work for nothing to get experience. Even for established artists, sometimes you had to swallow your pride and work without a guarantee, hoping drink sales would be enough to pay the band a small percentage or that customers would show some generosity with the virtual tip jar. She put the finishing touches on her little guidebook, eager to be done with it.

Her mind wandered back to the portal. She kept imagining what it would be like to find herself back in her own time.

Although she was apprehensive, she was drawn back to the doorway. Standing stock-still, she listened. Silence. She waited another moment, then entered the pass code and gave the door a shove. It swung wide open. She gazed into Natalie's living room for another long moment, alert for sounds of any kind. Nothing. She darted inside as if hiding from the enemy. When she thought about it, that's what she was doing. Younger Natalie was the enemy who had to be lured into a trap so Carly could reclaim her life. Even though the older version of Natalie had agreed to cooperate, it was like a tenuous peace treaty reached by opposing forces on the battlefield. There was always the fear of being double-crossed.

Closing the door, she meandered through the apartment, turning lights on as she went. On her two previous visits she had only seen the living room. This time, she continued into the bedroom. It was hard to believe this room was decorated by the same person she met in Philadelphia. The older Natalie's home was like the cottage of a gentle woman who liked gardening and needlepoint, and who decorated her living room with cream walls and furnishings in shades of pale green. This bedroom, like the living room, was done in red, black and stainless steel. The room's aura was aggressive, belligerent. Like the woman who lived here would do what she had to do in order to get what she wanted.

There were no photographs on the walls. There were abstract paintings in red, orange and black. But on the dresser, there were a few framed photos of Natalie when she was a young woman. In one, she stood between a middle-aged man and woman who had to be her parents. In another, she sat on the lap of a good-looking man with sandy hair. A boyfriend? A husband? And in the third photo, she was a young woman on stage singing into a microphone. Wearing short shorts, a halter top with long billowing sleeves and boots that reached her thighs, she had the look of a rocker. Which made Carly curious about whether Natalie seriously pursued her ambitions when she was in her twenties.

She noticed a laptop computer on the lower shelf of the nightstand. A dozen or so business cards were scattered around it. They were the same style business cards bar managers had given Carly as she visited them on Natalie's behalf. They had a QR code and a digital address for musicians trying to get bookings. It was plain now that Natalie had already gone through the process Carly had planned to recommend. She may have also uploaded videos. If so, presumably she'd already been turned down.

This meant older Natalie hoped Carly would leave a lot more than a how-to guide. She must be hoping for actual bookings, something Carly couldn't provide.

She checked her phone. Still no reply from Natalie. Since she agreed to the sublet, that must mean she would help coordinate the swap.

Back in Ian's place, she sat down at her laptop again, realizing most of what she included in her document was irrelevant. Natalie had bigger expectations. She sighed, feeling like she'd been played.

Shifting gears, it occurred to her that because she now had access to Natalie's apartment, she should move out of Ian's place. True, even a couple of days in that apartment held about as much appeal as spending time in a jail cell. But it would be a relief to Ian. He'd had enough of her.

She packed the few clothes she had in her suitcase and stacked the rest of her belongings on the couch. She was about to collect a few canned goods from the kitchen when Ian walked in.

"Where are you going?"

"I signed a sublet on Natalie's apartment."

"And you want to stay there?"

She looked down, unable to meet his gaze. "You've been the most generous man on earth and I appreciate it more than you'll ever know, but I've overstayed my welcome."

"You have *not* overstayed your welcome."

"Yes, I have."

"You can't move out." His words sounded like he was pleading, but there was aggravation in his tone as well.

"I hope it's okay if I take a few canned goods," she said, heading into the kitchen.

He followed, leaning against the fridge as she reached into a cabinet above the stove for a can of soup.

"Carly, the last thing I want is for you to clear out."

His voice had lost its edge.

She set the can on the counter.

"I'm sorry," he said. "I got mad because, well, because you're so focused on leaving. And I don't want you to leave."

She closed the cabinet door and opened another one where the coffee was stored. She didn't trust herself to speak. She had to keep him at arm's length.

"For the rest of your time here, I won't sulk," he said. "And I'll loan you as much money as you need since you'll be paying me back with interest. Compounded over thirty years, I guess I'll be set for life."

She put the bag of coffee on the counter, ignoring his little joke.

"You don't want to stay in that awful apartment," he went on. "You'd be all alone."

Her hands stilled.

"Besides, it would be like living in a fire station or a bad art gallery," he said.

Which made her smile.

Turning to face him, she had to resist the urge to wrap her arms around him. The love in his eyes didn't make it easy.

"How's your dad?" she said.

"He goes home tomorrow. A physical therapist will come to his apartment tomorrow afternoon to begin working with him. They're all about getting him moving."

She returned the coffee and soup, then headed for the living room to put her things away. While she was relieved she wouldn't have to stay in Natalie's hideous apartment, these last few days with Ian would be tricky. Why couldn't he be a self-absorbed asshole?

When the doorbell chimed, she was glad for once that it was Mona.

"Guess who I physically therapized at the hospital this morning?" she said as the door opened. "A good-looking older guy by the name of Thomas Seok Stewart."

"You're kidding," Ian said.

"He explained that Seok means stone or strength. Which is good because he's going to need strength. I start at-home PT sessions with him tomorrow."

Carly's phone vibrated. It was a message from Natalie. She turned away to read it. "That second week is fuzzy to me now. I went out every night and slept late every day. I sang with the band a couple of times but I don't remember which nights.

Friday night I went to the concert. That's as much as I can tell you."

Carly knew which nights the band played and which venues because she was the one who booked those gigs. She and Hawke planned a local tour to promote the new album. On Tuesday night of that week, they were scheduled to play The Full Moon Saloon. Thursday night they were booked at Faison's Pub. She had tried to nail down a show for Friday night but couldn't line up a good venue. Which left that night open, meaning she could attend the Stevie Nicks concert. She had printed the tickets as a backup and left them on her dresser. Natalie apparently found them and attended the show on Carly's dime.

"Any idea what time you left the apartment each night?" she typed.

She waited but got no answer. Still, she had a general idea of when Natalie would be leaving the mansion. She could start trying for a swap tonight. That thought sent a little zing through her chest.

She felt Ian watching but couldn't talk about it while Mona was there.

"I need food," she said. "Mona?"

"Now that you mention it, I do have hunger. That's how they say it in Spanish, I have hunger, tengo hambre. Did I mention Cruz is teaching me Spanish? I'm thinking of taking classes so I can eventually treat Spanish-speaking patients without an AI interpreter. I swear half the time they're wrong."

"I'm impressed," Ian said. "And it's timely that you planned your visit to coincide with lunch." Delivered deadpan but they both got the joke.

"You don't know how lucky you are to have a borrow-a-cup-of-sugar kind of neighbor!" Mona said.

He grinned. "No doubt it's also pure coincidence that Cruz is on his way over."

"Mierda! Fancy that!"

Cruz arrived as they fixed sandwiches, veggie sticks and fruit slices while music played in the background.

"Hey man," Cruz said. "You're always playing retro music these days. But that's okay. I like classics like Mariah Carey."

"Baby, baby, baby!" Mona said. "That's Whitney Houston!"

They paused to listen for a moment as "I Will Always Love You" filled the room. Carly could feel Ian's eyes on her.

The four of them sat at the bar, Cruz and Mona telling stories that made everyone laugh. Then Cruz described how a friend of his said he'd made a mistake getting involved with an older woman. He turned to Ian and said as an aside, "Like when you and Natalie had a fling until you told her she wasn't your brand of tequila." He laughed but Mona shook her head while Ian studied his sandwich and Carly pretended she wasn't shocked.

Besides being surprised, she was also annoyed that she was experiencing pangs of jealousy. It was ridiculous since whatever happened took place before she met Ian. It was entirely his business who he was intimate with, like it was her business that she was involved with Hawke before she was yanked out of her own time. In fact, if she hadn't been forcibly transported to the future, she would still be involved with Hawke. There was also the elephant in the room – her impending departure, which would leave Ian feeling abandoned. So who was she to pass judgment?

"I was flattered," Ian said, "but it took about fifteen seconds to realize she wasn't my type."

"Believe it or not, she came on to me too," Cruz said.

Mona responded with a possessive glare.

"Well, she winked at me one time at a party," Cruz explained. "But I told her I didn't date older women." He wiggled his eyebrows. "That pissed her off."

Mona blew him a kiss. "She flirted with your dad too, didn't she?" she said to Ian.

"For a millisecond. Until she noticed his cane."

"She's cheap wine in a champagne flute," Cruz said.

"You are so poetic, honey bun," Mona said.

When they finished eating, Mona and Cruz were walking through the living room to the front door when Mona spotted Carly's record album on a lamp table.

"Wow! That singer looks a lot like you, Katie!" she cried, grabbing the album and holding it for Cruz to see.

"Damn!" he said, looking from the album to Carly. "We know you can sing the pants off a gorilla, but we didn't know you already have an album."

"This really *is* you!" Mona said.

"No," Ian said, trying to take the load off Carly. "That's an album from thirty years ago. A band called Hawke & Carly."

"Then that must be your mother! Am I right?" Mona said.

"Yes," Carly said. "That's my mom – Carly Munro."

"Very cool!" Cruz said.

Mona turned the album over. "So you followed in your mother's footsteps. I guess she's retired now?"

This was the part Carly dreaded.

Ian jumped in again. "She already passed on."

"So sorry," Mona said.

"I better return this to my dad or he'll be upset," Ian said, taking the album from Mona's hands as he ushered her and Cruz out the door.

"My fault for leaving it out," Carly said once they were gone. "Can I ask you a question?"

"Sure."

"Cruz is right. You do play classic rock a lot. Did you do that before I came? Or is it for me?"

"I guess subconsciously I'm trying to make you feel at home."

"I like to hear current music too. You think I'm a relic?"

"Definitely not a relic."

"Can I ask you another question?" she said.

"Of course."

"Do Cruz and Mona have money problems?"

He sighed. "Mona, no. Cruz, yes. Why do you ask?"

"Well, they stop by a lot and eat half your groceries."

"Funny, I talked with him about it last week. I let him know it's not cool to sponge off Mona and me. I told him it's getting old and Mona is bound to feel the same way."

"So he's throwing his money away on?"

"Too many bars, restaurants, clothes, expensive cars – you name it. He's been making up for lost party-hearty time ever since college. Granted, he had to work to put himself through college and still ended up with some student loans to pay. But it's been eight years since he finished college. And it's always complain o'clock with him feeling like he was cheated out of a good time."

"Seems like Mona's in love with him. Hope he doesn't screw it up."

~

She used Ian's transit card again for the bus ride to the hospital. She found Tom alone in his room wearing a green hospital gown, sitting in a chair by the bed. She put a container of fresh peach slices on the nightstand.

"How's the physical therapy going?" she asked, taking a seat on the other side of the small room.

As she waited for him to reply, she noticed he wasn't looking too good. Besides the fact that his hair was flattened to his head, his face was pale and he needed a shave. When he spoke, his voice was weak.

"Of the many possibilities I considered as probable causes for my eventual demise, I never once considered death by physical therapy."

She smiled before noticing he wasn't kidding. "Sorry, Tom. It's that bad?"

"They insist I sit up, stand up, walk, do all these exercises, otherwise I won't have a complete recovery. But this new hip pain is piled on top of all the pain I already have and it's... it's..."

His voice cracked and he stared into his lap as he rubbed his thighs.

"Oh Tom."

"One of the medical assistants had the nerve to tell me today that I should try to see the glass half full, instead of half empty. I told her it would be easier if I had a glass!"

He shook his head.

"Not to mention the burning. It's unrelenting. And it's getting to the point where clothing hurts my skin. Even a slight wrinkle in the bedsheet beneath me causes pain." He brushed a tear away. "Sometimes I think the time has come when the best option might be..."

He didn't have to finish his sentence for her to know where he was going with that thought. Dragging her chair across the room to sit beside him, she slung her arm across his shoulders and gave him a gentle hug.

"Is there anything that gives you relief?"

"Sleep. But it's hard to come by."

"Besides sleep, is there anything that makes you forget the pain?"

He snorted dismissively.

"Even for a little bit?" she said.

"Sometimes when I'm painting."

"Yeah, I can see how that could help. Anything else?"

He rocked forward and backward.

"Listening to music helps sometimes."

"Like when you're totally into it?"

"Yeah."

"How about when you're hanging out with people?"

"Certain people."

"Who?"

"You."

"Who else?"

"Ian, sometimes. Sometimes not."

"Anyone else?"

"Naomi. She likes the same music I like."

"Yeah, she seems like a fun person to be around."

"Asher, usually."

He continued rocking.

"If I was your doctor, Tom, you know what I would prescribe?"

"A massage parlor that plays vintage rock, staffed by loose masseuses?"

She erupted in laughter. "Yep, yep. Exactly what I had in mind."

He glanced at her with a teary smile.

"What I would prescribe," she said, "is more frequent visits with people you like, regular painting sessions, someone to set up your paints and clean up afterwards, new speakers for your sound system and some creative sleep techniques."

Back to being serious, Tom explained that he tried to keep the pleasant activities going but it was easier said than done.

"Pain holds me back, slows me down, trips me up. It's hard to call someone when I feel like shit."

"I get it."

"Even when the pain recedes for a little while, it always comes roaring back. And I know I'll never be able-bodied again. I see pictures of me when I was younger and it makes me sad. It makes me wish I was normal again. When someone walks by me, I'm green with envy. That's how I used to move. Fast! They don't know how lucky they are to be able to walk without pain. I bailed on social media because so many of my friends post pictures and video of their travels around the world, or their weekend getaways to the mountains or the beach. It makes me jealous because I can't do those things. I can't stroll on the beach. I can't even walk from a hotel room to a restaurant. It's too far. Too painful. I'd give anything to be a regular sixty-something guy with arthritis, high blood pressure and cataracts. I feel sorry for myself and start crying. Then I can't bring myself to call someone or get my paintbrushes out."

He reached for a tissue.

It was easy to be glib about pain when you weren't trapped inside it. Easy to tell someone to think positive thoughts, look on the bright side, to see the glass full. His life had been taken from him and replaced with a hellish existence. And he was expected to grin and bear it while his doctors saw him as a prescription to write while forgetting he existed between appointments.

She couldn't help revisiting her idea of finding a way to change Tom's life for the better when she returned to 2024. Ian was convinced interfering could be catastrophic. But if she was extremely careful, if she kept her distance, perhaps she could help Tom avoid the terrible medical outcome that ruined his body – and his life – without screwing things up. She couldn't dismiss it out of hand.

16

"This is serious, Ian. He's deeply depressed."

They were sitting across from each other eating supper.

"I knew it would be worse after his fall. That's one of the reasons I got so bent out of shape. But Asher's his good buddy and he comes over a lot."

"Your dad isn't going to complain to Asher. I mean Asher is literally fighting for his life."

"Yeah. I'm aware." There was defensiveness in his tone.

"Tom needs help."

"He gets down sometimes. We all get down sometimes." Spoken like he knew something about that subject.

"Down? He's in the sub-basement! Besides dealing with all the pain, he's also grieving the loss of his identity. He feels like he's not the same person he was. He's talking suicide."

"Honestly, I don't believe he would—"

"He puts up a good front because he *wants* you to believe he's able to handle everything. He doesn't want to burden you any more than he already does. He feels guilty about ruining your life."

"He hasn't ruined my life."

"He thinks he has."

He was quiet for a minute as they continued eating. Then he returned to a topic she didn't want to discuss.

"Did he ask you to warn him about the surgery when you go back to your time?"

"No." She wasn't lying if she was referring to *today's* conversation. "I asked how his physical therapy was going and he said it's killing him. He broke down and told me how depressed he is. He sounds like he's considering—"

"It's all right. I'll help him."

"He told me he's distracted from the pain when he's around other people. And sometimes when he's painting or listening to music. But the pain and depression drag him so far down it's hard for him to organize those things, you know?"

"So he needs a scheduler? Is that what you're saying?"

"Yes. And, by the way, I think someone who should be brought into the mix is your brother. Why can't he call your dad every week?"

His expression was hard to read. She had a feeling he wasn't about to share his real feelings on that subject.

~

"Outta bed, you lazy choombas!" Mona cried, waltzing in the next morning.

The aroma of cinnamon trailed behind her as she made her way to the kitchen where she lifted a cloth from a plate of apple cinnamon muffins.

"Thought these would go perfect with a cup of your gourmet coffee," she said, plopping down on one of the bar stools.

"No argument there," Ian said, promptly fixing her a cup.

"I got another call from Natalie this morning. She was trying to reach Cruz but said he didn't answer his phone." She turned to Carly. "While we were talking, I told her about seeing your mom's record album. And about how you look like your mother's twin sister. I asked if she knew your mom was a rock singer from the old days. She laughed. Funny thing, though. She kept calling you Carly, not Katie. She's way too young for Alzheimer's, but it made me stop and think. She asked me if you've been clubbing since you got here. I told her the four of us went one night but you left in a hurry like you were skipping out on the bill."

Carly exchanged a quick glance with Ian.

"Where is Cruz anyway?" Ian asked. "He's supposed to be working on the Underwood project that's due, like, yesterday. I haven't heard from him this morning."

"He's incommunicado. Which is strange because he knew I was baking these muffins."

"When you hear from him, do me a favor and ask him to get in touch with me."

"Will do."

They enjoyed a muffin and coffee, then Mona hightailed it as Carly and Ian left for the hospital to bring Tom home.

~

By the time they got Tom into his apartment, his face was contorted with pain. Even being ferried in his wheelchair proved too much. All he wanted to do was lie down on his side with a cushion between his knees and a fan blowing on him so he could take a nap. Ian shut the blinds in his bedroom and turned off the lamp before closing the door.

"He'll need help when he wakes up," he told Carly. "I'll have to work from here today but you don't have to stay."

She chose to remain, sitting on the sofa with her laptop while Ian worked at the booth by the window.

They'd been busy for half an hour when his phone chimed. It was Cruz. Ian stepped into the hallway to take the call, barking a less than friendly greeting.

"Where the hell have you been, man? I'm having to pick up the slack because you're not pulling your weight."

While he was in the hallway, she heard a loud noise from Tom's bedroom. Rushing into his room without knocking, she was relieved to find him sitting on the side of his bed, elbows on his knees, eyes clamped shut. The lamp from his nightstand was lying on the floor.

"Need a pain pill," Tom hissed.

Carly had seen Ian set a small bag on the kitchen counter when they arrived.

"I'll find it."

She found the bag and took it, along with a big glass of water, to the bedroom.

He swallowed a capsule, taking several extra swigs of water.

"I need my walker," he said, pointing to where it was parked beside his dresser.

She brought it to him but when he got to his feet, he was so unsteady, she was afraid he would tumble over. She wrapped her arm around his waist, using her body to steady him.

"I'm fine!" he snapped.

"I think you need to sit down for a minute," she replied, her voice calm.

"I need to take a leak!"

Her eyes swept the room looking for a trash can, but all he had was a wicker waste paper basket.

"I'll get a bowl or something," she said. "The last thing you need to do is fall again!"

"Dammit!"

"You better behave yourself, Tom Stewart!" a woman's voice called out from the door.

Carly and Tom both looked up to find his favorite nurse standing there, a large hospital bag in her hand and a mock stern look on her face. Naomi Xu was wearing a green print summer dress and sandals, a far cry from the blue scrubs she wore at the hospital.

"She's right, you know," she said. "If you're not steady on your feet, the last thing you need to do is walk to the bathroom by yourself. Even with a walker. You could fall and break the other hip or re-fracture the one you already broke. Wouldn't that be a blast?"

Tom sat down on the bed again, conceding defeat.

"Okay. But please bring me something to pee in. My bladder doesn't have any patience or any manners."

Carly headed for the door but Naomi stopped her.

"That's why I'm here," she said. "Tom left an important item in his room."

She opened the hospital bag and withdrew a plastic jug designed as a portable men's urinal.

Ian returned then, assessing the situation in an instant. He stayed with his dad while the two women waited in the living room.

A few minutes later, the bedroom door opened and Tom emerged pushing his walker, Ian close behind him. With a bit of a wobble, he made his way to the booth, flinching as he sat down.

"Naomi," he said, "I can't believe you made a special trip to bring me a pee pitcher."

"I figured you'd need it the first few days."

"I'm glad I didn't have to pee in my cast iron skillet."

Naomi laughed.

Ian brought a bowl of orange wedges and two glasses of iced tea, his dad's tea once again in an insulated cup, Naomi's in a glass. He also brought the cooling slippers, placing them on the floor at Tom's feet. He left the two of them to visit sitting across the table from each other. Ian and Carly stayed out of the way, working on their laptops in the kitchen.

It wasn't long before classic rock was playing. Tom and Naomi discussed the history of each song and told stories about going to live concerts.

The music allowed Carly and Ian some privacy.

"What's up with Cruz?" she whispered.

"He's being very coy. Says he has to take care of a special job today, then he'll get back to work on our project."

Because Tom was enjoying Naomi's visit so much, he talked her into staying for lunch. But she had the smarts to leave right afterwards, telling him he needed to rest before the physical therapist arrived. Carly was encouraged by his improved mood. Naomi had to be the reason.

He took a brief nap, waking up in time to have a bowl of grapes before Mona arrived for physical therapy. While Mona was there, Ian drove Carly back to his apartment. Time was running out to find her way home.

After brushing her teeth, she looked in the mirror. There was something different about the way she looked. Her hair was the same, although she'd been wearing it pulled back a lot lately to disguise herself. It was also cooler that way. Her face was the same, although she hadn't been applying much makeup since she wasn't performing or going out with Hawke. Her clothes didn't have the style she always went for when she was in musician mode. Lately, she'd been wearing what she had on today – cheap, stretchy shorts and a T-shirt that Mona brought her. She hadn't worn her flowy shawl the whole time she'd been at Ian's place. But it was more than that. She couldn't put her finger on it.

Her existence had certainly been transformed since she arrived. She hadn't had the constant stress of booking gigs, doing shows, getting to and from venues, and everything else that went along with performing. While those stresses were eased, she had suffered from the constant anxiety of trying to go home. Still, she hadn't missed the lack of sleep, too much pub grub, too many drinks, empty talk with people she didn't want to hang out with and too much time wasted on a guy who was into her as long as she could elevate his career.

"Things are gonna change," she said. Another hook for a song. Who was she kidding? There were probably at least a dozen songs with that lyric.

She took off the shorts and T-shirt and put on the clothes she'd been wearing the night she was dragooned through the time portal. With her tight black pants and crop top on and her hair down on her shoulders, she felt more like her old self. The self who was ready to make music, the self who was ready to make some positive changes.

Stuffing her belongings in her suitcase, she rolled it beside her as she walked out of Ian's apartment the short distance to Natalie's door. Since it was Wednesday, there was no gig scheduled for the band tonight. Meaning Natalie's departure could be any time now. Or not. But Carly had to begin the process of detecting when she walked through the door. And she had to be ready to do her part. Thus, she would stand there and listen, waiting for the sound of someone approaching.

She entered the passcode into the keypad and pushed the door open. The room was dark. The apartment was empty. She positioned herself outside the door, ready to walk through it if she heard the telltale sounds. Holding onto the handle of her suitcase, with her purse hanging from her shoulder, she knew she would look suspicious to anyone in the hallway. She was ready to pretend she was looking for something in her purse if anyone took notice.

Five minutes went by without a sound. Ten minutes. Every once in a while she would hear a sound, but it wasn't what she was waiting for. After thirty minutes in the ready position she decided Natalie must be out and about. She likely slept in after last night's show, then went out for the afternoon. The evening too. There was no way of knowing.

When she'd been there nearly an hour, she closed the door again and returned to Ian's apartment. She didn't want to admit it, but she was relieved she hadn't heard anything. Her departure was postponed a while longer. The pain of separation was also postponed, for Ian and for herself.

Truth be told, this was a warmup. She had a feeling beforehand that it wouldn't be the real thing. It was the wrong time of day. Thus, it was safe to pretend she was ready to walk through that door to her own life. Twelve days ago when she first arrived, she was apoplectic and would've walked back through that door like a prize fighter ready to rumble. But the door was locked then. Now, she had to be brave to go through it. She had to remind herself that her world was on the other side. Not here.

She would try again around seven or eight. If Natalie was going bar hopping, that was a likely time for her to leave.

Too keyed up to cool her heels, she stored her suitcase in the rack by the door, changed back into shorts and headed to a nearby coffee shop. It wasn't as hot today and the walk would do her good. She used the cash card Ian gave her to pay for an iced mocha. For some reason the outing made her feel more in control. By the time she returned to the apartment, she was ready for a little AC.

When she opened the door, she was taken off guard at the sight of Cruz seated at Ian's desk, a laptop open in front of him. Playing above him on one of the large wall screens was video of a rock band performing. She couldn't hear music – he was getting sound through earbuds. In the two seconds it took him to see her and turn off the wall monitor, she saw that it was a video of a man and woman on stage sharing a mike with a band behind them. But her glimpse was brief.

With the screen now blank, Cruz closed the laptop, slid it into a case and tucked it under his arm. He headed straight for the door, sidestepping her as he hurried past.

"Catching up on some work. See you later!"

"Cruz? What were you…"

Ignoring her, he closed the door behind him and was gone.

She called Ian immediately.

"I saw video of a band onstage, and a man and a woman singing together. It could've been a video of my band – it resembled Hawke and me – but he shut it down before I got a good look."

"Did he say anything?"

"He said he was catching up on some work. Then he walked out. It can't be a coincidence that Natalie tried to reach him this morning, then this afternoon I catch him doing something with a video of a band. Possibly *my* band! Considering that he exposes deepfakes for a living, I'm guessing he has enough skills to *create* a deepfake."

"A deepfake of your band?"

"So he can make it look like a video of Natalie singing with my band."

"To send to club managers to get bookings."

"Correct."

"He was in my apartment, using the laptop I loaned him to do the upload. That way, if it's traced, it'll be traced to me."

"You need to get that computer back."

"He doesn't have another laptop and he's out of money. So he'll keep using it. Did you say anything to him?"

"I started to but he rushed off like he was dodging the police."

"Hey, gotta go! He's calling me."

She was shaken by the encounter. More specifically, she was upset by what it meant. If Natalie was paying Cruz to create a deepfake that would make it appear she was a competent singer, it meant she was going on offense and not waiting for Carly to create opportunities for her. It meant Natalie was savvy enough to know that Carly's help wouldn't be enough. Natalie had been hunky-dory with stealing Carly's life when she first went through the time portal. Now, even though it had been thirty years, it seemed that the older version of Natalie was still perfectly willing to put her own ambitions ahead of Carly's. Since they met in Philly, Carly thought Natalie had regrets about her behavior, but apparently not. Natalie's only regret was that her trickery hadn't been more successful. Now it looked like she was ready to use the plan for the reverse time travel swap to further her own cause, once again at Carly's expense.

17

"Did he threaten you?"

That was the first thing out of Ian's mouth as he walked through the door. He looked like he was ready to thrash someone.

"I think he was afraid of me attacking *him*," said Carly.

His response was a careful once-over, as though he needed to verify she was all right. With a bag of Chinese take-out in hand, he pulled her into an emotional embrace, the heat of the stir fry warm on her back.

"It's my fault," he said. "I should've paid more attention. He's been slacking off for weeks. I let it slide."

"I'm okay."

But he held onto her.

"Although I *am* getting hungry," she said.

"Right."

He let go and headed for the kitchen where he set the food on the bar, rounded up silverware and poured them both a near beer. Then he brought his laptop, sitting on the stool beside her so they could search as they ate.

"I didn't mention to Cruz when I loaned him the laptop that it's linked to my home network. I can see his files. I should've been keeping tabs on him. But when we first began working together, he was putting in the hours and getting a lot done." He sighed. "Here we go."

He had found the video Carly caught a glimpse of. He hit play and turned up the sound. Sure enough, it was a video of Hawke & Carly performing one of her songs, "Not Turning Back," from the album. It was a rocking good song with Carly singing lead, Hawke singing harmony, the two of them coming together on one mike. Except it wasn't Carly's face. Natalie's face had been added so it looked like she was singing.

"Natalie will be sending it to venue managers and booking agents."

Ian continued searching. "Cruz is also working on another of your music videos."

He opened it and hit play.

"That's the show your dad came to," she said.

In the video, Carly was singing her big hit, "Happenstance." She was at the keyboard, her hands busy on the keys as she sang. Several feet away, Hawke sang into another mike as he played guitar. Once again, Natalie's face had been superimposed over Carly's. It was so professional, average viewers wouldn't know it had been tampered with.

"He did a good job. Possibly good enough to avoid detection," Ian said.

"Older Natalie is uploading them to pave the way for when younger Natalie gets back Friday night."

Ian kept poking around for the next few minutes as they ate. It didn't take long for him to realize Cruz was not a beginner.

"He's got six videos."

He opened them one by one. They were political attack ads showing candidates saying things they likely never said.

"I don't believe it. He's gone into the deepfake business," Ian said. "He's making good money creating the kind of stuff we spend every day trying to shut down. He knows the ins and outs, knows how to fool anti-deepfake software."

While Ian wrapped his head around what Cruz's actions meant for him, Carly was already weighing how these phony videos might affect her. When she succeeded in returning to her own time, the tampered videos wouldn't exist yet. They wouldn't exist until they were created by Cruz in 2054 to help the younger Natalie get noticed. But if the younger Natalie returned to 2054, the older Natalie now living in Philadelphia would never exist. So she wouldn't be here in 2054 to hire Cruz to create the deepfakes. God, it was too complex to understand. But if Cruz created them and left them for the younger Natalie to find when she returned to her time, she would have possession of them, wouldn't she? Carly was getting a headache trying to comprehend it all.

Did it matter? If the faked videos weren't created until thirty years after the originals were shot, when Carly went back to her own time she would make more videos and copyright more songs. She could require anti-deepfake coding in her videos. She would have the advantage.

If, on the other hand, she failed to make it back through the time portal, then Natalie wouldn't return as her younger self to 2054. Her ill-fated attempt to break into the music business would be history. And the phony videos would be useless to the older Natalie living in Philadelphia.

With all that in mind, she didn't think there was a lot to worry about. Except for the stuff all musicians had to worry about – copyright theft, making a living, fair pay, being fleeced by Spotify which made billions while paying artists next to nothing, etcetera, etcetera, etcetera.

She relaxed so she could enjoy her stir fry.

"There's nothing I can do to save him," Ian said. "He's going to be fired. He could also be prosecuted for criminal wrongdoing. He is so done for."

With that, he closed his laptop and opened his untouched container of stir fry. He took a big bite like he was starving but couldn't stop shaking his head.

"Me and Cruz have been friends since we were in high school," he said. "I hate to see this happen to him. My ass is in a sling as well. I'm his immediate boss and his mentor. I recommended him for the job. I've given him nothing but good evaluations. Now they're going to think I've been doing this stuff too."

"Surely, they won't—"

"There's no 'surely' about it. I'll have to file an extensive report and be interviewed in person by company security. I'll have to take all my laptops in with me to undergo forensic inspection. They'll examine them with a fine-tooth comb. Although the laptop I loaned you belongs to me and not the company, I'd still like you to remove your personal files. They'll want a look-see at that one too."

She retrieved it immediately from underneath the bar. Taking a bite of egg roll, she attached the document she'd been working on to an email and sent it to the email address Natalie used before she went through the time gate and the one she had now. Then Carly deleted her files, closed the laptop and slid it over to Ian.

"You don't seem too upset," he said.

"To tell you the truth, I don't think the deepfakes will hurt me."

When she explained her reasoning, he seemed relieved.

"It's you I'm worried about," she said.

"Well, yeah, my boss could tell me to go jump in a Florida sinkhole. If he's genuinely pissed, he won't give me a reference for future jobs, which means my employment in deepfake detection is finished. I could kick myself." He pushed his plate away. "I have to call my boss in a few minutes and get in touch with Cruz. I need that laptop back and he's not going to want to give it to me. As much as I hate to say it, I think this may mean the end of my friendship with Cruz. First, though, I have to check on Dad. Asher is with him right now but I have to spend the night over there."

He left the kitchen, headed for the bedroom to make his calls.

Carly wished there was something she could do to help.

After cleaning up and moving to the living room, she could hear his voice from the bedroom. He sounded stressed. Had he been distracted while helping her these last couple of weeks? If she hadn't been living in his apartment, he might've caught on to what Cruz was doing.

Feeling antsy, she texted him that she was going outside to get some air. As soon as she entered the hallway, she heard a voice. She stopped when she reached Natalie's apartment, standing inches from the door. There it was again – a woman's voice. The words were unintelligible. But the tone was intense. She listened more closely.

"I have to go now," the woman said, like she was talking on the phone.

Then Carly heard a thump and a click, like the door was opening. There was a lurch in her stomach. If she tapped her code into the keypad right quick and opened the door from this side, she could walk into the apartment and cross through the time portal at the same moment Natalie passed through in the opposite direction. This was her chance! All she had to do was tap the code into the keypad to open the door.

She heard another noise. A muffled thump. Then another click and the squeaking of metal on metal. That was the familiar sound of the door closing in Carly's old apartment. Natalie had just exited into the hallway of the Vandermeer mansion. Carly had frozen, unprepared to take action, allowing this perfect opportunity to pass her by.

She should've already entered the passcode into the keypad and pushed the door open! What was wrong with her that she froze like that? She was infuriated with herself! If she heard a noise again, even if it didn't sound like someone from inside the apartment, she had to be prepared. If she'd been ready, she could've started through the doorway so she would occupy the threshold at the same time Natalie did.

Now that Natalie had left, there would be no other opportunity tonight. She would stay out late and not leave the apartment again until tomorrow afternoon at the earliest, and possibly not until she had to leave for tomorrow night's gig at Faison's Pub. Carly had to be primed for action. There would be no replay of this evening's fiasco!

She walked outside. As the sun set, she forced herself to do slow laps on the sidewalk rather than the fast, angry steps she wanted to do. She had to calm herself.

Fifteen minutes later, Ian found her. He sat down on the bench facing the street and raised his eyes toward the evening sky. She sat down too, leaving space between them.

"My boss didn't go ballistic like I expected. I think he'll stand up for me to management. But Cruz is another matter."

She was relieved and wanted to hug him.

"I've got to head back to Dad's now. Sorry to leave you on your own." He looked tired. "You know what I wish," he said, gazing at her. "I wish…" He paused, a wistful tone in his voice. Instead of continuing, though, he got to his feet and started toward the building.

"You wish?"

He kept walking, calling over his shoulder, "Doesn't matter."

She sat for a few minutes more, watching the cars go by, wishing Ian had finished his sentence. Wishing she had given him that hug.

She returned to the apartment which she had to herself now. Feeling that musical itch, she lowered the volume on the keyboard and began playing around on the keys – a little run, a syncopated melody, a glimmer of a song. She was feeling the passing of time, how time slips away, the loss, the self-reproach when it's gone and you haven't done what you intended, you haven't grabbed hold of what makes you happy.

"Time is stealing away," she sang softly, for her ears only. "Time steals away, baby." Which is what was happening to her. She had two days left before she had to leave. "Time steals away," she sang harmony this time, immersing herself in the music, closing her eyes. "Don't let time steal away." She was feeling lonesome and blue.

But Ian's predicament shoehorned its way back into her brain, diverting her energy away from her music. She was galled that Cruz had taken advantage of his friend. It occurred to her that while Mona said he was "incommunicado," it was possible she was covering up for him. She took off down the hallway, finding herself at Mona's door before she even had time to consider what she was doing.

Mona greeted her with a smile, but her hands were fidgety.

She led the way through her cluttered living room to the kitchen, ostensibly to make some popcorn and get a drink. Carly was suspicious, becoming more so with all the noise from the popcorn popping and Mona talking a mile a minute as loud as she could.

"I talked with Natalie again," she said. "All she could talk about is what you're up to. I told her you're getting ready to leave and will be staying at Ian's a couple more days. She asked if the two of you are close. I told her I think Ian's in love with you. But I told her I wasn't sure how you feel. I said it seems like there's chemistry. But I told her that if you loved him, you wouldn't go off and leave him. Am I right?"

Carly turned and darted from the kitchen into the living room in time to catch Cruz making for the door.

"Ian needs to speak with you," she said. "Considering all he's done for you, the least you can do is call him. He may lose his job because of your side hustle."

Hands on hips, she gave him an impatient look, Mona standing behind her.

"I tried, honey, but she—" Mona said.

Cruz waved her off.

"I'm in debt up to my pecs," he said. "I need the money."

"Yeah, well, you may have ruined Ian's life because you're too childish to live within your means."

Carly hadn't planned to say that but the words rushed out of her mouth.

He hung his head.

"Make it right," she said. "He's spending the night at his dad's because he can't leave him alone. But I know he'd be glad to get your call. You could start with 'I'm sorry.'"

"Cruz lost his apartment," Mona said.

"And whose fault is that?" Carly felt no sympathy. "Soon, he'll lose his car and his phone. Probably his girlfriend too."

She'd said enough and showed herself out. On her way back to the apartment, she texted Ian.

"Found Cruz hiding at Mona's place. He lost his apartment. Says he's deep in debt. I told him he should call you. Don't know if he will."

It took him a while to reply.

"I called him. He answered. I'll fill you in tomorrow. Dad is asleep. He's in a ton of pain. PT was a little too aggressive. I'll tell Mona to go easier on him."

A moment later, her phone vibrated again. Another text from Ian. A single heart emoji.

18

Carly was having coffee and cereal the next morning when Ian got home. After showering and changing clothes, he joined her in the kitchen, fixing himself a cup of coffee.

"Asher's staying with Dad for a while so I can meet with my boss. Cruz is going with me. He's supposed to be here in a few minutes. He was Mister Apologetic last night on the phone. He thinks he has an addiction."

"To what?"

"I guess you could call it an addiction to the party-down mode. He says he has to go out every night. He's maxed out three credit accounts and is almost maxed out on a fourth. No savings. And now, no apartment. He's living at Mona's. She's been spending too much because of him. But she's not as bad off as he is. Now he's about to be canned."

When his coffee was brewed, he poured himself a mug.

"You won't believe what he told me," he said, sitting down across from her. "He said because Carly Munro is dead, he didn't think anyone would be hurt by a deepfake of a thirty-year-old music video."

"Is he acquainted with the concept of right and wrong?"

"Ditto, Natalie. She's the one who hired him. And she knows you're very much alive."

She shook her head.

"I need to ask a favor," he said. "Asher can't stay long. He's going for a chemo treatment this morning. Can you hang out with Dad until I get back? I don't think he's quite ready to be alone."

"Of course."

"I'll drop you on my way to the office."

His phone chimed. "Mona's here," he said.

Mona walked in carrying a basket covered with a dish towel.

"Homemade cheese biscuits like my grandma used to make, hot from the oven." Her cheerful mode was set on max.

"Where is he?" Ian said.

She hesitated. "He changed his mind."

Ian pounded his fist on the bar, jumping up and whirling around like he was trying to keep from strangling the messenger.

"I'm sorry," Mona said, cringing. "He's afraid he'll be sent to prison or something."

She set the basket on the counter, then hugged herself.

"We talked about that stuff last night," Ian said. "If he wants to save himself he needs to come clean with Andy. Deleting the deepfakes is his best chance. Probably his only chance!"

When he pulled his phone out, Mona stopped him.

"He's not going to answer a call from you."

"Then *you* call him. Tell him what I said. Tell him if he wants to have a life, he needs to fix this now! You can also tell him if he doesn't show up today, it's not only *his* job on the line. It's *my* job too. He may not care if he never gets hired again. But I do. If I get canned because of him, my profession is wiped."

Mona began to cry.

"Now would be a good time," he said, louder than necessary.

"Ian," Carly whispered, giving him a look.

She hurried to Mona's side and wrapped her arm around her shoulders. "Ian's right," Carly said with a gentle voice. "You need to tell Cruz he'll screw up his life big time if he doesn't own up to what he's done. And it's not fair to wreck Ian's life too. Cruz owes him."

She handed Mona a napkin to wipe her eyes.

"I've been trying to tell him it's time to stop throwing money away and think about the future," Mona said. "He knows I'd like to have a family but he can't seem to—"

"Grow up?" Ian said.

Carly held her hand up, urging Ian to cool it.

"I get it," he said. "Cruz always complains he didn't get to be wild and crazy in college like I did. I had a scholarship and a dad who paid the rest. Cruz came away with a pile of student loans after working a bunch of crappy jobs. But he's made up for lost time. If he wants a decent life, he needs to start acting like an adult."

Carly turned her eyes on Mona. "Why don't you call him and tell him again how important this is to you."

Mona blotted her eyes. "I've got a history with needy guys," she mumbled, moving into the living room to make her call.

Ian looked like he wanted to pulverize someone.

Carly sat down on her stool again, taking a sip of coffee, straining to hear Mona's words. Mona told Cruz she loved him, but if they were going to have a life together he needed to fix the mess he created. She patiently pleaded with him. Then her tone changed.

"If you don't fix this right now, there's no way we can ever be together. You'll be hiding and you'll be miserable and you'll want to mooch off someone. But it's not gonna be me! I refuse to live with a moocher who thinks it's okay to earn a living creating deepfake lies! So, if you're not going with Ian right now, then you need to be gone by the time I walk back down the hallway, because you won't be welcome at my place anymore!"

There was silence.

Carly and Ian shared a stunned look.

Mona reappeared in the doorway, limp and teary-eyed. "I think I just flushed my life down the toilet."

No one moved. Finally Ian spoke.

"I've gotta go."

Mona stepped aside as he and Carly walked from the kitchen to the living room. He slid his two laptops in a carry bag while Carly put her shoes on. Mona stood holding the biscuits, unsure what to do, looking like she was afraid to go home, afraid of what she'd find.

"We have to leave," Ian said.

She shoved the basket into Carly's hands and followed them to the door. When Ian opened it, Cruz was there, laptop under his arm.

Mona rushed to him and wrapped her arms around him.

"I love you, baby," Cruz said, kissing her forehead.

~

Tom's friend answered the door wearing a straw fedora. Asher Blum was tall and angular with intelligent eyes and stylish glasses. He looked like the college professor he was. His complexion was sallow, though, reminding her that the reason he couldn't stay longer was his chemo appointment. She suspected the hat covered hair loss.

"Tom's taking a nap," he said, shaking her hand. "My name is Asher. You must be Katie. He talks about you like you're a rock star."

She chuckled, imagining what Tom had told him.

"How's he doing today?" she asked.

"He claims he's doing all right, but he lies to me all the time because I have cancer."

"Do you mind if I ask you a personal question?"

He was obviously taken by surprise.

"Sorry," she continued. "I've been wondering if you sometimes feel like your life has been stolen from you."

He hesitated before responding. "I'm guessing you're thinking about Tom. He used to tell me he felt like he was robbed of his life. But he stopped saying that when I was diagnosed. I understand where he's coming from. He followed what was considered sound medical advice and ended up in terrible pain as a result. It's easy to see why he's bitter. As for me, I'm one of millions of people who get cancer every year, not to mention other serious diseases. Because of that, I've never felt I was singled out. And while it's not fun, I'm thankful so many cancers, including mine, are treatable now. A hundred years ago, I wouldn't have stood a chance. So, to answer your question, I'm only human, which means I do get depressed, but I'm still kicking. And I have a fighting chance of beating this."

"Thanks. I didn't mean to be—"

"No problem."

"Ironic that you're battling cancer, yet you're here helping Tom."

"Well, I'm not in excruciating pain like Tom is. And Phil – my husband – takes good care of me. Tom doesn't have a good husband – or a good wife – to share his burden."

Right after he took off, Carly heard a sound from the bedroom. She paused to listen, hearing a low moan, then what sounded like a quiet sob. She rushed to his door, knocked and called out. When he didn't answer, she opened it, finding him sitting on the side of the bed, rocking forward and backward, eyes closed, a terrible frown on his face.

"Tom? Are you okay?"

He reached for a tissue from a box on his nightstand and blotted his eyes. Then he rubbed his thighs, working downward to rub his shins and calves before massaging one foot and then the other. He opened his eyes, looking at her with lowered brows.

"Another babysitter. Well, you're better looking than the last one

"How about I walk with you to the gentlemen's room?" She moved toward him.

"I've got grab bars in there."

"I'll walk you to the door."

She positioned herself beside him as he pulled himself to a standing position using his walker. She was thankful he was steadier today. She waited for him outside the bathroom and walked with him to the living room.

"I have to exercise my legs," he said.

He made one labored lap around the living room before taking a seat in the booth.

Carly brought him a cup of coffee and set Mona's re-warmed biscuits on the table along with two plates, knives, a small tub of butter and a jar of blackberry preserves. She sat across from him.

"Ian says you're leaving tomorrow," he said with questioning eyes.

What was she supposed to say?

"I'm not sure he'll survive," he said. "Do you have to go?"

"Tom, I…" But she stopped, waving her hand in dismay as she gazed out the window. "I don't belong here."

He sipped his coffee.

"I need some coffee too," she said, and fled to the kitchen.

When she returned they had their biscuits and coffee and talked about other things.

When Naomi arrived, Carly made tracks. It was a long walk home, but she needed the exercise and fresh air.

After a tepid shower she sat down at the keyboard, consumed with the new song she'd begun working on last night. Time flew as she played and sang, making notes as she went. She worked until her empty stomach nagged her into fixing herself some lunch.

When Ian arrived, she greeted him cheerfully, something she'd struggled with lately. She had the urge to share the song with him. On second thought, since it was about time slipping away, it would make him sadder. He seemed eager to tell her his news so she sat at the kitchen bar while he heated soup for his lunch.

"I thought Andy would fire him first thing, and maybe me too. But he was sympathetic about my situation. He said my success rate is higher than all but one of his employees and he doesn't want to lose me. He gave me a truckload of grief about not monitoring Cruz more closely. He wasn't as sympathetic with Cruz, but said if he can track the deepfakes and wipe them from the internet, he'll consider giving him another chance on a probationary basis. Cruz says he embedded a code in them, so he thinks he can do it. His customers won't be happy but they won't know who pulled the videos down. I don't think he's been dealing with dangerous people. At least I hope not."

"That's good news."

"Andy's mad, that's for sure," he said.

"I hope Mona doesn't blab to Natalie. She's talked with her several times and tells her things I wish she wouldn't."

"I could try talking with her but I don't know if she'll speak to me after I lost my cool this morning."

"I'll go see how she's doing. I'll be back."

She made her way to the other end of the hall. Mona looked nervous when she opened the door.

"Are you okay?" Carly asked.

"I'm happy Cruz made the right decision. But it's going to be hard. I hope we can make it."

"I hope so too. One thing I think you need to be careful about is telling Natalie too much. Cruz may have already mentioned this to you but it would be best not to tell her what happened to him. In fact, if she asks you about any videos, play dumb."

"My lips are padlocked."

"I'm afraid she'll cause him problems if she knows what's going on."

"You think she would do something bad?"

"I don't know, but I'd hate to find out."

"I get it."

"There's something else," Carly said. "I came to say goodbye."

"That's too bad. Ian is nuts about you. And me and Cruz like you a lot. I thought you might stick around."

"Thanks for treating me like a friend."

Carly gave her a hug, then walked back down the hallway. Ian was waiting for her.

"I need to go back over to Dad's. I'll see you tonight?"

She paused to think, realizing she had to be in position this evening for when Natalie left for the gig. If she accomplished her mission, she might never see Ian again. God, she couldn't think about that.

The softness in his eyes darkened into the kind of gloom that could make a person lose hope.

"You'll be standing outside that door, waiting to walk through it, won't you?" he said.

She almost said 'yes,' but didn't bother. It was a rhetorical question anyway.

Looking into his eyes, she could see the longing. She'd gotten so tangled up in his life, she didn't want to say goodbye.

"Will you think about me?" he said.

"If you only knew." Which would have to become a song.

He moved in close, his arms encircling her.

"A goodbye kiss," she whispered.

She lifted her mouth to his.

With his eyes fixed on hers, he whispered, "I want to make love to you."

Why did she have to feel so conflicted?

"If you don't want to call it making love, you can think of it as casual sex," he said, his eyes on fire.

Acutely aware that this could be the last time she saw him, she took his hand and led him to the bedroom. This was different from anything she'd experienced before. Because it was Ian, she knew she was loved.

They undressed each other and held each other close. Their caresses turned into much more, escalating with their heartbeats until they were intertwined in a tangle of passion. There was a roar in her ears as they reached a crescendo.

She had thought her craving for him might ease afterwards. But she would always want more. More of this man who filled her heart.

The look in his eyes was full of yearning and tenderness.

"Please stay."

"I can't," she said, her voice soft as feathers. "This is not my time. I don't belong here."

He raised himself on one elbow.

"Did you ever think you're here for a reason?"

"My life is back in my own time," she said, gently extricating herself.

"You can make a life wherever you are."

She covered herself with a sheet.

"Was this really just casual sex for you?" he said. "Or was this was your way of 'repaying' me?"

She gave him a wounded look.

"God, Carly, I love you. But you give yourself to me one minute and now you kick me aside?"

He slid off the bed, picked up his clothes and removed himself to get dressed in the bathroom.

She couldn't move. Instead of sharing a tender goodbye, she had twisted the knife she'd already plunged into his heart.

She never wanted to hurt this wonderful man. Now she had 'kicked him aside,' as he put it. *Oh, Ian.*

19

When Carly's phone chimed that afternoon, it was Mona. "Natalie called," she said.

Which made Carly's heart skip a beat. Mona must've tipped Natalie off and now wanted absolution for blabbing.

"Every time I turn around she's calling me again," Mona went on. "Well, maybe every *other* time I turn around. But don't worry, I didn't tell her what Cruz is up to. Anyway, she was calling to ask if you've left yet. I told her you said good-bye but you're still here."

Carly's phone chimed again. It was Natalie calling.

"I've gotta hang up," Carly said. "Talk with you later."

Although she was filled with trepidation, she had to answer. Even though Mona denied it, it's possible she let it slip about Cruz backtracking on the deepfakes. If so, there could be trouble.

"Checking to see if you're ready to go." Natalie's voice sounded unnaturally friendly.

"Yeah, I don't have much to take with me," Carly said, managing a small chuckle, hoping to keep things on a friendly bandwidth. "My arrival was somewhat unexpected."

"I wanted you to know I've been doing my part on this end. I paid a guy to edit some videos of my old stuff for me."

Carly wanted to point out that it wasn't some of *her* old stuff she'd asked Cruz to *edit*. It was music videos of Hawke & Carly stolen from the internet, then manipulated to look like Natalie singing. She had some nerve.

Why was she calling? That was the question. Was she hoping Carly would continue her efforts to jumpstart Natalie's music career right up to the last minute? At this stage, there was no more time. But that's when it occurred to her that when she returned to her own time, she would have three decades to prepare for Natalie's return to twenty fifty-four. The gears in her brain began to turn. If she were to intervene in Natalie's life when she was younger, there would be time to help her gain the experience she needed. Like a secret mentor, she could offer assistance. But would she want to mentor a woman who stole her career? And then stole her videos?

"Well, I should let you go," Natalie said. "I know you've got things to do."

"Yeah, thanks. And good luck."

"You too."

Later, she was rehearsing songs from the album, accompanying herself on keys when a text message came in from Tom.

"Can you please come over? I'll order you a car."

"Is Ian with you?"

"I sent him on an errand. His helpful son mode is wearing me out."

~

Tom served cookies as they sat across from each other in the booth. The cookies weren't half bad. The iced tea was way above average. Once again, he drank from an insulated cup.

"Being nosy," she said. "What's with the insulated glass?"

"Oh, it's one of the bonus problems I have – extreme sensitivity to cold. Touching a cold glass causes muscle spasms in my back."

"But you use ice packs on your feet."

"Yeah, ironic. Can't stand the cold but my feet are on fire so I have to use the ice packs." He shook his head.

Which heightened her guilt about refusing his plea for help.

"So you sent Ian out to run some errands?"

"He's driving me batty trying to help me, trying to motivate me, trying to console me, trying to convince me not to feel guilty about climbing up on that stool. I couldn't take it anymore. So I sent him to a Korean market an hour from here to get Napa cabbage, Korean radish and Persian cucumber so we can make my mother's homemade kimchi. I also gave him a regular grocery list so I'd get a long enough break."

That cracked her up.

"He's a good son," he added. "I don't know what I'd do without him."

Carly nibbled on her cookie, waiting for him to get to the reason for her visit.

"He says you may be leaving tonight. If not tonight, then tomorrow night. So I wanted to say goodbye." He paused, waving his finger back and forth. "Let me rephrase that – I don't *want* to say goodbye, but I guess I *need* to say goodbye. I'd rather not. I wish you'd stay. My boy will be devastated if you leave. When he got here this afternoon, he already looked like he was grieving."

She looked down at her plate.

"When you visited me in the hospital the other day, my pain was unbearable. I was desperate. I should never have asked you to warn me against having the surgery. I shifted my burden onto your shoulders. Which wasn't fair. I hereby cancel my selfish request. As you pointed out, even if you were able to convince me the surgery was a bad idea, I would see several surgeons who would convince me otherwise. Besides, without that surgery, it's possible I could end up worse off. Plus, I would never have met Naomi." He touched his heart with his fist. "So I want to make sure my shameful appeal is not a consideration as you weigh the pros and cons of returning to your own time. Please don't let my condition tip the scale. I should not have put pressure on you to go back." He stared into her eyes. "I want you to stay. If you do, my son will be happy. If you leave, well—"

"Thank you, Tom." She couldn't take any more of his pleading.

Changing the subject, he told her he'd seen a couple of monarch butterflies through his window. He called it a good omen. He had taken a couple of pictures to use as models for a new painting, the latest in a series of watercolors that he called, "From My Window." She insisted on seeing the paintings he'd already finished. Which included a Goldfinch considering his options, a squirrel taking a break, a cat on the lookout and a little girl being pulled in a wagon. They were beautiful, yet sad. In each of them, the point of view was of someone trapped inside, looking out the window.

When she got to her feet, he stood too.

"Good luck with your musical endeavors," he said. "I'll always be your biggest fan. Besides Ian, that is."

"Thanks, Tom. And good luck with your physical endeavors."

Which made him smile.

She gave him a hug. Amazing how fast this man had become like family to her. She would miss him.

~

It was three o'clock when she returned to her temporary home. The band would take the stage at nine on that Thursday night in 2024 at Faison's Pub. Which meant they'd get there by eight. Carly always arrived earlier to lower her stress, but she suspected Natalie was more casual. After all, since she didn't play an instrument, she didn't have anything to load in.

She wished she could see Ian again but had a feeling he would camp out at his dad's place to avoid a painful farewell. She hadn't intended for their lovemaking to be their goodbye, but perhaps it was better this way. In spite of his words, he knew she gave herself to him because she loved him.

With time to kill, she sat down at the keyboard to run through all the songs from the album. She'd been playing some music since Ian brought it home, but hadn't practiced daily. Although she was confident everything would come naturally as soon as she was on stage again, she didn't want to run the risk of being rusty.

Once she was in the groove, she felt so at home on the keyboard that she could sing and focus on the audience without having to concentrate on where her fingers were. To get her voice warmed up, she did some vocal exercises. Then she launched into one of her less demanding songs, not singing at full volume like she would on stage. As she went through the set list, she felt more confident, reaching the higher notes with ease. By the time she'd played them all, she was ready. God, she had missed performing.

After a light supper, she dressed in the outfit she was wearing when she arrived that night so she'd be ready for tonight's show. Then she applied her makeup. It had been a while since she'd used eye shadow, mascara, eyeliner, blush and glossy lipstick. She styled her hair so it draped nicely over the front of her shoulder and down her chest. She slipped her shawl over her top and added drop earrings. Last came her ankle boots.

The night she walked through the door into the future, she'd already loaded her new keyboard into her car. Assuming her car was where she left it, she could drive to Faison's Pub and haul it inside through the side door like she always did.

Naturally, Hawke would want to know where she'd been. He would press her for details. She needed to be ready with some reasonable answers. Not some ridiculous tale about being transported thirty years into the future through what amounted to a wormhole. He would be steamed that she hadn't contacted him.

She packed her extra clothes and toiletries in the suitcase and parked it in the hallway next to the bar stool she brought from the kitchen. Then she went back inside to check that she hadn't left anything important. She tidied up as she went, stacking her bedding in the laundry basket, wiping down the kitchen bar.

Checking her phone again, there was nothing from Ian. Should she text him? What would she say? I didn't mean to fall in love with you? Using a napkin, she dabbed at the corners of her eyes. It wouldn't do for her eye makeup to run.

Returning to the hallway, she opened the door to Natalie's apartment. This time she would move fast, crossing through the portal to travel to the past while the younger Natalie traveled to the future, both of them returning to where and when they belonged.

It could be a long evening. But she wouldn't allow herself to relax. She had to be ready to move. She started by pacing in a small circle in front of the door. Hearing nothing from inside the apartment, she moved the stool so it was positioned directly in front of the doorway. She sat down, took her borrowed tablet out and tried to read a book of short stories she'd downloaded. She gave up after finding herself reading and re-reading the same paragraph. Because she had to be on alert for voices or other noises, she couldn't listen to music. She considered playing around with some lyrics. But that didn't work either. With every muscle tight, she didn't feel the least bit creative.

She put the phone on the floor, which is where she would leave it for Ian to find. Her own phone would work again when she got home and charged it. Ian had paid for this "baby phone" like he paid for the keyboard, her food, her transportation, the bar thieves, you name it. He had been so generous, kind and supportive. As she'd told him repeatedly, she would repay him when she got home. She would set up an account in 2024, adding to it as she could afford to.

The evening dragged as she waited for any sound to indicate Natalie was leaving the apartment in the Vandermeer mansion. She strained to hear, moving closer until she was a hairsbreadth from the threshold. Maybe Natalie wasn't home.

She could be at Hawke's apartment or someone else's apartment, planning to go directly from there to the gig.

A noise startled her. It was a woman entering the hallway from the stairwell, coming home from work. She didn't turn in Carly's direction, never noticing she was camped out in the hallway.

Tired of sitting, she paced again, becoming even more antsy. If Natalie was inside the apartment, she had to be leaving soon for the show.

She stopped directly in front of the door, holding onto the wall to brace herself as she did leg lifts, first one side, then the other.

She was taken by surprise when Mona called out to her from the other end of the hallway.

"What's going on?"

An untimely visit from Mona was the last thing she needed.

"Sorry, Mona. Can't talk."

"What are you doing?"

Carly put her finger in front of her mouth, gesturing for her to be quiet.

"I saw—" Mona began.

"Shh!" Carly said, holding her hand up to silence her.

Mona stopped, putting her hands on her hips like she was miffed.

Carly refocused her attention on the open door as Mona gave up and returned to her apartment.

She checked the time. It was five till eight. She must've missed Natalie. Or she'd gone directly to the bar from a different location. Carly heaved a frustrated sigh.

That's when she heard a hint of laughter. It seemed to be emanating from Natalie's apartment. Carly tensed. She heard a woman's voice. Like she was talking on the phone to someone. It became louder as though she was moving toward the door. She grabbed the handle of her suitcase, ready to go.

There was the voice again saying, "who cares?" she took a step forward so her left foot was at the edge of the threshold.

"Don't worry, we'll get there in time." Definitely Natalie.

But then a man's voice answered her.

"We're gonna be late."

It was Hawke! He and Natalie were about to walk through the door together. Carly couldn't tell who was leading and who was following. What was she supposed to do? If she moved through the portal while two people were exiting, she had no clue who she would swap places with.

"Oh my God!" she cried, backing away as fast as she could move.

There was the squeaking sound again – the door of the mansion apartment opening. Then the voices were silenced as the two of them exited into the hallway. Natalie and Hawke were gone. They were on their way to Faison's Pub.

Carly slid to the floor, her back to the wall, legs bent. She closed her eyes and rested her head on her knees, trembling.

<u>20</u>

Carly had nearly wrecked everything. If she had passed through the portal at the same time Natalie and Hawke walked through from the other side, it was conceivable she could've swapped places with Hawke, not Natalie. Then she would've been back in 2024 but Natalie would've been there too. And Hawke? He would've arrived in 2054 as confused as she'd been two weeks ago. She groaned at the thought. The ramifications of what almost happened made her weak.

Now there would be one more chance – tomorrow night when Natalie left the apartment for the concert. That would be Carly's last opportunity to go home. After tomorrow night, the younger Natalie would no longer be living in the mansion.

She sat on the floor in a stupor, drained. There was the sound of someone rushing toward her.

"Katie, are you all right?" It was Mona. "What happened? Are you hurt?"

Mona squatted down beside her.

Carly shook her head without raising it. Mona's hand touched her shoulder as if to remind her she wasn't alone. Carly lifted her head and opened her eyes to find Mona studying her, a motherly expression of concern on her face.

"Can I get you some water?"

Carly shook her head.

Mona sat on the floor, apparently deciding it was best not to leave her new friend alone.

"You're in the same spot where Ian was sitting," she said, piquing Carly's interest. "It was a couple of hours ago. That's what I was going to tell you earlier. I almost asked him if he was okay but when I got closer, I could hear you singing and playing the piano inside the apartment. He was all ears. He definitely didn't want to be disturbed, so I left him alone. Funny, you both sat in this same spot. You had your head down on your knees. His head was leaning back against the wall with his eyes closed. What are the odds?"

Carly pictured Ian sitting here on the floor listening. He came home to speak with her, no doubt to plead with her again not to go. But he let her practice the music she'd be playing on stage. He knew it was vitally important to her that she make it back to her own time where her music career awaited.

Mona's phone chimed. "This is the third time she's contacted me today. Natalie is, like, pixilated on what you're up to. She wants to know if you've left yet."

She tapped out a reply.

"Boy, you sure can sing! You sound so much like your mom on that album," she said, raising her eyes from her phone.

Carly sighed.

"You could be in a cover band," Mona continued. "Retro music is ultra big. Old people love it. A lot of younger people dig it too. It's not like all the CGI songs cranked out these days with AI."

Carly felt the urge to correct her. CGI was for movies, not music. On second thought, it was the same thing, one for video and one for audio.

~

Alone now in the apartment, Ian's absence made her feel like a part of her was missing. She was going through what he'd experienced while she was at the hospital with Tom that afternoon when he told her he realized what it would be like after she left. Because Ian was spending the night at his Dad's, she wandered into his bedroom. Standing at the foot of the bed, she recalled their sweet lovemaking, the feel of his body, the touch of his hands on her skin, the pressure of his lips on her mouth. She didn't think he would mind if she slept in his bed. He'd been offering it from day one, guilty that she was sleeping on the couch.

Wearing a T-shirt borrowed from his dresser, she slid between the blue sheets wishing he was here too. "Oh, Ian," she whispered into the darkness.

Fatigue made her eyes close. She dreamed of a dark-haired man helping her do something. Something important.

When she awoke the next morning, sunshine peeked around the edges of the window shade, announcing that her final day on this unplanned visit to the future had arrived. She stretched her arms and legs, then sat up on the side of the bed. That's when she got a whiff of something sweet baking. She pulled on the shirt she'd been using as a robe, holding it closed in front as she opened the bedroom door. The combined aroma of coffee and cinnamon greeted her.

She stopped in the bathroom, taking a moment to splash water on her face, brush her teeth and twist her long hair into a messy chignon. After buttoning the makeshift robe, she padded through the living room to the kitchen.

With an oven mitt on, Ian pulled a square baking pan from the oven. In it was a golden brown coffee cake.

"Good timing," he said.

He poured each of them a mug of coffee, cut two squares of coffee cake and served them on plates. He sat across from her as though it was any other day.

She fought the urge to take his hand. She wanted to kiss it and thank him for his kindness. Instead, she ventured down a safe avenue of conversation.

"How's your dad?"

"He has a lot of pain but he's in better spirits than he's been in a long time. Naomi's gotta be the reason."

"Distraction."

"Precisely. She comes over every day after she gets off work. She asked Dad to teach her water colors. They're going outside tomorrow morning to paint together. He ordered a canopy tent to shade them from the sun. I'll set it up when it's delivered this afternoon."

Carly smiled as she took another sip of coffee.

"Naomi thinks Dad is witty," he went on. "And with her around, he *is* witty. Like his old self."

"That makes me happy."

"Dad told me something interesting about her. Remember she said she took a couple of classes from him in college?"

"Mm-hm."

"Well, she admitted to him that she had a crush on him back then. She signed up for those classes because she wanted to have him as her professor."

"Why am I not surprised?"

"Back then he was a young married man. Now he's—"

"...a handsome, unattached, senior hunk," she finished for him.

They exchanged a look of amusement.

"And, get this," he went on, "because they both love rock concerts, they're talking about getting tickets for a show this fall when a band they both like comes to town. I volunteered to go with them to push Dad in the wheelchair and help with logistics, but he ordered a motorized wheelchair, something he refused to do before now. He says he won't need my help. I was floored."

"Wow!"

"Yeah. He hasn't mentioned lately how his life was stolen."

Busying herself with another bite of coffee cake, she took his meaning. He was setting Tom up as a model for *her*. If his dad could see his life opening up to new opportunities even though he was still disabled and in pain, she should be able to grab on to a new life here rather than complaining that Natalie stole her place in the past. Message received. But it wasn't the same thing. Before she was hijacked through a time warp, she'd been on the cusp of success. She'd worked long and hard to get there. It was no simple matter replicating that achievement in a whole new environment.

She didn't want to discuss it again. Ian had other ideas.

"I know you're feeling a lot of stress today," he said. "And I don't want to add any more pressure, but I'm a hundred percent certain you would be equally successful in the 'here and now' as you would be in the 'there and then.'"

"Ian..."

"A hundred and fifty percent certain!"

She shook her head but that didn't stop him.

"I don't believe you have to choose between your music career and the man who loves you with his heart and soul, right down to his DNA."

"Ian, I'm sorry I have to leave."

"You don't have to!" he cried, hands slashing the air. "I'm not interested in being the inspiration for a song about lost love. I don't want to be your favorite mistake." An aggrieved reference to a Sheryl Crow song.

One of his flailing hands knocked her mug off the bar, its contents sloshing onto her chest like a rogue wave. Coffee drenched her shirt and everything underneath. Startled, she pulled the shirt away from her skin as she leapt from the stool. The tears that had been brimming in her eyes now overflowed.

"Shit!" he cried, rushing around the bar. He grabbed both sides of the shirt front and ripped it open, buttons flying as he stripped it from her body. She was left in an equally wet men's T-shirt, now stained brown.

"God, I'm so sorry!"

"I'm okay, I'm okay," she said. "It's lukewarm."

He dashed around the bar to the sink, wet a dishcloth under the faucet and grabbed the roll of paper towels. Meantime, she pulled the T-shirt over her head and dropped it on the bar, leaving the mess for him to clean up as she covered her breasts with her arms and dashed from the kitchen.

Upon reaching the bathroom, she remembered her clothes were packed in her suitcase, except for the stage outfit she had on last night. After washing coffee residue from her chest and arms, she dried off and scurried into Ian's bedroom. She found a faded shirt in his closet, slipped it on and made her way to the living room to retrieve her suitcase.

Ian was waiting for her.

"You weren't burned, were you?" he asked, rushing to her.

"No. I'm fine." She motioned for him to keep his distance.

"I'm so sorry. I never meant to attack you with hot coffee."

"Honestly, Ian. I'm good. The coffee wasn't hot."

"Lucky for you," he said, cross with himself.

She opened her suitcase on the floor, choosing a clean shorts outfit to wear.

"I know you wish I'd shut up," he said, "but you don't realize that if the songs on your album were coming out now, people would love them."

"Ian, I don't want to—"

"You have a genuine sound. People crave the kind of real music you create, not that synthetic garbage that passes for music in this hyper artificial day and age."

"Please—"

"And you're already getting offers here."

That made her stop and stare.

"I was wiping the counter," he said, "and a text message popped up on your phone. I didn't mean to pry, but couldn't help but notice it was from a bar manager offering you a gig."

"What?"

"That restaurant manager in Philly who offered you a job knows a local guy and messaged him about how good you are."

"I don't appreciate your snooping around—"

"I wasn't snooping. I was wiping up coffee. The words jumped out at me. I'm sorry."

Her forehead pinched as she hurried past him to get dressed in the bathroom. When she returned, he was sitting on the couch, elbows on his splayed knees, his head hanging down. He looked up when he heard her.

"Isn't there anything I can do to convince you to stay?" he said.

It was impossible not to be affected by the heartbroken look on his face knowing she was the cause.

He got to his feet and crossed the room to stand in front of her. When she didn't step back, he moved closer and wrapped his arms around her. Holding her tight, he kissed her hair.

"Stay," he whispered.

Burying her face in his chest, she breathed in the scent of him. He was making it very hard to do what she had to do. She was saved by the doorbell app on his phone.

"I don't have to answer," he whispered.

The visitor pounded on the door.

Carly stepped back and Ian opened the door.

"She's threatening me," Cruz said, charging into the apartment.

"Who?"

"Natalie! She's called me, like, I don't know, eight or ten times. But I didn't pick up. A few minutes ago she left a message."

He clicked on his phone to play the recording.

"Cruz, I'm hoping the reason you haven't taken my calls is that your phone is screwed up. Because, I'm sure you wouldn't ignore me after I paid you serious money to do that job for me. The video is gone. Call me back ASAP."

"She didn't threaten you," Ian said.

"Sounded like it to me," Cruz replied.

"Okay, so she's irritated but I didn't hear a threat. I thought you were going to tell her you didn't know what happened, that you would check into it."

Cruz rubbed the back of his neck. "Yeah, that was the plan. But when I saw it was her calling, I couldn't bring myself to answer. I guess I was afraid she'd know I was lying."

"Let's have a cup of coffee." Ian led the way to the kitchen so the two of them would have a bit of privacy.

Although Carly remained in the living room, she could hear their conversation as Ian started another pot of coffee.

"Why don't you tell her the truth? Or at least part of the truth."

There was no reply.

"Tell her it was me who detected the deepfake and then the boss fired you," Ian went on. "You don't have to mention the boss is giving you a second chance if you find and delete the video."

"I don't know," Cruz said.

"If she pressures you, you can explain that with deepfakes, there's always a risk of detection. If she demands her money back, it's up to you how you answer. Depends on what you told her when she hired you. If you made a hundred percent guarantee, you could offer a partial refund."

"With what?"

"You could say you'll repay her on the installment plan. Or ask your parents for a loan."

Silence.

"I'd give you a loan," Ian said, "except I've already given you two loans. And you haven't yet paid me back a dime."

While the two of them talked, Carly left the apartment to get some exercise. She didn't get far. Mona was walking out her door and called out.

"I tell you what – I used to like Natalie. She was funny and friendly. No more though! She's getting on my nerves."

"What now?"

"Well, she's been driving Cruz insane calling his number a bazillion times. I told you last night she texted me yesterday, like, three or four times, asking about you over and over. Now, she's already texted me twice this morning. She wants to know where you are and what you're doing."

Carly shook her head. "I guess the latest news bulletin about me is that I'm heading outside right now to walk some laps before it gets too hot."

Mona grinned.

"You haven't told her anything about Cruz, have you?" Carly asked.

"I've sealed my lips like a fighter jet dematerializing in the Bermuda Triangle."

Carly smiled.

"I need to get some exercise too," Mona said. "I'll join you."

They made their way to the front lawn. Staying in the shade where possible, they walked at a moderate pace.

"I'm going over to do physical therapy with Tom this afternoon," Mona said. "Ian asked me to make sure his dad doesn't get carried away. Tom is one motivated patient, I'll give him that. I think having a girlfriend helps."

"Have you met Naomi?"

"Oh yeah. She's like the best thing that could've happened to him. I used to wonder why he didn't have a lady friend. I guess he wasn't in the mood until now." Then she shifted her attention to Carly. "So you're leaving tonight?"

"Correct. You can tell Natalie my suitcase is packed and I'm ready to go."

"I'll tell her right now. Hopefully, she'll back off."

They parted ways and Carly returned to the apartment to find Cruz gone and Ian about to leave. Without a word, he pulled her into an embrace, holding her tight against him. Then he planted a kiss on her lips, released her and was gone.

She put her hand on her heart and stared into space until she was able to move again.

With him at his dad's to install the new yard canopy, Carly had the privacy she needed to record the song she'd written for him. But first, she wanted to make an important phone call. She'd given it a lot of thought, deciding she was the best person to do it since she wasn't a member of the family. She would call Ian's brother and give him a gentle talking to about keeping in touch with his dad. Which, of course, would help lighten Ian's load.

She knew Zack wouldn't answer an unknown number so she was ready to leave a message. She had written down what she wanted to say to avoid rambling. As she spoke, she pictured Zack in her mind from the photos she'd seen on the wall in the kitchen. There was definitely a family resemblance but he didn't have the warm teasing look in his eyes that Ian did.

"Hi Zack, I'm a friend of Ian's. I'm a friend of your dad's too. The name is Katie Gambill. I want to let you know your dad needs you to give him some attention. It would seriously lift his spirits. Which is very important with all the pain he's in since he fell and broke his hip and had surgery. It would also take some of the burden off of Ian's shoulders to try to keep your dad's spirits up. My impression is that neither of them wants to ask you for help. But they could definitely use it. If they deny needing help, they're lying because they don't want to nag you. So I'm doing it on the sly. They don't know I'm calling. Thanks. Bye."

Clicking off the call, she was relieved that little chore was done. Now, on with recording Ian's song.

It still needed polishing, but she would do that when she got home and then record it eventually. She would also include it on her next album so he would get to hear it in its finished form. But she wanted him to listen to it now when the emotions were raw, in a version sung especially for him. It was called "Time Steals Away."

When she finished, she got teary-eyed listening to it one last time. Then she attached the audio file to a message which she set up to be auto-delivered at midnight, by which time she would be gone.

Natalie had told her she headed out for the concert after re-heating leftover pizza for supper in the apartment. Because it was her last opportunity for the time travel exchange, Carly wanted to be early. She took a kitchen stool and her suitcase into the hallway at six o'clock.

If she'd been nervous the night before, tonight she was a basket case. Every little creak of the building made her jump. Every whisper of water passing through the pipes caused her to lurch toward the open door. No exercises tonight. She was intent on being ready to leap into action.

Hearing a noise in the distance, her head jerked around to scan the hallway. It was a man coming through the stairs door, heading in the other direction. She breathed a sigh of relief.

The gears in her brain chugged away as she imagined going home. Of course, that was contingent on the time portal working. She was counting on it to function as it did before, transporting the two women as they simultaneously passed each other in the doorway. There was no guidebook though. She was going by her own theory, a theory she believed was logical based on everything that had happened. Still, there was no guarantee.

If it *did* work, she would arrive in her old apartment in her own time with three decades to prepare for Natalie's return.

That thought sparked an insight. With the reality of those thirty years stretching out before her, it occurred to her that after resuming her music career and living day by day and year by year, she would eventually arrive once again in 2054. For the last half of July of that year, there would be two Carlys – the one she would become at the age of 61 and the younger Carly staying with Ian as she tried to find her way home through the time portal. When her 31-year-old self successfully returned to the past, her older self would be free to find Ian again. As hard as it was to fully comprehend, that day would be tomorrow.

Why hadn't she thought of this before? All those times Ian asked her not to leave, she could've told him she would return before he even knew she was gone. In fact, her older self would have to bide her time until this two-week interlude was over, allowing them to meet and fall in love.

And there was an important bonus. She would also have time to find a way to help Tom avoid that damn surgery. There had to be a means by which she could educate him about the possibility of failure without him ever knowing she was involved. At the very least, she would have time to research the possibilities and find specialists to help Tom without altering other aspects of his life.

She pulled her phone out to send Ian a text. "Ian, You won't have time to miss me. I'll be back tomorrow!"

21

Carly's finger hovered over 'send.' It was the solution to her dilemma. Instead of having to choose, she could do both – pursue her music career *and* continue her relationship with Ian. First one, then the other. Music was her life. But Ian, well, she was deeply in love with Ian.

It was strange to contemplate. For her, thirty years would've elapsed. As she lived those three decades, she could imagine not being able to resist seeking him out as he was growing up – watching him on the playground at elementary school, taking a peek when he was in high school and college, checking on him as he started his career, always maintaining her distance. But what would it be like yearning to be with the man he would become while watching him grow up?

And if she was intent on avoiding any other relationships as she waited for the day she could walk back into Ian's life, it meant she was headed for a life focused entirely on her music with no one to share her joys and sorrows with.

For Ian, one night would've passed since she left. That sounded like a good thing. Still, what would it be like for him to go to sleep tonight, then wake up tomorrow to have the woman he loved return to him, not as she was when she left,

255

but as a sixty-one year old? What a shock that would be. And it begged the question – would he still want her when she was old enough to be his mother?

As for her, perhaps some might say she could have her cake and eat it too – that she could go back to her own time and bust her ass creating and performing music, then return to Ian when she was older to spend the rest of her days with him. Yet the more she thought about it, the more it sounded like having your cake and waiting until it was green with mold to eat it. She'd be older and wiser when they reunited, but it's possible she would also be sad and bitter after all those years of solitude.

The alternative was to allow herself to have superficial relationships while she clung to her love for Ian. She didn't like that idea at all.

She stared into the darkened apartment. There was a noise. Was it from the apartment? She barely breathed as she strained to hear. No, it was nothing.

If she was intent on returning to her own time to pursue her music career, then she had to be certain that was the most important thing to her. She should throw herself into it and forget about Ian. Because if she left him now, it would be unfair to return at the age of sixty-one to resume their romance as though nothing had happened.

Ian had supported her from the moment she arrived confused and bewildered, not understanding what happened to her. He had helped her and encouraged her. Somewhere along the way, he had fallen in love with her and she, with him. The difference being that he was open and honest about his feelings. She was not. In truth, she loved him and wanted to share her life with him. But she also wanted the creative life of a musician. He insisted he wasn't asking her to choose between the two. Was it possible he was right? That she could have him *and* her music career if she opened her heart and mind to all the possibilities? Without even trying, she already felt like a member of his family. Without trying, she had already proven she could thrive here.

There was an important consideration she mustn't lose sight of. Finding true love was so special that ignoring it would be to cast aside one of life's greatest gifts. The tightness in her back eased as she considered making a life with him, considered pursuing her dream here in this time with Ian as her partner. She had already discovered he was the man who made her heart sing. Perhaps, as he kept insisting, she could build a life wherever and whenever she wanted.

One thing was certain. She didn't owe Natalie a return ticket to this time and place. She left of her own free will and did so with malicious intent. Then, just when Carly was ready to forgive her, she showed her true colors by once again trying to stack the cards in her favor at Carly's expense.

She erased her text and set her phone aside.

That's when she heard another noise. It didn't come through the open door in front of her. It came from further down the hallway. She was stunned to see the grey-haired Natalie step through the stairwell door, a tall man behind her the size of an NFL defensive lineman.

"Glad to see you're ready to go," Natalie called out with a smile.

"Yeah," Carly replied, feeling a little prickle on the back of her neck. "Do you know what time you left the apartment?"

"I remember it like it was yesterday. I dropped a slice of pizza on my outfit as I was hurrying to leave for the concert.

So I had to change clothes at the last minute. I threw on some shorts and a fresh top. When I walked through the living room the clock said seven fifteen. I was in a mad rush and almost forgot the suitcase I packed."

Carly's phone said seven thirteen. She peered into the darkened apartment but heard nothing.

"I'm surprised to see you," Carly said.

"I wanted to thank you for finding me and convincing me to do the swap, as you call it. I also wanted to see you off."

The muscleman's body language was calm on the surface, but he was like a tennis player receiving a serve, ready to lunge in either direction to return the ball over the net like a bullet.

"Looks like you know what you're doing," Natalie said as the two of them reached her.

Carly did her best to hide the uneasy feeling in her gut. She heard a distant noise but didn't take her eyes from Natalie and the intimidating giant beside her, not wanting to alert them that the portal was about to open. She answered in a loud voice, hoping they didn't hear the telltale sound.

"Yeah, I packed all the stuff I had with me the night I left my apartment to go to our big album launch show. Little did I know I would never reach the Triple Vee that night, but would end up here thirty years in the future!"

"Now you get to return so you can climb the ladder to the big time," Natalie said with a half-smile that held no warmth.

There was another sound, like someone clearing her throat. Without a doubt, it was coming from inside the apartment. She could see it in Natalie's eyes that she heard it too.

"That's what I'm hoping," Carly said. "To make it to the big time."

"Did you hear that?" Natalie asked, her eyes flicking toward the doorway.

Carly played dumb, turning her head as if to listen.

"Time to go," Natalie said, stepping too close for comfort.

Carly's desire to travel back to her own time had melted away. She wanted to stay with Ian. This was where she should be. Waiting thirty years to be with him would lacerate her heart.

There was a sound of movement from the apartment. Then a voice mumbling. It was younger Natalie.

Older Natalie heard it too.

"Go!" Natalie shouted, waving her hand at Carly.

Carly edged away. Despite all her planning and preparation, despite all of her heart-wrenching conversations with Ian, she had no intention of walking through that door after all.

"TJ!" Natalie cried, signaling her partner.

Acting as one, she and her strongman grabbed Carly's arms, one on either side, and pushed her toward the door.

"You fucking traitor!" Natalie cried. "We had a deal!"

Carly dug in her heels, refusing to be forced through the time portal. But it was two against one and the thug had the strength of a backhoe. She instinctively dropped to the floor, trying to avoid their grasp, but they succeeded in pushing her several inches closer. In desperation, she planted one foot on either side of the door and locked her knees.

"You're going, like it or not!" Natalie hissed.

Carly groaned as she strained to hold her position.

"Take your hands off her!" It was Ian.

With that, the pressure behind her vanished.

She spun to the right, catching sight of Ian as he reached Natalie's hired gorilla. She also saw Tom heading toward them at a fast clip in a motorized wheelchair. He didn't slow down either, plowing into Natalie from behind. The impact lifted her off her feet, her butt landing in his lap, causing them both to cry out.

TJ threw a hard right, striking Ian in the jaw, sending him sprawling backwards to the floor. The goon then lurched toward Carly again, grabbing her by both shoulders this time, determined to propel her across the threshold.

A woman's scream echoed along the hallway. Carly didn't know where it came from. Meantime, Natalie tried to raise herself from Tom's lap. Despite being disabled, Tom managed to wrap his arms around her waist, preventing her from standing up.

Carly dodged the thug's grasp. But he and Ian were now engaged in close combat inches from the doorway. And the strongman had the upper hand.

"No!" Carly screamed at the top of her lungs, realizing Ian would be forced through the time gate.

The gorilla was about to shove Ian across the threshold. Desperate to save him, Carly charged into the fray, knocking Ian aside.

That's when Raj's voice boomed through the hallway. She recognized his British accent.

"What is going on here?"

Off balance, Carly tried to regain her footing. But the muscled henchman used the momentary distraction to bulldoze her full force. She fell so fast she didn't have time to get her hands out in front of her, landing face first on the floor, gasping in shock. Her chin felt like she'd been hit by a hammer. She lay there, trying to gather her wits, vaguely aware of clamorous voices behind her. A woman cried out, "let me go!"

Carly rolled onto her side, her eyes squeezed tight against the pain. "Ian?" she said.

"No!" It was a woman's voice.

Carly had to get up off the floor before someone stepped on her. She opened her eyes as she pulled herself to a sitting position, wincing in pain. The lights had dimmed. Where was everybody?

"Ian?"

No answer.

With a creeping sense of dread, she peered around her. She was alone in a darkened room. One small nightlight somewhere on the far wall provided enough light for her to get to her feet and flip a light switch beside the door.

She had arrived in the last place she wanted to be. She was in her apartment in the Vandermeer mansion, her lamps covered by scarves, the window draped with mauve curtains. She was back in 2024. Natalie's hired hand had rammed her through the time portal. She felt like she'd been robbed a second time.

"No, no, no!" she cried.

22

The door stood wide open. She stepped through it, finding the hallway empty. She noticed the familiar dark green walls and wainscoting, the antique light fixtures on the ceiling. Remembering that Ian wouldn't be born until next year, her eyes brimmed with tears.

If she was here, that must mean she and Natalie had once again traded places. As she was shoved through the doorway by the big thug, the younger Natalie must've arrived in the chaotic hallway of the apartment building where Ian lived. She would be struggling with her shift in time like Carly was. Oh, the irony. Both of them were back in their own time and fit to be tied.

Trying to imagine the scene in the hallway as younger Natalie appeared, Carly couldn't help but wonder what happened to the older Natalie and her hired hand. Then it occurred to her that if a furious younger Natalie was trying to return through the time portal to 2024, then she should do the same from her end of the wormhole. Carly needed to walk through the doorway from the inside of her apartment to the hallway so that she and younger Natalie could exchange places all over again.

She rushed back into the apartment, turning around to walk again through the door to the hallway. She repeated herself fifteen times, going back into the apartment, turning around and walking into the hallway, hoping to find herself returned to Ian's time. She tried over and over to catch the younger Natalie coming through the portal in the opposite direction so they could generate another time travel exchange. Nothing. Had the younger Natalie chosen to stay in her own time? Or was she being prevented from returning?

Carly had caused this by charging into the fray as the muscled brute wrestled with Ian. But if she hadn't thrown herself between them, it would be Ian standing here now in her old apartment, alone and in the wrong time. There's no way she could've let that happen. At least she had saved him. But now she was here and he was three decades in the future. She knuckled a tear away.

Moving closer to the door, she listened for voices. After all the time she had plotted to engineer a time travel swap so she could return to the past, now she needed to do the same thing to return to the future. Unfortunately, there was no way to communicate with Natalie.

Based on what older Natalie had told her, if left to her own devices, younger Natalie would try to return to 2024 because two weeks after she arrived, she still believed she could make it in the music business. Whether Carly and Natalie could walk through the time portal simultaneously was a question mark the size of Central Park.

Exhaustion and pain caught up with her. She went to the bathroom to check the mirror. Her chin was swelling up from where it slammed into the floor. She looked in the freezer for something to use as an ice pack. There was a single frozen entrée – chicken fried rice – which she wrapped in a dish towel and held on her chin. Returning to the living room, she opened the door, staking out a position in a chair inches from the threshold.

At length, she returned to the kitchen where she heated the frozen dinner, carrying it with her to the living room to eat. After a couple of hours, she heard a noise from the hallway. It was Jessica, her neighbor across the hall. She called out to Carly as she unlocked her door.

"Did your aunt go home?"

So that's what Natalie told everyone.

"Yeah. She had to go."

"Glad to have you back. She said you guys swapped apartments and you were staying in her place in Boston to do some shows there."

Carly was too drained to make up a story.

"I saw your hot boyfriend when I got home from work yesterday."

The insinuation was plain that something was going on between Hawke and Natalie. Which Carly already knew.

"See you later," Jessica said in cheerleader mode, then retreated into her apartment.

Silence returned. The hours dragged. Sitting so long by the open door, she dozed off. She didn't awaken until the next morning when a noise caused her to spring to her feet, nearly losing her balance. It was her neighbor Jessica again, slamming the door as she left for work. She gave Carly a pitying look.

"This won't do," Carly muttered to herself, heading to the bathroom to wash up.

She had to come up with a plan. What were her options? She could resume her career and try to forget about returning to Ian. She could live her life and plan on returning to Ian when 2054 arrived as a 61-year-old woman. Or she could try to return to the future sooner rather than later. But with no way to communicate with anyone, how was that possible? Unless she could somehow send a message to 2054.

Which jogged a memory. She'd seen a report not long ago about people sending messages to the future. She needed to do a search on the internet. When she left her apartment two weeks ago en route to the album launch show, her laptop was sitting on the kitchen table. It was no longer there. Checking the other rooms, she came up empty handed. Natalie must've taken it. She didn't have her phone with her either. It was in her purse on the hallway floor by her suitcase in Ian's time. Which meant she didn't have her driver's license and most of her cards. But she had a spare car key in a shoebox in the back of her closet. Also in the box was an extra credit card she had never signed. She did so now, then found her car in the front parking lot – with her Roland keyboard still loaded in the back – and headed for the library.

She searched online, finding several companies that claimed to send emails to the future, assuming you knew what email address to send it to and assuming the recipient would still have that email address when your message arrived. There was no way to confirm how reliable those services were. There were no Yelp reviews. You'd have to receive one of these messages in the future to know if it worked. Despite deep misgivings, she paid a fee with three separate online services and sent an email to Natalie. She told her that if she wanted to return to 2024, to walk through the door from the hallway into Apartment 113 over and over again, explaining that *she* would be doing the same thing in the opposite direction as she tried to return to the future. She told Natalie that she wanted to get back to 2054 as much as Natalie wanted to get back to 2024.

Then she paid three more times to send an email to Ian. She told him she wanted desperately to return to him. She said she would keep walking through the door from inside her apartment to the hallway. She asked him to help younger Natalie do the opposite, if he could, to walk from the hallway into Apartment 113 so they could create another time travel swap. She closed by telling him she loved him, then hit "send," praying he would get at least one of the messages.

As soon as she got home, she did as promised, walking through the door to the hallway every few minutes, hoping to hear noises that meant younger Natalie was trying to do her part in the future. She was crushed when she heard nothing and ended up in the same dark green hallway every time. It was like waiting for a train that had been taken out of service. Her messages to the future had evaporated into the ether. Although deeply disheartened, she resumed walking out the door, then returning. She didn't know what else to do.

Unwilling to give up, she carried on with her futile exercise into the evening hours. It was nearing midnight when she stopped, unable to take another step. Uncomfortable sleeping in her bed so far from the door, she sacked out on the couch in the living room. At the first hint of movement or noise, she would charge through the open door. But there were no sounds. There was no movement.

The next morning she was jerked awake by a loud noise. Leaping from the couch, she staggered forward, ready to charge through the door. But the noise was merely Jessica coming out of her apartment again.

Keys in hand, Jessica stared at Carly, who was tangled in a sheet with her disheveled hair falling in her face. She thought her neighbor was about to say something, but she changed her mind. She had undoubtedly concluded Carly was crazy. Not good. This could lead to something negative like a call to the authorities to report a mentally unstable woman in the apartment overlooking the big oak. That scenario had already played out in the past according to the article she found. Carly couldn't afford for it to happen again. She nodded at Jessica and closed the door.

There was precious little food in the kitchen but she found some crackers and a jar of peanut butter. That was her breakfast along with some horrible coffee. She'd been spoiled while staying with Ian to gourmet coffee that she now missed. More importantly, she missed having Ian across from her at the breakfast bar. Missed his witty comments and his lovey-dovey eyes. Missed the vibration of his vocal cords that seemed to produce a corresponding vibration somewhere inside her.

As much as she hated to admit it, she needed to face the possibility that she could be stuck here, that she wouldn't be able to return to Ian until she'd lived the next thirty years. Thus, she would arrive the way people normally arrived in the future, one day, one week, one month and one year at a time. Could he love her when she had grey hair? Who would she be then? Would she be the same Carly she was now? Would she have the energy and drive she had now? The creativity? Would she have the same heart she had now?

Ian deserved more. He deserved a woman with passion who wasn't hoping to slow down after a life spent in high gear on stage. Her vision blurred again.

Another noise in the hallway! She jumped up, knocking her coffee over as she raced across the room. Yanking the door open, she saw the black poodle that belonged to a neighbor from the other end of the hallway.

"Come here, Sydney!" her owner called.

Carly used to stick her head out the door and exchange pleasantries with the woman. Not today. She closed her door and covered her face in her hands.

She cleaned up the coffee spill, listening as her neighbor repeatedly called the poodle. It took a while for her to corral the dog.

Should she get in touch with Hawke? She didn't have her phone. She could take an Uber to his place. The prospect made her feel ill. She wasn't ready to give up. Not yet.

She showered and put on clean clothes before walking through the door again. There were no sounds to suggest Natalie was in the hallway of the apartment building that would one day sit on this lot. Like yesterday, she walked through the door repeatedly, hoping Natalie would be passing through in the opposite direction. But to no avail.

Late that afternoon she got her hopes up again when Jessica arrived home from work. As before, Carly's door was standing open, prompting her neighbor to give her another suspicious look.

Was this how it would be from now on? Jumping at every noise? Rushing to the door thinking now was the time for another time travel swap? Pining for Ian.

It's possible Natalie had accepted her fate, staying in her own time to try her luck at music again. Or she may have washed her hands of the music business to find something else to do. Maybe that's what Carly should do as well. Get in touch with Hawke. Tackle damage control after the disastrous album release show. It was exhausting to contemplate.

She started walking through the door to the hallway again, then returning to the apartment. Over and over. A couple of times, neighbors saw her but no one paid much attention. That's how it was these days.

Following another interminable day, she succumbed to fatigue at midnight. She grabbed some bedding for the couch, leaving the door open. Once she rested her head on the pillow, she took some deep breaths to calm herself. Like it or not, she would have to move on very soon. She needed money. There was no Ian to pay her way. Eventually she drifted off.

As before, a noise jostled her awake. She stumbled and fell trying to stand, landing on her knees. Which wrenched her into full wakefulness as she struggled to get to her feet. Someone called her name.

"Carly?" It was a woman's voice. "Are you there?"

Carly limped to the open door and peered into the hallway. It was dark and empty.

"Carly! Are you ready?"

Her stomach knotted up.

"I'm here!" the voice cried.

"Natalie?" Carly said.

"I'm ready! It's now or never. Older Natalie is coming."

Was this truly happening? She had to act. Now!

"I'm coming through the door!" Carly shouted.

Natalie said something in reply but her words were unintelligible.

Heart racing, Carly stepped tentatively through the doorway, hoping the timing was right. Moving one foot, then the other she crossed the threshold. When she reached the other side, she held her breath, afraid to look around her. Then tears of relief welled up as she recognized the cream walls in the long hallway that had become so familiar. She heard Natalie's voice faintly through the open door from inside the apartment but couldn't understand the words.

Then there was another voice. A man's voice. Turning, she saw Ian standing outside his apartment door, in the very same spot where she'd first laid eyes on him. Wearing only a pair of boxers with a terrible bedhead and glassy eyes, he was the sun rising after a long, dark night.

A slow smile spread across his face. "Damn, you're a sight for lovesick eyes."

Only someone hopelessly in love would see her that way with her witchy woman hair and the dark circles under eyes.

He hurried forward, his arms encircling her.

"I love you," she whispered.

"And I adore you."

She wrapped her arms around him and held him tight. After fearing she'd lost him, now she didn't want to let him go. It took a moment before she was able loosen her grip so she could look into his eyes.

He responded by touching her swollen, discolored chin.

"I landed on my face when that gorilla shoved me through the door."

He was injured too. She touched his jaw where there was a bruise and broken skin. That's where Natalie's accomplice punched him.

"I'm fine," he said, wiping his eyes.

Then he kissed her, a long, slow kiss.

When they were able to put a little space between them, he slid his arm around her waist and walked her into his apartment where he tended to her bruises and scrapes with tender loving care. When that was done, he looked like he wanted to adjourn to the bedroom. Instead, he fixed a big breakfast, pouring coffee before sitting down next to her at the bar. He pushed his stool closer until it was touching hers. That way he could kiss her and rub his hand over her back as they ate.

She savored the coffee as she gazed into his eyes.

Curious, she asked him why he came back Friday evening.

"To beg you one last time not to go. I was stunned to find you battling Natalie and her oversized wingman."

"I wish I'd come to my senses sooner."

"When he shoved you through the door, I was in a state of shock. Everyone was yelling and screaming. You were gone and younger Natalie was there with a suitcase, looking totally disoriented. Then she caught on and whirled around, ready to charge back into the apartment. That's when Raj slapped his hand on the keypad and closed the door. She reached out to put her hand on the keypad to open it again, but – and you won't believe this – the older Natalie grabbed her and wouldn't let go."

"Both Natalies were there?"

"Yeah, it was bonkers."

"That doesn't make sense."

"It didn't make sense at the time but maybe now it does."

She thought about it. If the older Natalie had disappeared when the younger Natalie returned to 2054, that would've meant the younger Natalie would *not* have lived out her life in the past, that she would've stayed in 2054. But if the younger Natalie returned to the past a second time to remain there, that meant she *would* live out her days there. Meaning the older Natalie would continue to exist as Carly had met her in Philadelphia.

Ian continued with his dramatic recounting of the hallway confrontation.

"The older Natalie started telling her younger self that she needed to stay here and not go back to the past. She kept saying 'bad things happen if you go back there.' She told her, 'you never make it big in the past, you end up being a big nothing.' But the younger Natalie looked like she'd been dumped at a looney bin. I almost felt sorry for her. She kept trying to reach the door but the older Natalie and her hired hulk forced her to leave with them."

"That is so weird."

"No kidding! Mona showed up asking if she should call the police. Man, it got louder and louder! Raj demanded to know what was going on. I couldn't answer because, well, because I..." His voice caught in his throat. "You saved me from being pushed through the time gate, then that big asshole forced *you* through the door instead." He paused, shaking his head, taking a moment to regain his composure. She squeezed his hand. Then he continued.

"The two Natalies and the hired hand were nowhere to be found. I guessed they drove back to Philly. So I went after them."

"You drove to Philadelphia?"

"But nobody was home. I banged on the door and yelled for her to open up, but nobody answered. A neighbor next door threatened to call the cops if I didn't shut up. I figured they holed up in a hotel somewhere so I drove home."

"Did you get the email I sent you?"

"Yeah, I found it after I got back from Philly. It made me so sad listening to that song. And I was so confused at first."

"Oh – I forgot about that one. I set it up to auto-deliver."

"Was there another email?"

"Yeah, I asked you to help Natalie come back through the portal. I paid to send it through three of those websites that promise to deliver emails in the future."

"I think you got taken."

"I sent one to Natalie too."

"Well, maybe that's how she knew you were trying to come back through the door. When I heard her shouting in the hallway, I came out in time to hear her say she was ready. Looked like she was having an insane conversation with an invisible somebody."

"I was that invisible somebody."

"Man, does that make me happy."

He pulled her close and kissed her softly. The kiss quickly escalated into something much more amorous. Pulling her up from the stool, he wrapped his arm around her waist and walked her to his unmade bed.

Their lovemaking was like a ballet of kisses and caresses that carried messages of passion, commitment and joy. She would never comprehend the force that brought them together, but she understood what would keep them together. It was love.

23

One year later

She was ready. And her band was ready. They had polished her new songs for several months playing hole-in-the-wall bars before heading into the recording studio. Tonight was the big album release show. The album was called *Carly Munro: Time is of the Essence*. They would perform before a sold-out crowd at the Bellevue Theater.

She was beyond happy that audiences and critics were responding with enthusiasm to her new music. The single that was released from the album a month ago – "Time Steals Away" – was climbing the charts and racking up streams. It was the song she'd written for Ian when she thought she was leaving. But she'd re-written it since then, changing it from a melancholy ballad into a propulsive rock song about making the most of their time together.

She'd been invited to perform at three high-profile music festivals and was juggling requests for interviews. She wasn't naïve though. A big part of her appeal flowed from her notoriety as "the time traveling rock singer."

After choosing to stay with Ian, she fully expected to face major challenges. It turned out to be a rougher ride than she imagined. She and her sister and brother had to have DNA testing done to prove she was indeed their sister, the same Carly Munro who went missing in 2024. Confirmation of her identity allowed her to use her Social Security number, open a bank account, get a new driver's license, and, very importantly, to claim her song copyrights. Everyone had been understandably skeptical, forcing her to jump through endless hoops to prove herself legit.

She had called Natalie ahead of time to let her know she was about to spill the beans. Natalie was more than happy to tell her version of the time travel swap so she could monetize her fifteen minutes of fame. With the help of a ghost writer, she penned a quick memoir that cast her as an innocent victim of the time portal. Her story was then fact-checked on talk shows that invited her to defend her claims. She made a tidy sum from book sales, videos and appearances.

One of the most popular interview questions was why she didn't use her knowledge of the future to make money. She said she tried to do so but wasn't savvy enough. She claimed that because her trip through time happened suddenly, she didn't have the chance to prepare.

One thing she didn't mention in the book was euthanizing her cat. Before Carly went public with her story, she and Ian learned that unpleasant fact from Raj who got a message from a veterinary practice asking for assistance tracking Natalie down. They wanted her to pay the balance owed for euthanasia services a month before she traveled to the past. Ian said she must not have wanted him or anyone else to know what she was up to as she prepared to travel through time. Putting the cat to sleep eliminated what she apparently viewed as a loose end. That way no one would have any reason to come into the apartment. Ian was livid, pointing out how easy it would've been to find Boots a home.

Needless to say, various government agencies examined Apartment 113, as well as the hallway and the entire apartment building. After numerous inspections and intense scrutiny, the eventual conclusion was that a temporary wormhole had existed, enabling Carly and Natalie to swap places through time. They also concluded the wormhole had closed. Even so, the government contended the portal was a national security risk and gutted the building, replacing it with a secure bunker protected with a system of signals that obfuscated the precise location of the overlapping doorways and prevented electronic intrusion. The apartment complex was acquired by the feds through eminent domain and all four buildings were razed. The owners were reimbursed and residents were given a stipend for relocation expenses. There were those who accused the feds of lying, claiming such tight security wouldn't be needed if the portal no longer existed.

Carly received a flood of messages from old acquaintances, including people she'd known in the music business. Hawke was one of the first to reach out, suggesting they resurrect Hawke & Carly and do a reunion tour. He was certain they could make big money. She wanted to laugh in his face. Instead, she arranged what turned out to be an awkward video call to tell him she would be ironing out the copyright issue for her songs. He had an awestruck expression on his face the whole time, finding it hard to believe she looked precisely as she did when he knew her in his younger days. No threats were made, but he got the message loud and clear. He agreed to withdraw his claim, realizing he'd lose the battle if it went to court. Which meant she had a small income stream since her old songs were selling on retail platforms and getting a lot of airplay with all the stories about the time traveler.

She reflected on the challenging year since she chose to stay. There was still some disagreement about whether to use her actual birth date, which would make her sixty-two. That was unhelpful since she'd been alive for thirty-two years.

There was also the tabloid frenzy that percolated through mainstream media as well. The publicity had been a nightmare at times. Ian helped her maintain her sanity even when the paparazzi tracked her down. Fortunately, it was easy to disguise herself when she went out. She hoped the media fascination would fade.

She shook her head, trying to keep her mind focused on tonight's show. Leaning into her persona as a rocker from the past, her clothes reflected elements of earlier decades. She was wearing a short, fringed jacket, distressed jean short shorts, a black top, sparkly stockings and ankle boots.

"Wow!" Ian said, as he joined her in the bedroom, taking in her long legs.

"Do ya think I'm sexy?" she said, quoting a Rod Stewart song from way back.

He grinned. "Every guy and gal in there will think you're sexy."

"You don't look too bad, yourself," she said, eyeing his trendy grey slacks and jacket. No tie though. He was too cool for a tie. "You could be the first James Bond with spiky hair."

He laughed as she pulled him in for a kiss, leaving lipstick on his mouth.

On the limo drive to the venue, she found herself thinking about the people who were part of her new life.

Tom and Naomi had moved in together. In addition to painting watercolors together, Tom played his autoharp a lot these days as the two of them sang folk songs and traditional Korean and Chinese songs. He still had terrible pain and burning. That was her sole regret about not staying in the past – she wasn't able to help him avoid the path that led to all his pain. Of course, there was no guarantee she could've made a difference. She would never know. Now, Naomi's presence in his life brought him a lot of happiness. That, coupled with her regular massages and daily diaphragmatic breathing, seemed to reduce his suffering. Luckily, Naomi was as much in love with Tom as he was with her.

After cleaning up the mess he made with the deepfakes, Cruz had segued into video production, making use of his AI skills. He had a real talent and was helping Carly create music videos. He and Mona were paying off their debt and Mona had started dropping hints about having a baby.

Tom's friend Asher Blum continued to battle cancer, but he did so with a positive outlook and a determination to live in the moment.

Following Carly's secret phone call, Ian's brother Zack stepped up, calling his dad every week and coming to visit more often.

Ian's Uncle Hwan and cousin Joey welcomed Carly to the family by telling embarrassing stories about Ian as a kid. And they began bringing the old family Monopoly game over now and then for wild and wooly tournaments.

It was Raj who found a new apartment for Carly and Ian after he and Priya moved in so Raj could be the complex's on-site manager. The free rent made it possible for him to continue working from home and taking care of Veda while

Priya worked at the hospital. They were saving to buy a house.

Having gotten pretty good at being a roadie, Ian hauled her keyboard through the back door of the theater and helped with setup. After telling everyone to "kick some musical ass," he gave Carly a kiss and headed upstairs to the first balcony.

Since this was their first big show, the entire band arrived at the venue way ahead of time. They checked that their instruments were in place to speed the transition from the opening act to their own set. Which left them with time to warm up, change clothes and touch up their hair and makeup.

~

As the building reverberated with loud rock music, Carly and the band made their way from the dressing rooms to the backstage area. Waiting in the wings during Big Bender's last song, she gave her bandmates a thumbs up. There was a flutter in her stomach, but it was a good flutter. She was hungry to make some music.

She had found a talented woman bass player named Sadie with a flair for vocal harmonies that contributed mightily to the band's sound. Leo, their virtuoso guitarist, was a natural at backup vocals too. What a gift. Mick, the drummer, kept his eye on Carly, taking his cues as if reading her mind.

They worked well together. Sometimes one or the other of them had an opinion about how a song should be played, but they respected Carly as the leader and abided by her decisions without any of the knock-down-drag-out arguments she used to have with Hawke in the old days. She paid them a generous gig rate and made sure they were fairly compensated for recording sessions – a flat rate for each session plus a percentage of record profits.

Peeking out front, she was thrilled at the packed house. The Bellevue Theater held 2500 people with standing space on the main floor in front of the raised stage, and seating in a lower level wraparound balcony as well as an upper level balcony. It was the biggest audience she had played for and, with luck, a preview of even bigger things to come. The show was billed as "Carly Munro, Live in Concert."

She'd hired three videographers to shoot footage to be used in music videos. Like most performance venues these days, The Bellevue broadcast a frequency that blocked phones and other devices from recording audio or video. Which meant there wouldn't be a sea of smartphones waving in the air. Instead, they'd be looking into a sea of faces belonging to fired-up fans. She was stoked!

When Big Bender played the last note, the audience cheered and whistled. They took their bows and trotted off stage in triumph.

The announcer cranked the audience up another notch in her introduction. "The time has come! Time is now on your side! Give it up for the world's only time traveling rock star – New York's own Carly Munro!"

Flashing hundred-thousand-watt smiles, Carly and the band bounded onstage, taking their positions, double checking that their in-ear monitors were snug and their instruments were plugged in and ready. Her new bandmates focused on Carly as she counted down. Then they cranked out a red hot opening number as she belted out the evocative lyrics of "Fair Weather Lover" while pounding the keyboard.

What a night! Fueled by the audience's energy, the band was like a basketball team when every player has a hot hand. It was far removed from anything she'd done before. Being a ticketed event, fans had paid to see her perform. And they roared their approval after every song.

Looking up into the first balcony, she spotted Ian on his feet, applauding like a madman. She introduced a song she wrote for him, "A Sight for Lovesick Eyes," inspired by the first thing out of his mouth when she returned from the past. She blew him a kiss during the chorus.

Tom and Naomi sat by his side, the two of them looking on like doting parents. Asher and his husband Phil were seated behind them. Zack was there too, close to his dad and brother. Even Uncle Hwan and cousin Joey showed up. Carly's sister Mia, her husband and two teenagers sat nearby along with Carly's brother Brian, his girlfriend and their daughter. To her surprise, Raj and Priya showed up as well.

Mona and Cruz were somewhere in the sea of bodies in the pit, always up for the thrill of rubbing shoulders – and other body parts – with strangers, and perhaps joining in the body surfing as the evening wore on. No doubt, they had already taken selfies before the show began to share online.

Following several tunes from her new album, she slipped in a couple of her old songs from the 2024 Hawke & Carly album, reminding everyone she wasn't exactly an overnight sensation. When she sang "Happenstance," she was struck by how prophetic it seemed as she cast her eyes toward Ian again. "It was fate, baby, that brought us together, not happenstance that brought you to me." The second time through, she switched the lyric to, "…not happenstance that brought me to you." Ian made a heart with his hands.

As the set list turned again to her new songs, she gave a shout out to each member of her band, knowing how important it was that they get to share the limelight with her.

She dedicated the next song to Ian.

"Although he didn't know it at the time, this one was co-written by the guy I share my life with. When Ian said these words to yours truly, I knew he was the man for me. I turned his words into a tune called 'You're a Song.'"

The funky drum intro had the audience moving even before she began to sing. "Sometimes you're like a hard-driving rock song with a pounding rhythm and a wild guitar. But sometimes you're like a heartfelt ballad with lyrics that stay in my head forever."

It was thrilling when the crowd responded with so much energy.

Among the tunes on the set list was one that grew out of her frustration during the first couple of weeks after she arrived in the future. She wrote it as she was falling for Ian and wishing she wasn't. Sadie started it off with a kick-ass bassline before Carly gave it her all, singing "Don't Need No Complications." It was a hard rockin' song that laid bare the frustration and pain of trying, but failing, to stop love in its tracks. The audience ate it up.

She saved "Time Steals Away" for last. She was on an emotional wave crashing over the crowd, her powerful voice intertwining with the throbbing music. There was cheering and screaming as fans swayed and waved their arms above their heads.

After one encore – a song called "If You Only Knew" – and a second shout-out to the band, she left the stage floating higher than a jetliner. Excited about the future, she hugged Sadie, Leo and Mick, letting them know how important they were to her.

Writers from several online music mags cornered her backstage afterwards, doing their best to make her feel guilty about "unfairly" climbing the rock 'n' roll ladder of fame based on a freak accident of nature. She didn't take it personally, telling them her music would speak for itself. She reminded them there were plenty of celebrities who never made it as rock performers because their music fell short. She also told them she had established her bona fides, working her way up like everybody else did.

Not everyone was so cynical. The merch table sold all the vinyl LPs she brought – five hundred records.

To show her appreciation to her band, she invited them and their partners and friends for drinks and food at a cool bar close by. Ian, Tom, Naomi and other family and friends joined in as the exuberant group reveled in the wildly successful show.

If there was one thing Carly knew she wanted and needed, it was a band with chemistry. She'd done her best from the start, knowing audiences would sense it and that the music would be the better for it. By the laughter and hugs being passed around tonight, it looked like she had achieved that objective. Which gave her so much satisfaction.

She took the opportunity to sing Ian's praises, telling her bandmates and friends how he supported her creativity and independence from day one, including paying all of her expenses as she re-launched her music career.

"Now it looks like I'll finally be able to pay him back," she said, blowing him a kiss.

~

Three enthusiastic reviews were posted by the following morning. In one of them the reviewer said she was skeptical of the time traveler and expected to be unimpressed, but found the songs to be meaningful, yet a blast to listen to. Another reviewer praised Carly's voice, saying it reminded her of "vintage rockers Christine McVie of Fleetwood Mac, Annie Lennox with the Eurythmics, and Ann Wilson, lead singer of the rock band Heart." The third one said the best thing about Carly's music was that it sounded like the real deal, not another AI production. "Carly Munro just might be a success because she's brave enough to walk the highwire without a net. Hopefully, her success will help spur a resurgence of real singers and real musicians putting out real music."

After checking the reviews, she and Ian enjoyed their morning coffee in the new apartment. She was still walking on puffy white clouds of happiness. She was also filled with wonder that she had accidentally traveled to this time and place to find the love of her life. She openly admired him sitting next to her at the kitchen bar. He noticed.

"Do you ever question your decision?" he said.

"Not once." She knew which decision he was referring to. "You're the love of my life."

Setting his mug down, he scooted closer. Then he leaned in and kissed her, holding her face in his hands.

"Although I thought you might be missing a marble or three the first time I laid eyes on you," he said, "I knew even then I was going to fall in love with you. It was like you magically materialized out of my dreams. What I didn't know at first, but I do now, is that I'm gonna love you till the end of time."

He was speaking in song titles again.

"Even if I'm a rock musician?" she said, teasing.

"You've gotta know by now I'm strong enough to be your man."

Impressive that he was familiar with that particular Sheryl Crow song.

She laughed and kissed his lips, heat rising through her body.

"Have you ever heard Aretha Franklin's 'Baby, I Love You?'"

He shook his head.

"You need to give it a listen. In the song, she tells her man if he snaps his fingers, she'll come running, because…" then she caressed his cheek as she sang the refrain, "baby, baby, baby, I love you."

The End

Review it

Thank you for reading *Time Travel Swap*. If you enjoyed it, please help spread the word by posting a star rating or a brief customer review. Or tell your friends, in person or on social media. Thanks very much!

About the author

Connie Lacy writes time travel fiction, speculative fiction and historical fiction, all with a dollop of romance. She worked for many years in radio news as a reporter and news anchor. She and her husband live in Atlanta.

Acknowledgements

Special thanks to my musician son Kyle Lacy for proofing my manuscript for music references and descriptions of a musician's existence. He provided helpful feedback and suggestions. Any mistakes or misrepresentations are my own.

Much appreciation to the four talented New York City-based musicians I interviewed to learn what their professional lives are like. Their insights and anecdotes helped me create a main character who is a singer, songwriter and musician. Thanks to Mel Johnston, Yannie Beliziano, Amanda D'Amico and my son Kyle Lacy for helping me understand the creative process, what it's like performing on stage and many of the behind-the-scenes chores involved. And thanks to the women musicians for sharing their experiences working in a field dominated by men. Brief bios are below.

Mel Johnston is a vocalist, songwriter and teaching artist based in Bushwick, Brooklyn in New York City. She's the leader of the rock and blues band Mel and the Tall Boys. In addition to her work as a band leader and songwriter, Mel has also performed extensively all over the country as a background vocalist. When not performing or writing new work, she provides instruction and songwriting mentorship to students of all ages. Look for Mel and the Tall Boys on Spotify and find Mel on Instagram: Instagram.com/mel_johnstonx

Yannie Beliziano is a multi-instrumentalist performer, songwriter and vocalist from New Jersey. She got her start in TV and film, being featured in Sesame Street episodes and starring in the movie "Dragon Tales; Let's start a Band" when she was 4 years old. When she was 20 she had her off-Broadway debut in "The Office! A Musical Parody," moving on to originate roles in a National Tour and Regional show. Raised in a household with both Belizean and Italian cultures, Yannie fell in love with every aspect of music at a very young age and honors her cultural identity in a unique sound. She's been releasing a consistent stream of singles which you can find on Spotify. She performs at venues all over New York City.
Find her on Linktree: linktr.ee/YannieBeliziano

Amanda D'Amico is a multi-faceted performer with a degree in Musical Theatre. She's been seen onstage regionally in roles such as Julia Sullivan *(The Wedding Singer)* and Jeanie *(HAIR)*. She also performed aboard

Disney Cruise Line as part of the Mainstage Cast. While auditioning and waiting tables, she sings regularly at weddings and popular live-music venues in New York City, including singing lead and backup vocals with a rock band. More on her website: www.aedamico.com and Instagram: www.Instagram.com/aedamics

Kyle Lacy is a guitarist/singer/songwriter from Atlanta, Georgia, but his time machine made a quick refueling stop in 1956 and he was quickly infected with the DNA that gave birth to Rock 'n' Roll. His debut album *The Road to Tomorrow* was released in 2020 by Brooklyn-based Dala Records. The album was described as "A fine mix of soul, blues, gospel and rock 'n' roll that deserves a larger audience." (AddtoWantlist) The single "Low and Slow" earned multiple spins on The Craig Charles Funk and Soul show (BBC). His 2nd solo album, *Pleasurecraft*, is available everywhere. He recently completed a full band tour to support his release of *The Record Hop EP* in March of 2025. Kyle is also currently the musical director and touring guitarist for the Harlem Gospel Travelers (Colemine Records).
Website: www.kylelacymusic.com/epk
Links to social media & streaming platforms on website.

The song "Happenstance" ©2025 Kyle Lacy & Connie Lacy. Used with permission.

Sign up for newsletter

Get your FREE copy *The Engagement Ring, A short story.*
When Ethan pops the question, Lydia pops some
questions of her own. A 21st century take on a marriage
proposal with a pinch of humor and a dash of the
unexpected. Sign up: www.connielacy.com

Also by Connie Lacy

The October That Changed Everything
As the world teeters on the brink of nuclear war, Cheryl
Donovan falls for an Army helicopter pilot. A story of
love, friendship, family and courage set during the Cuban
Missile Crisis of 1962.

Livvy and the Enchanted Woodland
Rural Georgia 1930. Pursued by a wealthy neighbor as
she dreams of a mysterious Englishman, Livvy escapes
to her secret woodland where everything may not be as
it seems. Historical fantasy, magical realism, romance.

A Suffragette in Time
Thrown back in time to the 1850s, Sarah Burns becomes
a suffragette who finds danger and romance where she
least expects to.

The Time Capsule
An unlikely journey through time brings Hannah Myers
face to face with a man like no other. But she doesn't
belong in 1918 with a killer flu epidemic raging and the

KKK targeting the newspaper reporter she's fallen for. Can she rewrite history to protect the man she loves?

The Going Back Portal
She avoided the Trail of Tears. But can a young Cherokee Indian woman of 1840 survive the white man intent on owning her? Can a time traveler from the future help?

The Time Telephone
What if you could save your mother's life by calling her in the past on a time telephone? An intriguing coming of age story. Teen/Young Adult Fiction

A Daffodil for Angie
It's 1966. Angie's got a lot on her plate – the women's rights movement, school integration, the Vietnam War, a cocky anti-war activist and a sexy quarterback. A coming of age story that drops you right into the social upheaval of the 1960s. Teen/Young Adult Fiction

VisionSight: a Novel
Seeing the future is a curse for Jenna Stevens. A heartfelt novel of secrets and unexpected love.

The Shade Ring Trilogy
A compelling Climate Fiction trilogy in the year 2117, a time of runaway global warming. A love story in a hotter, more dangerous world.
The Shade Ring, Book 1
Albedo Effect, Book 2
Aerosol Sky, Book 3

Contact/follow

Newsletter sign-up: www.connielacy.com

www.connielacy.com
www.amazon.com/author/connie.lacy
www.Facebook.com/ConnieLacyBooks
www.Goodreads.com/ConnieLacy
www.instagram.com/connielacy_author/
www.pinterest.com/cdlacy0736/
www.tiktok.com/@connielacyauthor
www.youtube.com/@connielacybooks
Email:

WildFallsPublishing@outlook.com
connielacy@connielacy.com